At Home with Miss Vanesa

E. A. MARKHAM was born on the volcanic Caribbean island of Montserrat – which bears a strong resemblance to his invented neighbouring territory of St Caesare – and went to school in 1950s London. After working in theatre in London and the Eastern Caribbean, he lived mainly in continental Europe in the 1970s, where he was a member of the *Coopérative Ouvrière du Bâtiment*, building and restoring houses in the Alpes Maritimes.

Markham now lives in Paris. He is Professor Emeritus of Creative Writing at Sheffield Hallam University, where he headed the Creative Writing programme for fourteen years, introducing the highly successful MA in Writing. In 2006, Markham is International Writing Fellow at Trinity College Dublin. He is a member of the Royal Society of Literature.

Markham has worked in all the literary genres; his publications include nine collections of poetry, four collections of short stories, a novel and a memoir. His 2002 book of verse, *A Rough Climate*, was shortlisted for the T. S. Eliot Prize for Poetry. In 2005 Tindal Street Press published his critically acclaimed stories, *Meet Me in Mozambique*.

Praise for
Meet Me in Mozambique
(Tindal Street Press, 2005)

'This is a very funny and sometimes moving book, its dead-pan wit embedded in almost every line'   *Independent*

'E. A. Markham moves freely between unserious topical references and the serious comedy of metafiction. Whichever it is, it is always beautifully written and, in the end, oriented towards the unknown, the lure of what lies beyond'   *TLS*

'All are observed with dry humour and eye for detail, and each offers a different account of that most contemporary of experiences – being an exile. Reminiscent of the writings of V. S. Naipaul, these stories are both less literary in form and more relaxed in tone than his work, but are none the worse for that'   *The Times*

'In defying the rules, Markham has produced a book which has a wonderfully original, eccentric charm . . . [His] prose is often quirkily conversational, rather like the musings of an absent-minded professor whose speech is full of playful literary references, private jokes and little epiphanies . . . All serve to build up a picture of Pewter's complex life: a life which defies easy racial stereotyping and oversimplified categorisation. And this is the real achievement of this excellent book'   *Guardian*

'Pewter is at work on a play based on his life, and at other times is aware of his own status as a fictional construct, so we have more than one level of reality to contend with in Markham's fictions too. Thankfully, the indulgent reader's hard work is rewarded with socio-political insights offered from an unfamiliar perspective, and all manner of arch, intellectual in-jokes'   *Independent on Sunday*

At Home
with Miss Vanesa

E. A. Markham

**Tindal
Street
Press**

First published in October 2006
by Tindal Street Press Ltd
217 The Custard Factory, Gibb Street, Birmingham, B9 4AA
www.tindalstreet.co.uk

A CIP catalogue reference for this book is available
from the British Library

ISBN-10: 0 9551384 0 X
ISBN-13: 0 978 0 9551384 0 9

Typeset by Country Setting, Kingsdown, Kent
Printed and bound in Great Britain by Clays Ltd, St Ives PLC

For Mimi

'When your children invite you out to dinner, you accept.'

Professor James Meade
(*Montserratian-born Canadian academic*)

Contents

One

I

Bookmarks for John La Rose

or The Restoration of Scotland
to the Commonwealth

The sound spread like the heat being switched on and the chill started to drain back into the ground; for it was damp in the cemetery, dank March in England; and you checked yourself, embarrassed for making connections between rebirth and its opposites; and everyone was so well dressed, so rightly dressed; and that rightness still chimed with events earlier, the singing in the church; with the tributes – tributes both shaming and uplifting. Uplifting, because they were appropriate: everything I knew about the man who had died said that the tributes were appropriate (and I had known him for nearly forty years). But shaming, too, because it threw a sort of light on your own life, and made you uneasy about what you saw suddenly lit up there; not that it was a surprise, but it made you uneasy, nevertheless. For when your time comes, you thought – you tried to banish the thought, but that merely encouraged it; like a tiresome companion on a long journey; and this was not helped by sitting next to a man who was clearly losing it – when your time comes, you feared that those who would do the eulogy, who would pay tribute, would have to lie on your behalf. Maybe they wouldn't lie outright; but would have to de-emphasize certain traits and overstress others, the effect of which would be to lie. *A man is dead, that is the truth; call a lie a lie.* And you were sitting there thinking, while the Twenty-third Psalm was being sung, beautifully sung, and a poem by Martin Carter read, and a new poem by Kamau Brathwaite performed to perfection by the author, and the steel pan played – poem and steel pan done so expertly – you were sitting there thinking: I owe it to those who might give the eulogy on my behalf, who might pay tribute to the absent me, not to have to lie or go into contortions; so, in deference to them if nothing else, I would have to adjust the *balance* of my life, starting now. So that those folk – it would be better if they didn't know me too well – so that they wouldn't have to lie. And the thing to do now to effect that adjustment would be to stop thinking about myself for a moment and surrender to the present occasion; associate myself with the tributes paid to a friend who – ah – already wouldn't know that it was a sharp but pleasant spring morning in north London, not even raining.

And then at the graveyard ('yard'. Why 'yard'?) – at the graveyard, more tributes; the songs, the hymns. The selection was balanced; mildly surprising, initially, but not in retrospect, and, on reflection, there was a rightness to it, the tone faultless; the departed would have approved: there were the hymns, the carols ('Swing Low, Sweet Chariot'); but also there was Marley. And then after 'We would meet by the river some day' and the 'Union Song' and 'The International' (our man was a trades unionist, too), there was 'The Red Flag'.

II

That's when the warmth began to issue from the ground, countering the dampness. That's when – as I was thinking how right the 'sweet' in 'sweet chariot' seemed – that's when the sap from the ground started receding from shoes, stopped rising through feet; and after a quick glance at the prickling sound from nearby, I tried not to gaze at my new neighbour, whose voice was what the electric switch had suddenly turned on: the effect was a prickly blanket thrown over you, welcome but encouraging an itch. 'The people's flag is deepest red', had come to the rescue.

The accent was Scottish; the full-throated gush of the vowels making 'red' and 'dead' more than the tired old rhymes you remembered, a surging wave-like memory of something from the deep ocean urging itself against the shore; the fear and excitement like something expected but unknown made me chime in, like a student on a demonstration, with 'Then raise the scarlet standard high . . .' etc.

And yes, our man being buried, the radical Marxist, had once studied to be a Catholic priest (we had been reminded about that in the church: was his legendary even temper, then, more than personality?) and that added to the piquancy. But new, revised images of him had already crowded that out: the realization that he was not just a grandfather but a great-grandfather; his well-behaved-seeming great-grandchildren led up to the casket to say a dignified goodbye, prompting you to think that part of this man's luck was that he had founded a – what? – a tribe, a village, a community; and a man who had done so much might be expected to have some of his more familiar achievements – his knowledge of Spanish, of French, of Latin; his founding of a bookshop and a publishing house; his inauguration of a book fair – slip by you without undue reflection.

And so I embarrassed myself in the graveyard; and sang. I gave myself the usual silent telling-off for having fallen down so quickly on a resolution made an hour or so before in the church, not to appropriate this event; and, as usual, shifted the blame. I was lucky to put down this lapse in taste to glimpsing a tall man I hadn't seen in thirty years, maybe, also singing the chorus to 'The Red Flag'.

(So we need our funerals to bring us together, and I was thinking of a story by the Japanese writer, Haruki Murakami, a story about chance: the man in the story thinks of things and then they happen. He goes to a jazz club and wants the musician to play a couple of numbers not usually played, and without his requesting them, the musician duly plays the numbers. Then, in the same story, a man goes to a shopping mall one morning each week [this is in America] and spends part of the time quietly reading *Bleak House* in the café, and discovers that the woman sitting opposite him is also reading *Bleak House* [*she* discovers it, but the point that's being made is one of *chance*], and so on: the woman is about to have an operation for breast cancer; the man's sister – from whom he has been long estranged, no contact between them for years – then reveals, when he rings her on the spur of the moment, that *she* is about to have an operation for breast cancer, etc. All this came to me as I stood in the graveyard, and heard the Scottish [female] open-vowelled chimes of 'red' and 'dead', and glimpsed the tall man – a man I had not seen in perhaps thirty years – doing his best to upstage us all.)

Afterwards, we said the right things to each other – the man from the past whom we used to call Balham, and myself. Neither of us now lived in this country, I across the channel, he further afield; so it was no longer necessary to play the game of host and be seen through; and we could both take credit for that. We praised the other's health and bearing and robust look, perhaps not lying; and said the usual things of needing to meet on occasions not like this. And as we parted we knew that each was reviewing the last thirty years, weighing up the balance of advantage to himself.

This is like a footnote inserted in the story about a funeral. I had known Balham for close to fifty years; we had been to school together; we had done our GCEs at the same college in Kilburn. He wasn't part of the group that you hung out with after school, the unofficial 'reading club' in the common room where you had a go at Shakespeare, and were relieved that some of the jokes in that early part of The Tempest *were* attempts you might improve on; though you were impressed, you remember, by old Gonzalo's definition of 'Commonwealth' to his sceptical mates. No, Balham was less of a friend, then, more someone you sought out on occasion because he came, originally, from your part of the world. He was tall (yes, and he had aged well) and his pal – also from my part of the world, and doing his GCEs – was an amateur boxer; the combination of tall man and putative boxer giving them a certain – not cachet – a certain presence *in* the school. Tall man and boxer admired my wrestling with Latin verbs (conjugation conjugation) and, perhaps, my knowingness about Dickens and Chaucer; and they invited me to play tennis at their table. I always lost. That they occupied one of the communal tables longer than was appropriate was my argument, not always voiced, to explain away my losing; the embarrassment of hogging the table undermining my resolve. But it wasn't the table tennis that tested my loyalty to friends to whom I wasn't particularly close, it was the saying of grace at meal times.

Some of the boys at school pulled rank, hinting that fathers and uncles were paid monthly – or paid themselves monthly – rather than weekly and therefore had salaries, rather than wages. Or that an older brother or cousin at this or that college had already been fined for walking on the sacred grass in the quad, laid down centuries before; and that even those reading non-Classics at the university had to fall in line and say Latin grace at dinner time. Our

7

friends' response to this – our friends the tall man and the boxer – was to make a show of doing grace, at their lunch table in Kilburn, before tucking into their whatever-it-was and chips. The grace was sung. The first line of that particular song of praise was usually 'The people's flag was deepest red . . .' I, a loser at table tennis, accepted the loser's penalty and, at the dinner table, sang along. End of footnote.

When I collected myself in the graveyard and looked round at what had originated all this, the Scottish temptress had gone. (*She's on the train to Scotland. From London to Scotland. She will be on the train from Waterloo to Paris. No, she's on that earlier train from Sheffield to Edinburgh. I am sitting opposite, making a note for a story that won't get written. She's reading her book. At some point when the train stops at a station – Newcastle? Berwick? – she looks up . . .*)

III

At the reception – it may have been called something else – at the reception in another part of London, excellent curried goat was served, among other things; rice, so much food, what must it cost? At the reception more introductions with old friends; people looking splendid in their best clothes, pity about the occasion (though the thought had occurred, earlier, outside the church, that so many black people on the street, tastefully dressed, was a sort of statement that shouldn't be ignored). But here at the reception, duty done, the day 'enjoyed', I had started to say goodbye to the gathering – to head for bus, tube, train and home across the channel, hopefully in time for a late supper – when I again ran into Balham, only now coming in. He is smug, I think; there is something of the Cheshire cat on his face; he will make you work for an explanation. So instead of pressing, I point to the appropriate room and recommend the curried goat. *What could he have been up to?*

So, time to retract some of the goodbyes and to talk (again) of general matters. (Hours earlier, in the church, one had been drawing up pros and cons: imagine never again seeing a woman's smile? *That was worth dying for. That was worth, surely, all the opposites of dying for; never again choosing your toothpaste, packing, in anticipation to visit a new place; or just identifying strange shapes in the clouds with your grandchildren: surely, the fellows who wrote, who told the Bible stories must have led sad lives.* But then again, imagine never having to worry about money, about taking your medicines, about how Africa is to be irrigated, is to be governed; about whether your partner loved [loves] someone else? *That's consolation of sorts.* Now, the discipline was to avoid praising each others' achievements or to crow about the new more-distant places of residence.)

So we praise (again) the organization of this event.

We approve of the *balance* achieved: music, tributes, poetry, hymns, the Gregorian chant; the 'flawless' Latin.

We are impressed by the *rhythm* of the journeying: the move from church to graveyard to food, colonizing not just different bits of London *but so much space. (Reversing earlier journeyings? Mounting a subtle resistance against the too-easy move from life to death? Don't push it.)*

We praise the singing (and optimism) of black people (*who will not be deterred from burying their dead*).

We praise the singing (and fatalism) of black people (*who seem at their best on these occasions*).

We celebrate a remarkable man whose first public legacy in dying is to bring so many talents together. More than that, to occasion an event so huge in cultural import cutting across the absurdities of class and race, that this was, itself, the ultimate tribute. (*Would he were here to enjoy it.*)

At which point Balham reappears, with his plastic plate and fork, nodding approval of the curried goat.

We praise the curried goat; and apologize again for venturing a comment on the financial cost of funerals.

I had done enough. I had played the game. I had, symbolically, lost at table tennis again. So what had Balham been up to?

This is the story. Between the graveyard and the reception Balham went on a quest. He wormed his way – no, let's not be mean-spirited – he made his way back to the house of our dead friend: there were people there, of course, some family, friends, others helping to coordinate the event, to give directions on the phone; and maybe the odd person who didn't feel up to the graveyard, though the widow (a cruel, new word, new condition) – the widow turned out and commanded herself to be gracious.

So Balham had found his way back to the house, infiltrated the couple's library and rifled the man's private stock of books; at the end of which he had formulated a plan. The plan was to complete our friend's unfinished reading material. Balham had gone through the shelves, identified bookmarks and resolved to get to the end of those books – presumably, he selected some and rejected others – those books that our friend who had died had been unable (or unwilling) to complete. It was elegant, it was imaginative, it was *appropriate*. Not for the first time in my life I envied this ('lesser') man. He was no longer the somewhat embarrassing tall boy at school hogging the tennis table; he was no longer the dubious character reading sociology at university in Leicester and thinking himself a poet; he was now a man with a *conceit* that I envied. I wanted more detail about his programme of action.

His stratagem made us look conventional; all those earlier platitudes for a friend who was not that much older

than us; that mention of a father-figure, even as we resisted the notion of the father-figure for we were at the age
when such an idea was worryingly close to the trans-
cendental. It had been easy to agree that he had been a
substantial presence *out there*, in the vanguard, as we say.
If it was true that he had not exactly shielded us, not quite
making us more secure or safe, hadn't he at least made us
more confident in our temptation to articulate a contrary
view, to protest against the unacceptable? And with his
removal didn't we now all have to inch forward and fill a
little gap that had opened up; and didn't that put on us the
onus to speak out more confidently, in our own voice?
Yes, yes and *yes*. But these were the normal things you
said on these occasions. Now Balham had gone further.

And still he made me leave without satisfaction. I couldn't
directly ask about authors and titles he might now be reading
– as a form of what? More than remembrance. Maybe bene-
diction. So I left without a clear list of books he proposed to
read to complete our friend's cycle of literary interest. I
had no wish to emulate Balham. (I would, perhaps, have
preferred to choose to read, in remembrance, something
that the man must have enjoyed, *Anna Karenina*, say.) But
I felt my curiosity about titles and authors somewhat vulgar in the light of the tall man's more magisterial concept.
He did let slip that there was 'a thing on Hugo Chávez and
Castro and the New American Revolution' as one of the
unfinished books. Difficult to establish whether that was a
title or a description of a political monograph. Then there
was mention of the pile of political pamphlets by the bedside table, presumably not yet read. (He didn't reveal the
titles of those pamphlets which would now be read in case
they had not been read.) Another book casually mentioned
in this context was something about travellers across *cultures* but he didn't name an author. He mentioned Heidegger
and Sartre, but not whether philosophy or biography; and

other authors he named included Naipaul, Monica Ali and Robert Antoni: he didn't specify the books. And did the clutch of random-seeming names – Martin Carter, Dickens, the Holy Bible – mean that there would be no form of selection by the reader? An interesting detail was the mention of the diaries of an Englishman who had run the National Trust. (I was later to identify him as James Lees-Milne. Curious.) But then again: could the Dickens have been *Bleak House*?

On the way to the station I found that the original excitement of Balham's idea started to fade: there were too many unanswered questions. Bookmarks are sometimes left in books by accident. What then? How did we know that our friend had intended to read those books to completion? He was a publisher, after all; he may have been just checking things in some of the books. Or parking the bookmark accidentally. Also, he wasn't alone in the house: what of the wife's, the widow's taste in reading: some of the marked books might be hers. Would it be ethical to be reading *her* books through to the end while she was alive? Wasn't that akin to finishing her sentences?

Even though I told myself that none of this might matter – the concept being the thing – that what Balham had initiated was something generous, different in spirit from the thing that a musician, say, might do in completing someone else's score, for that was public collaboration, your name was on the finished product, it was paying homage, but also self-serving. The same as with an architect finishing someone else's great building, for the building would be there as witness. So though Balham's homage would be altogether more subtle than that, yet . . . there was still something that smacked of imposing your will on the dead man. What if he had decided that he had had enough of the book in question and didn't want to pursue it? To force a man to read to the end, by proxy, a book of which he is already bored, is to play a trick on someone who can't defend himself; worse, really, than forcing a child to eat his greens; for the child's protests are likely to be loud. Was this really as generous as it seemed?

It would be against the spirit of the resolution made in the church to compete with Balham (to upstage or undermine him); that early resolution about the reining in of 'self' had to mean something.

I was at home, scanning my own shelves, checking the bookmarks: I would complete *Moby Dick*, I had always promised to complete *Moby Dick*, and would do so, whether a friend were alive or dead: that extraordinary sermon early on, and the image of Queequeg, first encountered forty years ago, needed to be re-engaged with. But what of *Britain's Royal Families* with the bookmark on page 178? In the middle of a chapter on 'The Kings and Queens of Scotland'? The bookmark was between the penultimate and last pages suggesting that the chapter hadn't been quite completed (or the bookmark would be over the page; though I had presumably got through the kings, from Alpin to Kenneth II, for whatever reason). What else? The bookmark in the hardback copy of Philip Roth's hugely anticipated *The Plot Against America* was recent and temporary, soon to be moved forward; the one in Boccaccio lodged at the 'Seventh Story' (which one was that?) brought nothing back to mind, though, with Plato, the marker between the much-read *Symposium* and the examined-in-the-distant-past *Republic* was one I would wish my bearer of tributes to pass comment on. What did this tell us: that one's random reading was relatively broad but that one's attention span was possibly short? Would completing these books be akin to tidying, to cleaning up the life? Was the dead man's life as untidy as mine? And was that a lesson for me to get on with it and get my act together? The small panic is with the books not started. *Dr Johnson's Dictionary: The Extraordinary Story of the Book that Defined the World* by Henry Hitchings, long on my desk, must be started just in case, as with Michael Holroyd's much-deferred biography of Augustus John. What of the five-volume *A History of Women*, a decade on the shelves, only glanced at, shifted from one address to another, perhaps to demonstrate that the interest was long-standing. *This must not be overlooked by the one bearing tribute* . . . Oh, this is crazy.

In the bookshop yesterday I bought a copy of Ortega y Gasset's *The Revolt of the Masses*. (In my half-hearted attempt to represent that 'pile of political pamphlets by the bedside', I had pulled from . . . here and there, Terry Eagleton's *The Crisis of Contemporary Culture*, and *Africa in the Shadow of Clash of Civilizations*, by Ali Mazrui, along with *United States Intervention in Jamaica: How Washington Toppled the Manley Government* [by someone called Ernest Harsch], and a few others: it had all seemed so insubstantial.) I had once heard a colleague at work mention that Ortega y Gasset had anticipated both Sartre and before him, Heidegger. That was a sort of interest my friend, who had died, might have wished to pursue. (I had heard him talk quite knowledgeably, to a charming Italian friend, about Gramsci.) So, I'll add Ortega y Gasset to my list, if only to concentrate someone's mind. This is not an entirely attractive train of thought to encourage, given its more elevated beginnings, so I'll disguise it for anyone eavesdropping by pretending it to be a game. I'll give it a misleading working title, something like, 'The Restoration of Scotland to the Commonwealth', to buy a bit of breathing space.

Two

2

At Home with Miss Vanesa

THE FIRST SONG

*O*h, it wasn't a song in the usual sense, no lyrics, no warbling from the verandah into the night air; just the necessary singing, singing for your supper. So what was not put to music that first night was the theme of death, death made lyrical. And Miss Vanesa would set the lead by saying that, yes, in England, we were running into a time when all our friends were dying, and even if they weren't our friends, as they had come to the country more or less the same time as we had – the 1950s – and were at the age now when they were dying . . .

Funerals, funerals everywhere.

Funerals, funerals everywhere . . .

As that was happening you had to see those who were dying as friends, you had to think of them as part of the extended family; you had to be sorry, indeed, that they had chosen to end their days in a country that had never taken them to its heart.

If it ever had a heart.

If it ever had a heart.

And don't get her wrong, Miss Vanesa was not sentimental; no one had ever accused her of being sentimental –

they had even badmouthed her for putting her father into a Home in England. And, yes, you had to be buried – buried, cremated, whatever – disposed of somehow, if only in the interest of hygiene. And that was a sad end to something as demanding as a human body.

And Pewter, agreeing, told a story of visiting a hospital for a minor matter; and there was he sitting on the bench, waiting, with all these sick people. For you don't realize that you're really sick until you go to the hospital and find yourself among all those sick people. There should be a better way in these places, to separate the slightly sick from the really sick.

There should be a better way.

Short of segregation in a . . .

No, not in a fascist way.

No, that's not our way.

And this old man, West Indian, big, solid, but old, slow and stiff-legged, comes in and sits next to Pewter on the bench; and they have a little chat – as you do. And after their little chat the old guy sighs and says to him – thinks for a bit and says to him:

Yes, sah: when we came here we were young men.

When we came here we were young men.

Even the women were young men.

At least you still have your sense of humour.

When on the island Pewter had arranged to stay with Miss Vanesa; he wasn't a particular friend of hers, though he had known her early on; but it seemed discourteous to decline the offer of accommodation; it would only be for about four days, on his way to Barbados, or on his way back from Barbados. And Miss Vanesa lived in one of those popular Heritage houses that Pewter, too, had been associated with. His sister, on another island, herself a returnee, also lived in a Heritage house. Miss Vanesa wrote plays but insisted on being called a novelist, and had started a reading group on the island, a book club. She had had a play published but her mind was set on being a novelist. That's why Pewter prepared himself – knowing he'd be spending four days with her – by tracking down her novel manuscript in Birmingham, and having a read of it. He imagined their conversations, on the verandah of her house on the island, comparing successful and less successful novelists, as well as the playwrights, and being shamelessly bitchy. That's his idea of what should take place on the verandah of a Heritage house.

The novel manuscript was still held at her old university, pending revision. It had been supervised – either supervised or assessed – by someone Pewter knew, but he probably wouldn't admit this to Miss Vanesa.

So the novel existed. This was not the case of someone sitting here on her verandah all the while claiming to have been Queen of England without giving any hint of the date of your accession or the year of your state funeral. Though, of course, Miss Vanesa was very much alive – and not even an old woman at that. And talk of her being a fraud was unkind in another sense because bits of the novel had been published in a magazine in England and in a couple of places back home. So the evidence was there. But Miss Vanesa wasn't out to persuade: either you accepted that she was a novelist or you didn't. She had never kowtowed to people in England during her long years of residence in that country; nor was she prepared to do that now to the jackarses on the island. (Here you had to live a life of censorship: if you were driving along a country road, in the afternoon after the rain, and you happened to be in a reflective mood at the too-sexual greenness of everything; and you were with a friend, and you expressed your feelings about the greenness of things, and wondered if it wasn't better to live in places where leaves changed colour and fell in the autumn, they would look at you as if this was a woman thing, and you were in need of counselling.) But then the jackarses here were no worse than the Secret Racist Society at the university over there who, when they read her novel, having run out of excuses for failing it, had charged her with an excess of sensibility. In the days when she bothered to discuss these things she would pose the simple question: how does a woman, sensitive to lewd glances and conversations inside the heads of strangers and passers-by, aware of the glances as she went about her business, and the silent conversations she had no difficulty providing a voice-over for – how was she not to be in a heightened state of awareness *as her normal mode*? She was a woman. And colour would be a feature in this: to internalize and acknowledge all that 'consciousness' didn't seem to her as 'excess'.

He wasn't put in the spare room but in the second bedroom. The spare room where the iron was, was an all-purpose storeroom, with prints (and some original paintings) stacked against the wall, unopened boxes; a bookcase, obviously reflecting something of Miss Vanesa's past literary life: Portuguese novels, plays in English, including one well-annotated copy of Brecht's *The Caucasian Chalk Circle*, with copious acting notes, presumably in Miss Vanesa's hand. In one corner, on the floor, was a magnificent chess set, made of whitish glass.

But he was wary of asking Miss Vanesa too many questions because of a casual remark she had made earlier. They had been having a drink on the verandah with Pewter admiring the view, the sea in the distance – all that; and Miss Vanesa told him he would be the guest of honour at the monthly gathering of the reading group, in a couple of days' time. But she had expressed in passing the need for people in the islands to respect themselves, not in the foolish old-time way of boasting about living in a big house, or being light skinned, but in a new way of not being taken in by the charlatans who came swanning in from the big cities, from the metropolitan centres. She had been impressed by her visit to the St Lucian Reading Group to find them totally relaxed about having had in their midst the likes of Walcott and Garth St Omer, so the little forceripe boys coming in with their PhDs from America and Canada didn't confuse anyone. Pewter had thought to add Arthur Lewis, the 'Nobel' economist, to the list of distinguished St Lucians insulating the people against the wideboys from North America; but he didn't want to appropriate Miss Vanesa's argument. So they talked a bit more about the reading groups. The members took it in turns to host the meetings every month, and Miss Vanesa warned Pewter he would be expected to say a few words to them, as her guest.

'Pity you'll be missing Fred,' she said, somewhat tauntingly.

'Fred?'

'Yes, my good friend, Winifred. She's active with the Tourist Board. She –'

'Ah! A lady!'

'Winifred. Member of the book club. Knows a lot about plants and science. She's visiting family down in Martinique. Nice-looking woman, Fred; French background; you'd love her.'

And they talked a bit about Fred.

Before going to see his sister Pewter would be heading south for Barbados to give a bit of moral support to an old friend who was struggling to recover his library, destroyed by hurricane and flood, so even though these visits were private now he felt almost as stressed as when he used to come through to do this or that at the university centres. Apparently, these were now struggling to find audiences because people complained about the security situation, with their having to come out at night, in the dark.

*

In England, Miss Vanesa had taken one of those creative writing degree courses. Having got through the MA she had embarked on the practice-based PhD, where you had to produce a full-length literary work as well as a substantial theoretical commentary to show how the scholarly and the imaginative disciplines complemented each other. She had, as Pewter found out, fallen down on both parts. The mark-sheets, though generous in praising aspects of the novel, were nevertheless quite unambiguous about its defects. And, yes, one phrase that was used was 'excess of sensibility'. It is said that an incensed Miss Vanesa had asked her tutor if the same examiners, given the chance, would have accused the great Virginia Woolf of excess of sensibility. But then Miss Vanesa was a black woman, and before that a black girl growing up in England, and everyone knows such a person was not allowed 'sensibility'. She made a vow to herself not to mention the injustice in Pewter Stapleton's hearing but just to treat it as water, water flowing off her back, as if she were a duck.

They didn't know the simplest things, like how, at school, she had had to negotiate what to feel when they pronounced her name. She had been born in the West Indies, in the Caribbean, and had always been called Vanessa. It was not until she went to school in England and they discovered that her name was spelt Vanesa – one 's' not two – that the teachers insisted that she be called by something else. You couldn't tell them at home that her name had changed, and you couldn't own up at school that maybe someone in your house couldn't spell your name;

so at school she answered to one sound and at home to another. She had written about this in her MA novel (alas, unpublished). She had written about the dilemma of liking the name her mother called her but of accepting that the teacher knew best: and was that, too, 'excess of sensibility'?

She had explored her two identities, a Vanesa at school who believed that there was a reason for everything that happened, good or bad, so that when you were raped and mugged and killed in the street, you should ask the reason why people who were otherwise normal were doing this to you. And then at home she would accept the Vanessa who said that when you were raped and mugged and killed you should find a way to punish the abuser.

Beat him. Put him in prison. And then hang him. An eye for an eye, as in the Bible.

After she had been mugged in England – and in broad daylight – she had no hesitation in going along with that Vanessa.

II

Miss Vanesa played chess; for there was a second set in the sitting room. But what exercised Pewter was this arbitrary 'remake' of the house, as if assembling its furnishings was something you did on your various wanderings round the world, grabbing what came to hand. And he began to wonder if that's what Heritage meant to him, too – a chess set as a declaration of intent. As if you were saying the game played here wasn't cards or, whatever, dominoes by the old men – the young men – outside the rumshops in your youth. Then he lost the thought.

And he was thinking of rejection letters; not in a sense of anger or bitterness, for this was a lyrical moment on the verandah, though they were inside, relaxing in Miss Vanesa's comfortable chairs – 'Made by a little man here, y'know, little rasta man who knows his carpentry, his joinery; you don't have to play the arse and import everything.'

He was thinking of rejection slips he'd had over the years, over the decades, wondering when a mass of rejection slips got to the point when it was no longer interesting to count them. Then they acquired critical mass, changed from number to amount. *And did he then wear that amount on his sleeve, in his posture, his gait – in the sound of his voice, the sharpness of his reply? Or did he just let rejection slips slip themselves into his name, Pewter Rejection Slips Stapleton, to show he could live with the condition, to show that his back was as broad as – broad as his host's ill-defined discontent.*

Sorry I . . .

What would you do?

So he had to suffer the embarrassment of asking her to repeat the question, which she did, as if she were accustomed not to be listened to.

So if he went to the hospital to visit someone, a neighbour, say, and he couldn't remember the man's second name; but it was, y'know, one of those places that wouldn't let you in to the ward without the patient's name; so he had to make up a name on the spur of the moment; and then he was admitted, and shown to the bed of a perfect stranger: would he be relieved that there were people enough in the world so that any name you thought up would fit someone? Or would you be depressed that all the names in the world were already taken?

And Pewter had to think about that; and he thought if

she were a different kind of person that question would be
an invitation to having sex now that the supper was over;
but they would have to work to steer clear of that. So in
the end he said, yes, it was depressing that not only were
the names taken, but that the one you conjured up was
likely to be lying in a hospital bed, near where you lived.

And Miss Vanesa looked at him for an extra second and
called him a philosopher.

The names you called people. A lot of people had been
reduced to ordinariness by taking on safer names when
they left the island. Take Pam*ela*. Pam*ela* would have
grown up, grown to womanhood, and made love with
someone calling her by that name. Suddenly, she finds
herself in England where everyone called her something
else, *Pam*ela, as if she were something sanitized and coming out of Jane Austen – or, if you like, Samuel Richard-
son: surely, after that she would have to make love – she
would expect to make love – *differently*. Just because the
racists didn't want to talk about these things it didn't
mean that they weren't real to the people living them. And
she reckoned that was the problem between her generation
and the younger ones. People of the nieces' generation,
born in England, not caring about heritage, except some
nonsense coming out of black America – as if, among their
many handicaps, what a black person needed to take on
was the burden of being 'ethnic'. But coming back to the
nieces: if you asked them who their friends were and you
found out they were people with low IQ – or low self-
esteem – who didn't respect themselves; in academic terms,
they were the sorts of people who limped through university (if that!) with a low 2.ii or a Third, and if you
merely said to the girls, 'You can't do a little better than
that?' they were going to turn round and *cuss* you.

Because they're English people; though their skin is

black. They look at you as if you're strange, foreign; they call you names behind your back. When your own called you names behind your back why shouldn't the enemy call you names to your face?

The first to arrive at Miss Vanesa's open-air gathering were the Professor and Arwell, a returnee, like Miss Vanesa, repatriated from St Caesare. The Professor was in his own place, a man of stately gait, carrying a couple of plastic bags. Miss Vanesa greeted them as they fiddled with the gate and told them to come in, come in.

'Where's Janine today?' she asked the Professor.

'She staying at home, she . . . she not feeling too well.'

'I sorry to hear it.'

They came in, shut the gate and welcomed Pewter to the island. The Professor paused and looked around with a proprietorial air and again commended Miss Vanesa's view – of the hills, the sea – from the terrace.

'This is what we leave England for.' A vague but wide gesture. 'No millionaire nor prime minister in England wake up to a view like this.'

As they walked, flat-heeled, up the verandah to where Miss Vanesa and Pewter stood, the Professor suddenly did what Pewter could only describe as the Ali scuffle.

'You still doing that foolishness, Barrington?'

'Natural flow.'

'Once in the army, always in the army,' the other man said, obviously his party-line.

'Always used to have to do that when you crossing the bridge. Break the stride.' This seemed to be for Pewter's benefit. 'And when you come down to it, you know, a gallery, a verandah this high off the ground, is just another bridge subject to natural flow.'

'Yes, we all know about the Tacoma Bridge,' Miss Vanesa said.

'Washington State. 1940.'

'Now you've got that off your chest, you can all come in.'

Pewter was lost in all of this, though he knew the man by reputation. The Professor had handed over the two plastic bags, one with a couple of bottles of alcohol and the other, clearly with some sort of food, in a dish.

'Janine can't come,' he said to Miss Vanesa, 'so she send this.'

'She shouldn't have bothered; is her company we want. She's down with something?'

'Oh, just the hip and . . . the pills not working too well.'

'I'm sorry.'

And then it was time for introductions. The Professor turned to Pewter.

'So what's your story, young man? You look to me like a man who knows the answer to a conundrum.'

Among the other returnees to arrive was Nora, a rather distinguished woman from Montserrat. She, too, brought something for the kitchen; and warned Miss Vanesa not to overdo it with the food, as there were some low-life people around who only came to your place to eat you out of house and home. And then someone, a member of the book club, asked Pewter if he had read Toni Morrison's *The Bluest Eye*. He soon began to feel a bit of a fraud as he was being introduced to these people as if he had something new to tell them. He couldn't help noticing, though, the distinctness of everyone's accents – and idiom; and he filed away a little note for himself to do better with his written dialogue.

The tables laid out on the verandah were occupied, but down in the garden the guests were relaxing and exchanging pleasantries. Pewter had helped a bit but Miss Vanesa had

had a woman there since early morning, who was seeing to things. Millie was said to have had a son at university in England studying medicine, but she downplayed Pewter's attempts to talk too much about it. Earlier that morning Pewter had heard some music, a guitar, someone playing chords. And he had looked out and seen Millie in the yard hanging up some wet clothes on the line. As the music had stopped by then, Pewter had had a few surreal moments putting two and two together.

There was also help for Miss Vanesa from an unlikely quarter: two lads who had been clearing the patch of land next door were pressed into service to help Millie lay out the chairs and tables in the garden. They brought their cut-lasses with them, and Pewter wondered if he was the only one who didn't much like the look of that.

People arrived with cooked dishes, so Miss Vanesa and Millie didn't have to spend half the day in the kitchen.

'Is how they does do it in Italy,' someone said, referring to the bringing of food to the party, 'in writing circles over there. Everyone bring a favourite dish.'

Someone agreed but said that this wasn't a million miles away from the old Maroon system they used to have when he was a child growing up here; people coming to clear a piece of land, and the man of the house, or the woman of the house preparing a big cook-up for everyone.

A banquet.

We had lost that sense of togetherness, someone said.

Once you lose that there's no way you can get it back.

But the Italian theme was taken up. Someone, a woman, was explaining about Chianti. It was a wine, of course, but it was also a place; it was in the place they called Tus-cany, which is where Tony Blair used to go on holiday with his family. But though the wines were all labelled Chianti, they weren't all the same wine. Just as not all rum is the same rum.

Someone said that that's what they drank in that film, *The Silence of the Lambs.* Chianti. And everyone gave a little shudder and changed the subject.

Pewter circulated, hovered to listen, sometimes joined in, saying that this was, indeed, the narrative verandah idea in action. Now, they were talking about who should or should not be allowed to vote in the British elections, and the Euro-elections; or why Iran and South Africa should not be denied their nuclear ambitions, though people here didn't trust North Korea; and someone was pointing out that, since 1945, America had made war only on dark-skinned people, so it was important for dark-skinned people to have their bomb – and did they hear about the latest, the Grenadian boy from Ipswich who was killed in Iraq? By a suicide bomber. Pewter went past two women sharing confidences, asserting very loudly their private fears, talking about 'the terror' of discovering something in the bathroom mirror and taking the anxiety to your doctor, and having to wait for the doctor to send abroad for a second opinion. But though loudly expressed this was not for Pewter's ears, for when he hesitated, not sure whether to join in the conversation, the body language shifted, and Nora, whom he had met earlier, acknowledged him with great courtesy, smoothly introducing a new subject for his benefit. So he took the hint and soon moved on. Somewhere in his hearing was the Professor reflecting on what seemed mediaeval punishments for wife-beaters and other vicious criminals that they were sending back to the islands from abroad: if the state was too timid to hang them, they should at least keep them in the big countries so that they couldn't contaminate the entire island population: what was Pewter's view?

If Miss Vanesa wanted him to say something to this gathering, he had to be sure to get the tone right, he was thinking to himself.

But he wasn't allowed reflection. It was the Professor, again. Though it was the man with the Professor, the one they called Arwell, Pewter's fellow islander who seemed to be eyeing him quizzically. Though Arwell said very little, he seemed judgemental; so, what was it now?

This time it was a question about the Trojan Horse. Was it the horse or the men inside the horse who were Trojan?

'It had a fella in these parts they used to call Trojan,' someone said. A preacher.

Someone corrected him, claiming that the preacher's name was Legon, not Trojan.

Pewter found himself saying something vague about Troy and Greece, without straying into name-calling, no Hector, no Achilles. And hoped, in the end, he had made a passable joke about it.

The boys who had been clearing the land next door and had helped with setting out the furniture now formally joined the party, and one of them was asked to play the guitar. They were quiet and respectful, listening to the adults talking about their experience abroad, and the fact that most of them from England had free passes on the London Underground because they hadn't sold their properties in London and visited regularly impressed the lads, who listened quietly and stuck to soft drinks, mainly Cokes, and modest helpings of food.

Pewter paused at one table where a youngish, pretty woman was explaining to her companions why she had had to leave England.

'Is when you have to throw way the second chicken, I can't take it.'

'What you mean, throw way the second chicken?'

'You know, like when you go to the supermarket, they give you two for the price of one.'

'Oh, when it's near the sell-by date.'

'That or whatever. When they have them and they have to get rid of them, and they offer you two for the price of one.'

'They do that with the women in Poland and –'

'Behave youself, man.'

'Shut up, Barry.'

'Sorry I open my mouth.' So the woman was allowed to continue her story about shopping at the supermarket.

'Two for the price of one. Or two for five pounds or something like that, when one would have cost you £3.95. And is always too much, when you're cooking for one; or even for two. Or if it have a case where there's a vegetarian in the house.'

'Lot of young people now turn vegetarian, you know; is the fashion. Not like the old days.'

'Old days gone, boy.'

'Old days gone.'

'And I say to myself,' the woman with the chicken story continued. 'Girl, what wickedness is this? Twice in two weeks, you know, I have to throw way the second chicken.'

'I know the feeling, child; it make you feel like a criminal who abuse children.'

'I have to throw it away. Because no point eating bad food just because you want to save the planet.'

'Those societies are out of order, man.'

'I had food poisoning once, boy,' a man interjected. 'If you can survive that you're a better man than me.'

'But you survive it, Barry; you survive.'

'No, I don't survive.' The man was indignant. 'The body not made to survive a thing like that.'

'And I say to myself' – the woman hadn't finished telling her chicken story – 'I say, Pearl, what sort of society are you living in, where I have a perfectly good chicken, and I don't have anybody to give that chicken to so they could cook it and eat it before it spoil? Even if you know your neighbours in England you can't insult them by giving them the extra chicken. They goin' cuss you, you know.'

'They cuss you, cuss you back to where you come from.'

'And I say to myself, Pearl: with all the starvation and misery in this world, here I am, twice in two weeks throwing away a chicken because they say you mustn't eat it after a certain date. And I think what sort of evil thing is this that I'm doing; and I tell you I shame to be acting so much like a brute. And I know I have to get out of that society. However hard it going to be over here. People bad-minded and worthless over here, I know that. They grudge you because you have maybe one or two little things to put in your house that they don't have. But I say to myself, if I have a extra chicken here, nobody going cuss you if you say to them: I make a mistake and buy two chicken for the price of one, you better take this home and cook it before it spoil.'

'When things get that bad, you know,' someone agreed, 'you have to leave. You just have to come home.'

'You have to come home.'

'You have to come home.'

But this was interrupted by some sort of contretemps at another table – the tables were being constantly moved around to keep the guests in the shade – and, again, it was the Professor and Arwell in their new position, with the two young boys from the field next door; still in respectful attendance.

The raised voices seemed insistent enough, even after they returned to natural pitch, so everybody was aware that something had happened; and Miss Vanesa appeared at the edge of the verandah and urged the boy to play something on the guitar. That immediately eased the tension, someone urging the boy to sing for his supper. And the boy, doing what he was told, took up the guitar and started to tune up.

But Arwell was speaking to Pewter: he had a book with lots of common phrases like 'Singing for your supper', and a lot of them were coined by black people. Though the racist people over in England liked to give them all to Shakespeare: wasn't that right, Professor? (This was directed at Pewter.) But Pewter was again wary, because someone said that Arwell had been into local politics in England and Pewter felt an edge of competition. So he answered with an ambiguous but friendly gesture. Meanwhile, others were calling out requests to the guitar player.

'You know the one by the Platters: "The Great Pretender"?'

'Wrong generation, man.'

'Generation gap.'

Someone else started to hum, 'Goodnight Irene', a tune that was taken up by a couple of others. '*Irene goodnight. I'll see you in my dreams.*'

'That's old-time song, man.'

'How about the Krueger warehouse song? The calypso. After the hurricane.'

'Miss Vanesa don't want no nastiness and criminality in she place, man.'

Someone was already singing the line: '*Mister Krueger, what HAVE you got in your warehouse, Sah? Tell me Mister Krueger.*'

'Krueger is something else, boy.'

And the boy, having tuned up, started to accompany himself, light and easy, with a song no one seemed to know. He sang: '*My father always promised us that we would live in France . . .*'

He was listened to in respectful silence. Then someone said, approvingly: 'Judy Collins.' After which the boy sang: 'Bridge over Troubled Water'.

And the applause at the end seemed reflective.

'Boy serious, man,' was the verdict that no one contested.

At the start of the next number, which was the Beatles' 'Let it Be', Miss Vanesa sidled over to Pewter and demanded: 'Maas Pewter, you going dance with me?'

'They make a nice couple,' Nora was heard to say.

So, on the verandah, they started to dance to the number; everyone applauded. At the end, the dancing couple was praised; and the musicians, too (his friend having joined in); everyone agreeing they should have a recording contract in England. (The person calling for Miss Dynamite was ignored.)

And now Pewter couldn't get out of saying a few words to the gathering. He was still not sure how to pitch it: would a reference to Eric Williams and the University of Woodford Square, back in the days before Trinidad independence, be in order? When he was last in France friends were talking of the new *café-philo* phenomenon – a gathering of like-minded people in the café to make intelligent conversation. But what was happening here was more – what? More *something in the making*. He was on the verandah looking down; so he'd just better get on with it; he cleared his throat:

'As you can see, I'm not a dancer.' He basked in the protests and started again. 'Miss Vanesa says I must say something. And the first thing to say is to thank Miss Vanesa for arranging this magnificent gathering.' And to this there were 'hear hear's and claps. 'Including the musical accompaniment.'

More applause.

'I feel a bit of a fraud,' Pewter continued, 'standing up here, y'know . . . with people who, in one way or other have been successful in their life. Brought up their children. Suffered the . . . ah, challenge of having lived abroad. So. So don't expect, y'know . . . words of wisdom or . . . wild adventures where I end up at the top of the mountain . . .'

'We've been to the mountain top.' From the Professor.

Pewter thought, briefly, of a friend of his, now in Mozambique, who had flown Concorde; but turning to the audience, he found himself again upstaged.

'We've been to the mountain top.'

'Yes. Y'know, even if you were talking of something simple like . . . climbing Everest. Like I've never claimed to have ended up prime minister of this or that country.'

'You qualify.'

'You are qualified.'

'Thank you; thank you. Or anything like that. But I'm sensitive to the fact that, y'know, this is a Heritage house. A Heritage house is supposed to remind us of some link with the past. Links with the past we're in danger of . . . well, we're supposed to have lost. Yes. So our house isn't just an up-market bit of . . . reinforced concrete, however nice-looking. We have an old phrase, don't we? The narrative verandah, which is where you used to sit out at night and tell stories. Remember, even in your imagination, you're doing that. Some of you will recall Mr Biswas in Mr Naipaul's *A House for Mr Biswas*. When he dreams of his house the verandah is the first thing that he sees: it's the space that links all the other areas of the house. There's a rocking-chair on the verandah. It's like the one prop on the stage, where you sit down and tell the story. But to come back to us. When you're a child growing up here, you remember listening to the adults telling their stories. We didn't have that in London or Birmingham or Leeds or . . . Toronto. And those who stayed here were conscious all the time of living out our friend Andrew Salkey's 'sea-split family' syndrome, getting more and more resentful. Feeling left out. Back then the grown-ups would talk about family abroad. Family in Cuba and Haiti. And occasionally when one of those who were abroad visited, you'd say: Say something in Spanish, Uncle George. Uncle Mike. In Spanish. In French. Even in Dutch, because some went down to Curaçao. Aruba. It was usually the father. Or an uncle. Sometimes a great uncle. And there was a romance to being abroad in the days before we ourselves experienced "abroad".'

'England was a lot of things but it wasn't romance,' someone said.

'I thought you had a good time over there with the ladies,' his partner observed.

'I hear you.'

'Is what I hear.'

'I hear you.'

Pewter tried to get a grip on his theme. 'But I'm not here to complain,' he said. 'I told Miss Vanesa that I'd try to tell a story that I hope to write down one day. About a little island here. A hurricane. A volcano. People scattered. People fleeing. Leaving house and everything behind. The yard they grow up in with the fruit trees, the grafted mango and breadfruit and sugarapple. Guava. You're bound to leave the odd chicken that's going to be laying eggs after you've gone. All that.' He could hear himself talking; he forgot what he was saying. Oh yes. People fleeing natural disaster.

'But some staying put.' He hoped that that would sound like a bit of dialect. 'Refusing to go, despite the advice of the experts. And the way people managed to come through without . . . in a sense . . . coming through.' He should stop now.

He stopped: he was in danger of becoming one of those visiting wideboys with their PhDs. He had to recapture their attention. With a joke.

'Some people say that a story should always have a title. So I'm calling this one "The Loss of Naples". Most of us have lived abroad and come back. Whatever our experiences there's a little bit of nostalgia for over there. And I like to think Naples – y'know "See Naples and Die" . . . I like to think "Naples" represents not just Italy but that little bit of nostalgia for us, whether we've been to Italy or not. Of course, in Miss Vanesa's case it was Lisbon – apart from England.

'But, you know, we're not naïve people, we're too old for that. If we follow the poet and divide experience into Before and After; between Innocence and Experience . . .'

'Like the poet.'

'Like the poet . . . well, then, we represent the Experience wing of things. So, you know, when I think of Naples and all the good things, I also think of the volcano they had there many centuries ago which turned the villages of Pompeii and Herculaneum at the foot of the hill into a museum. Museums.'

'Like what happen in Montserrat and St Caesare.'

'Like what happened in Montserrat and St Caesare.'

He was drifting; he was talking nonsense like the nonsense others talked. He was talking about a Heritage house as if the homes built for people after the hurricane and volcano were designs laid out in the architectural schools of some university department far away that had studied the effects of hurricane and volcano. His mind flitted to something Miss Vanesa had said about the spare room and her pictures – which were mainly classical prints of the Impressionists and whatnot: had Pewter noticed that so many of the art galleries in England and Europe had black men and women guarding the treasures? So where was the literature of all these, in effect, black trainee-curators sitting down there day after day absorbing the world's art? Black cooks were popping up all over the place on television telling us how to cook – as if we didn't know how to cook: where were the black people from the galleries talking about art? Pewter had a wicked thought that this must be the subject of Miss Vanesa's next novel. He had to

*check himself and think back to a real situation, his visit
to the island a week after the hurricane, in 1989. He had
walked out of his friend's villa and into the wreckage, and
confronted this woman whom he knew; someone who had
worked for the family. And turned on his tape-recorder. It
was Nellie: she was getting ready for church, it was a
Saturday; but she was in good humour. The roof and one
side of her house had been severely damaged; but the dress
for church, fluttering on the line outside, was spotless,
creaseless. Was this when the Heritage house idea took
shape in his mind?*

We don't have any water yet. (The woman wasn't aware
of the tape-recorder hidden in the carrier-bag.) *We have to
carry little water in bottles and buckets and so . . . and
then we have to boil it. Otherwise to that we praise God.
The next morning, the morning after the hurricane, you
know, when I saw the plane and helicopter flying flat, low
down to see what is happening, we can't believe – even
one lady who see it on the TV in England and come here
and say the same thing – we can't believe it's Codrington
that . . . Some of them get plastic to put on the roof. But
me don't have anybody to get me plastic. I get a little help
to pick up some old galvanize, and pound them out; and
we use a little tar to block up the holes, and that have to
do till we get some help. But me thank God that we still
alive. It could have been worse.*

'Liming.'
　'What?'
　'Liming, boy. Semilime. Liming.' An old hand, back to
the present.
　'Lewe listen to what the man saying.'
　That jogged Pewter back into his story about the loss of
Naples. He would put Pliny the Elder in his story, and

quote from the *Historia Naturalis* but he wouldn't talk about that now.

'So this is a post-volcano story,' he said self-consciously. 'I think a place should be found in the story for . . . Miss Frances, forget her name, who took care of all the animals.'

'Tuitt.'

'That's it; Miss Frances Tuitt who started the rounding up of the domestic pets so that they could be shipped off to Canada for safe keeping.'

'She wanted to take lizard as well, you know; she eccentric.'

'Course, she eccentric.'

'All them woman who live on they own eccentric.'

'There's room in the story for eccentric people,' Pewter said. Then he modified it. 'For an eccentric person.'

'Is the wild dogs they should be shipping out.'

'It have a lot of wild dogs round the place; the place not safe.'

'And some of the wild dogs, they walking round on two feet.'

'But it gives the lie,' Pewter continued, 'that it's only the English who care about their domestic animals.' And it was really time to wind up.

'So it's good that we can get together from time to time like this,' Pewter wound down, 'not to have one person preaching at the rest of us as if we're in church, but just to chat, to share experiences.'

'To lime.'

'To lime. We've all been through the . . . storm one way or other and come out the other side. And it's good to get together from time to time – like this – to have a little drink to our escape.'

The suggestion of applause saved him; he stopped, and heard more applause.

Miss Vanesa applauded, came forward, kissed him on

the cheek and thanked him. Then she sprang a surprise. 'It's a little verandah play,' she said. 'Just a sketch. A little dialogue that the young people have put together. Just to show we're not all old . . . fuddy-duddy people who've passed our sell-by date.'

And while she was speaking two young people, a boy and a girl, brought out a table and two chairs and set them up in the shaded space at the front of the verandah, and waited discreetly while people reassembled, forming a new audience; during which time iced tea was served.

'So let the play commence,' Miss Vanesa commanded, at last; and the audience applauded.

THE THIRD SONG

The Sea, the Sea, or some such nonsense.

Though it's good to have sea-salt all over the skin. Pity Neanderthal man, who probably couldn't swim. Or people who lived in the middle of a continent, no lake in sight, aeons before swimming pools. So we must vote against those who poison our waters.

He was back from the sea, impressed by Miss Vanesa's magnificent body in her swimming-suit, and he wished her many lovers and lots of family. She had praised his body, too; like a good host.

And here was he, relaxing after the swim, weighing up the claims of Miss Vanesa, his host, and his sister, still to be visited on another island. He had brought presents for both, and hadn't handed over Miss Vanesa's yet, as that would affect what he would give to his sister. He was travelling light, so the books were small. But small didn't mean small in anything but what they weighed. He had supplied countless Heritage houses in the region with the contents of their bookcase; so he was expected to bring books; that's why he chose very carefully for his sister and for Miss Vanesa.

The eight books for Miss Vanesa were from a new mini-Penguin series – easy-to-read extracts from people whose names we know, stories by García Márquez and Truman Capote, a little bit of reflection by Camus, on growing up in Algiers; some short short stories by someone he'd never read; a bit of philosophy by our friend, Alain de Botton, Ian Kershaw's 'Hitler' book, Death in the Bunker. *That, and a couple of magazines.*

For his sister – her set was chosen earlier – a 'heavier' run of Penguins: these had to do with Great Ideas extracted from the bigger texts which had contained them: Rousseau's The Social Contract, *Gibbon's* The Christians and the Fall of Rome *(from the great book), Charles Darwin* On Natural Selection, *Freud's* Civilization and Its Discontents, *George Orwell's* Why I Write *and Virginia Woolf's* A Room of One's Own. *And none of these was over 176 pages long. (He had already given Miss Vanesa a couple of magazines – issues of* Wasafiri: *he didn't know if she was a subscriber; so he brought her the special issue of Fanon and the one on Lusophone literature.)*

And he justified the degree of seriousness accorded to his sister to the fact that she had grown up with a large library in St Caesare and had lost it; and the long challenge of restoring that bit of heritage required them to think differently about it, different from the decorating of Vanesa's clean, new concrete box; so the decision was made. (The fact that his Barbados trip was to help an old friend there preserve what was left of his library – wrecked by hurricane and flood – in the face of official indifference, made Pewter see this trip in part as his self-appointed role to protect the Book.*)*

When they were lazing in the drawing room later (she wasn't allowed to help with the clearing up; nor was Pewter, as the guest), Pewter felt that they had relaxed into a state where watchfulness was no longer required. They had talked a bit about the reading groups, about the politics of the reading group, about Dr Dodds' Slow Reading Group in St Vincent, a deliberate decision to respect the reading process, against all this skimming business you got in the West – all these adverts everywhere in the papers to improve your reading speed – back to the way those rasta boys did it in the seventies, slowly, when they used to talk about 'penetrating' the text. And Pewter and Miss Vanesa talked more conventionally about the wide range of reading material that people were blessed with nowadays.

Pewter knew that Miss Vanesa had sometimes got into trouble because of the reading material of her groups. And it was even rumoured that Miss Vanesa, who was very prim and proper on the island, was a lot more adventurous in her personal life when she was off-island visiting the reading groups. So he didn't reveal what was on his mind. Instead, he complimented her on one of her authors, Japan's Haruki Murakami. Pewter was interested because some of the Murakami stories were informed by earthquake. More than that, they took earthquake as their leaping off point – as their sort of psychic pulse; and Pewter had been hoping to do something similar for St Caesare and its volcano in 'The Loss of Naples'. Though as he was saying this he decided to come straight out with the question.

'All that stuff at the table, earlier. The little contretemps in the garden . . .'

'Oh, the men having to defend . . . manhood. It's the culture, as you know. My wife and daughter might be secretly gay but I'm all man. With plenty pickney. That'll never change.' She seemed to be absolving him.

That, for some reason, made it easier to refer back to their brief meetings in London thirty-five years ago when she was a struggling actress. They talked, with a pleasing lack of strain, of the group they had known in West London staging plays and doing music; and then they started talking of people nearer home. Nora, for instance, from Montserrat. Nora, with the hyphenated name.

'Nora married her aristocrat in England. Had a serious business there. If you had Nora running this country we'd all be rich.' And Miss Vanesa brought him up to date with some of the other guests. Pewter was wondering if the story he heard that Miss Vanesa was herself gay was true; but he wasn't close enough to her to pursue it. So he came back to an earlier subject.

'And you play chess, too,' he said.

'Fancy a game?'

No, he didn't play. The best he'd ever done was to learn the rules enough to interpret the odd work of literature, like Thomas Middleton's seventeenth-century play, *A Game At Chess*, when he was a student, fascinated by what it said about European diplomacy at the time: the *Dramatis Personae* were all WHITE KING, BLACK KNIGHT, etc.

She didn't respond to the joke. Then she said: 'Is the only memory of my father I want to preserve in this house.' (Was she talking about the chess set? Her father as a chess champion?) He was prepared to leave it.

And then Miss Vanesa had second thoughts and told him a story.

She had been in a play years and years ago; she was a novelist, but she had done the theatre thing, as he knew, years ago, she'd even done something with the old Caribbean Theatre Workshop, with Michael. Ah, but those were the days when she was still young and not-too-bad-looking.

So he told her that she was still young and not-too-bad-looking.

And she thanked him, and called him an Anancyman.

And said he had been well-trained by the white ladies in England. And continued her story, to Pewter's relief.

This had happened in an island not too many miles away from here. And there was a scene in the play where the young wife who had been left on the island could tell her critics – her bad-minded neighbours – that she had not been abandoned because a parcel always came from the man abroad, on her birthday, and at Christmas, whatever. Until the parcels stopped coming. How is the woman to face her persecutors on this small island? So she simply got a mail order catalogue and ordered herself a treat, in good time, for the days that mattered to her.

Anyway, she said, after she had packed the old bastard off to the Home before leaving England – and she wouldn't lose a moment's sleep if that Home was run by a gang of racists – she went out and bought a chess set, to remind herself that the man whom she called a father had had no more emotional connection with her than pieces on a board of a game she didn't play.

To answer Pewter's question, no, she didn't play chess.

And so to bed.

*

He was up in the middle of the night, with a hot drink, trying not to disturb the house, wondering what he could do, where he could go to escape what had to be night-mares. Except that this one wasn't so bad; it was like a continuation – it *was* a continuation – of that scene after the hurricane with Nellie, the woman he had interviewed, what must be ten years ago now; and it was crystal clear: you didn't need film to preserve the past if you had access to this sort of recall.

. . . *You see, we had come out of the house – me, and me daughter, grand-daughter – come out of the house and go*

44

under the floor: you see that patch up there? Is where we were, and then the water come and wet all we down underneath the floor there. Man, it was something. Before that we decide to hide inside, to go behind the bed and all we can hear is rukutunduruk *and the child say: 'Mamma, come out, come out.' And all we run out and stand up there inside the front door, so so, and hold on. And this door fly back out, man; and the wind, man, it start to pitch we all back; and all we ease forward and try to hold it back, and all we hook on and hug up together and hold that latch there to prevent it open out again. Because the wind wicked, the wind fling out one big-size girl up at Hill and stick the girl to one post up there. And the mother say, 'Oh, me daughter gone, now.' They say she side a hurt her still. But she alive; I saw her. Another child at the north – I don't know if it was a boy or a girl, but however the story go – the child was in the water swimming when the storm struck . . .*

And after this he woke up in a panic fearful for himself, and he was thinking not of the woman who had lost everything: something drenched him in perspiration, and after trying to calm himself, without success, he reached for this or that prop, and eventually settled on an old fav-ourite, a poem, Elizabeth Bishop's 'One Art', a statement of loss he could relate to – he had introduced it to students, over the years, pretending that it was the form that was interesting – *that's the way to do the villanelle*, sort of thing. And after that he was able to drag his mind up from his own buried concerns to the woman who had lost her house in the hurricane.

And this woman had ended up in a refugee camp in Anti-gua, and never got a Heritage house. Over-compensating now, he was driven to contrasting her fate with those of the criminal types – also returnees – who were being deported from America, and were now living in identikit Heritage houses.

'You insomniac, like me.' Miss Vanesa had joined him on the verandah, dressing-gowned and slippered, also with a drink. She had a packet in her hand.

'If you're insomniac, you might want something to read.'

And immediately it dawned on him that she was offering her novel manuscript. He didn't want to own up to having read it; so he expressed the right sort of surprise and said that he had read an extract, some years ago, in the Longman's anthology.

She said she didn't think he'd like it because it was, perhaps, a woman's novel with an excess . . .

'An excess of fine feeling?'

She looked at him with new interest and said, yes, he could say that.

And Pewter recalled the portrait of the father from his recent reading of the manuscript, and how unconvincing it was. There they were in this house in, wherever it was, East London, and the man seemed to have no job. He was retired but his life contained little trace of the job he had presumably done for forty years; and all he did, except to exploit the women in the house – apart from trips to the pub to meet his mates and watch sport on Sky TV – all he seemed to do was to fantasize about women with white skin and blue eyes and silken hair; and day after day he humiliated the women in the house, in a covert way, because they didn't have white skin and blue eyes and silken hair – and there were whole riffs of internal monologue about this – while on the other side mother and daughter, and visiting female relatives, fantasized about appropriate ways to punish him. And there was no verbal disagreement in the house, they were perfectly polite to one another at breakfast, and the novel ends with us not knowing whether the women would succeed in punishing the father in the end. It was OK as an idea, but as narrative it lacked tension; it was just as if the minds of the main characters were being laid out for the reader's inspection. It needed work.

So, sitting here on the verandah in the middle of the night, Pewter accepted the manuscript and promised to read it and give the author an opinion.

Miss Vanesa reminded him that she was tough; he didn't have to be kind.

IV

THE FOURTH SONG

She's not bitter, why should she be bitter? She's back here in reasonably good health, and not old; she's back here living in her Heritage house, which is paid for. Of course she now has to guard against the thieves who would begrudge you what you have, because you've lived abroad, and that means you have money which you didn't work for. You just turned up at the Social Security Office in London or wherever, and said: Give me the money. Give me the free money. And when you spent a lifetime accumulating enough free money you then came home and distributed it to every Tom, Dick and . . . Vasco da Gama because is their money too, and you just went abroad to collect it for them; like you're a delegate for some poor country – one of those fatbellymen coming to the World Bank and saying: 'Give me money. My people are starving.' So though life is no easier here than there, she is not bitter: she consoles herself by saying, despite everything, this is a lyrical moment; and she's in control of the mood; she's learnt not to let the mood control her. Despite the bad-mindedness. She once made the mistake of saying to somebody that she approved of hanging, and she's never been allowed to live it down; even though everyone else she knows believes the same thing. Don't get her wrong, she's not talking of America, where they use hanging to punish black people. Nor is she talking about some unspeakable, corrupt country out there where those in power, whole families of them, who should be strung up, do it out of savagery. But the terrorists and drug dealers standing outside the infant school gates – they should be strung up, too.

No no, she isn't a fanatic; she believes in moderation. She doesn't even believe that hanging should be brought in as a policy, because like everyone else she's uneasy with the idea of judicial murder as the norm, only as an exception. She couldn't have been a schoolteacher all these years if she didn't have those reservations. But she believes in the ten-minute rule, when things get so out of hand, when the murderers and wife-beaters and child-killers get too brazen and feisty and thumb their nose at you, and lick you down in the street and rape you in broad daylight, and chop off your hand for your gold bracelet and ring – there comes a time when you say: Enough is Enough. Are You Thinking What We're Thinking? And that's when she would bring in the ten-minute rule. And say, even though we don't believe in hanging, or the chair, or whatever, in this crisis we're suspending the normal rule for ten minutes. And in those ten minutes this and that species of scum will learn what it is like to thumb their nose at decent people. That's all she's saying, not seeking to change the rule, just to bring in an exception from time to time.

(When Miss Vanesa said that, Pewter thought of something in Camus, in The Outsider, towards the end of the little book when the fellow, whatever his name was – Meursault – is reflecting after being sentenced to death for the shooting of the Arab; and he reckons that the condemned man should be given a chance. Instead of the guillotine – the

48

certainty of the guillotine – the murderer should be given a chemical compound which kills him nine times out of ten – giving him a 10% chance of escape. Pewter wasn't sure if Miss Vanesa's system was more or less sophisticated than that.) So what he said was:

It's got you a pretty bad press.

But already he was thinking of something else. Pewter was thinking of his latest faux-pas, just a few weeks ago. He was down with the flu, and his students were having a production of A Midsummer Night's Dream which one young woman, a second-year student, had adapted. And he felt he should go to the performance. He wanted to go. And on the night in question he wrapped himself in a warm coat, armed himself with sweet lozenges and a flagon of orange juice to still the coughing. And he was sitting there, near the back, congratulating himself that he had controlled the coughing pretty well. Every time there was a suggestion of a cough he either popped a sweet into his mouth or took a swig from the flagon. And the rumble he let out could barely be heard by the person sitting next to him. Then he let it all out during the interval. But towards the end of the play – maybe it was his trying not to laugh at an OK Bottom – or to be angered at doormat Helena's lines – all the evening's suppressed cough was rushing to get out, so he thought, he'd given it a good run, he'd put in an appearance and felt good about himself – ill, but good about himself. He didn't have to sit it out.

At the foyer he told a couple of young stagehands to give his best to the students in the cast and explain that he was poorly, so had to head home, and couldn't stay for a drink. It was then that one turned to him and said, 'Were you the one coughing through the performance?'

And he was gutted, as they say; because he thought he had avoided coughing through the performance: clearly,

*he had given no thought to the play, just to his heroic act
in sitting through it, uncoughing.*

*What prompted this thinking now was the memory of
Miss Vanesa's novel. The wash of feeling that she drenched
everyone in the house in East London with didn't issue from
their characters, or even from their situation. It was interesting to read, but it was fake.*

*If she were a different sort of woman Pewter would
have welcomed Miss Vanesa to his own world of fakery.*

*

At breakfast he asked her a question on his mind. Why
come back; why return now?

Miss Vanesa wasn't fazed.

'The camel's back,' she said. 'It's true, you know, what
they say about that last straw.'

'And the last straw?'

And here she paused for a long time, smearing jam on
her toast, pouring herself another glass of fresh orange
juice. Had he crossed some boundary?

'I remember . . .' and Miss Vanesa paused as if she were
trying to remember. 'I remember going into the chemist
one day. I didn't even plan to go into the chemist; I'd been
to the bank and . . . Anyway. So I popped into the chemist
next door because I had a bit of a cough. One of those stub-
born things you can't get rid of. Irritating as the weather
was good and everybody was saying that it was spring.'

'Yes, I know.'

'So I bought the . . . the cough mixture. I'd already been
on a course of antibiotics and they had to check that I
wasn't allergic to anything. And while I was waiting, I
remembered I was low on toothpaste. And then I realized I
had a little abscess – nothing big – on my gum; so I bought
the mouthwash. And I remember clearly it all came to
£9.37. That's a lot of money just to spend in passing, just

to try to keep yourself clean. And then I had this friend who came round later. Old friend, did biochemistry at Imperial, and works in the laboratory at Boots; and as we were sitting there chatting, she read out the labels on my stuff from the chemist, and read out what everything contained, sorbital this, macrogolgycerol hydoxystearate that. And you think: I've just paid £9.37 for this. And you need to be an educational witchdoctor even to say it. You can't win against this level of pollution. And I started thinking of coming home. Right there and then.'

He thought of many things to say. In the end he said, 'Miss Vanesa, it's been an education.'

3

From the Narrative Verandah

Miss Vanesa ended up wiping the tiles and decided to take a rest: she could do things at her own pace again; she didn't have to press on if she didn't want to, she wasn't anyone's maid or servant, or slave. Before she had time to reflect on this an image flashed through her mind: it was of the man inside the house, in the bedroom, sprawlingly awake in that smug way that men have as if expecting praise or credit for a job well done. She would have to be prepared to work to keep that air of satisfaction on his lordship's face – by doing the smaller things a woman was released to doing without being asked. Keeping the dust down. By bouncing up out of the bed as if she had been given a new lease of life, bouncing up and going out to face the morning and the dew, to mop the gallery, the tiles, the whole verandah and then putting out the table for breakfast. Wiping that free of dust, too, of dead insects. Then she would take the shower so that she could be dust-free. Just in case.

She banished the thought (thoughts); and her sigh was one of relief; there was no man in her bedroom, no master in her house, her home. So she was keeping the dust down for herself, she was doing it now before it got too hot and sticky; and she would have the shower before breakfast, to feel comfortable in her clothes. Miss Vanesa sighed – this felt like a sigh: she wished – she sort of wished it were different.

She was doing all of this two days before she needed to.

Miss Vanesa was expecting not one but two male guests: they were famous, sort of famous, so you had to be careful not to hurt their pride. She had had something less than an affair with one of them; and she was content that it had become so fuzzy in her mind that she barely registered which one it was she had had the affair with. Not quite; but things had receded as these things do, so she no longer minded, in memory, whether it was Michael Carrington or Pewter Stapleton who would claim the right to see through her clothes to her nakedness. She was and wasn't looking forward to her house guests.

So, she turned back inside to have her shower.

And now the white man was on the verandah admiring the view. His voice sounded like Michael Carrington's and when he turned to face her the face was Carrington's. He was wearing a white suit and that struck her as – not odd, exactly, just something you couldn't help noticing. She had a mad thought of how he would get the dust off his suit; though the film of white sand might not be too noticeable, might blend in; was it a statement? Maybe he was bringing something heroic into her home. This was the challenge of these men who visited: they forced you to think of things a little outside your normal grasp or range; and she wasn't sure if that helped you or if it made you feel as if you were pretending to be someone else. (This straining and stretching was, they said, good for the soul.) Before long you ended up matching their own way of thinking; and they praised you for that. You could talk to them, then; and everyone would agree that the conversation was

54

interesting. ('There are no countries in the West Indies, just communities.' *Interesting?*) One of the men – the one who hadn't yet arrived; he had passed through a year ago – had called it Singing for your Supper. She didn't have the will to pursue that thought now, though she wasn't sure she approved of it, of singing for your supper; her attention was demanded by the man who was here, talking to her and expecting an answer.

Carrington was at his most genial, giving the low-down on his friend, Pewter Stapleton, who hadn't yet arrived from Sheffield. Or from Paris. Upmanship. One-upmanship. Already this man had changed her way of thinking, 'low-down' seeming a closer fit, a more natural turn of phrase for a man who had lived in America, and had become cool. (And divorced.) He had done what he could for his old friend, Carrington said, urging Pewter away from the no-blame aesthetic of England. But, you could only take a man so far out of his Englishness, etc. ('No-blame aesthetic'?)

II

Her resentment against the missing Pewter Stapleton was generic. The fact that they – the Pewter Stapletons of this world – lived all their lives in places that at best patronized them and casually rejected them as being less than the preferred breeding stock was something they colluded with the enemy in not wanting to talk about. So they must hold forth instead about Pliny the Elder and General de Gaulle coming to power in France in 1958, and the constitution of the Fifth Republic, and the lack of democracy, today, in Uzbekistan.

Her resentment against Pewter Stapleton grew to recognizable levels after he had sent her a book about women.

For of course he was a feminist, and she had to learn about the rights and needs of women from him. True, he had to protect himself against *his* women – some called them the White Ladies' Ethnic Conquering Army (WLECA) – among whom he lived, but that was not Miss Vanesa's problem. Maybe someone who was not a member of the WLECA was deemed to be impressed by a book on women.

And even now, yes, she found herself defending Pewter Stapleton from attacks of the man in the white suit. (He was athletic: would he throw a spear, would he reach for a concealed gun? No.) He recited snatches of an obscene poem to make his point; a poem which included what the Americans call the 'N– word'. He made a point about the quotation but Miss Vanesa wasn't clear what it was.

In the end she returned to bed with a headache, which is what women are allowed to do. It took the visit of one important man to her home to remind her of her headaches. She wondered if this constituted an accident in the home, less visible than those involving the man's limbs or rages or silences. But maybe she was being unfair to her guest, who was full of appreciation and, really, already singing for his supper.

She mustn't get this out of perspective. They weren't here to see her. As cultural ambassadors to the island (from the islands and now to the island) they conferred lustre by staying in her home. And observing them at close quarters was the pay-off, might just be what she needed to make herself visible.

They would deny this was the relationship they had with her, and be hurt; and would spend awkward time taking care of her feelings. One of the men was moving house, moving from one country in Europe to another country in Europe, very near the first country. He had been packing boxes for months (over a year, apparently):

did the victorious generals of history ever pack so many boxes with their loot? One university had taken some of the boxes (important man!). A woman friend had stored some boxes. Another woman friend had stored some boxes. (How large was the sex of these women friends?) And there was a car load or a van load of boxes due for the new address. Miss Vanesa found it interesting, of course, but she couldn't help reflecting that her own move from one continent to another, over several years, was assumed by her considerate house guests to have taken place, as it were, without visible effort on her part.

Was she complaining? She was planning her strategy. First, she would keep a diary. So that her bad moods would not be edited out: she would keep a diary, if for nothing else, to put back into her home what the men had taken out. The diary would explain why, for the duration, her visitors had forced her to act in a certain way. They filled the house with a different noise and something normally there had to be taken out to make room for that noise. And she might even note down the noise she might miss when they eventually vacated her house.

For the house didn't seem empty to her. Ordinarily, she didn't feel the need to go from room to room filling the space with her sound. And last time when she suddenly felt, on the verandah, that she was strangely alone, she had gone indoors and rung someone and talked about something that didn't matter much; and her breathing had returned to normal.

'What's keeping our friend?' she asked now, as if submitting herself, again, to the present.

The man in the white suit had a complicated answer; and listening to him Miss Vanesa thought of men in white suits speaking from the podium; only that he was facing in, addressing her, his only audience, not facing out, at the crowd. And his voice was not like an actor's. Maybe it was the heat of her own body but looking at him, so coated in white, she wondered if sponging him down was something she should propose.

She agreed that the absent Pewter Stapleton was full of himself, that this had something to do with his habitual late arrival. (Apparently, the late President Mitterrand of France used to come in late at EC summits; and now the 'comic', Jacques Chirac, had maintained the tradition; so maybe Pewter was president of something that his friends didn't know about.) Ah, but there's the phone, to the rescue.

III

They were having a fight, the important men, here on the verandah, as if this were an old play someone had forgotten to revise. The dialogue was a boast clearly to put Miss Vanesa in her place; for Miss Vanesa was at the stage where she aspired to be associated with the rogue managements and publications dissected and damned for her benefit. Apparently, some major magazines paid derisory sums for the work of her guests and left errors in the text uncorrected; so she duly matched their manufactured outrage. Stop writing, seemed to be the message communicated to her; stop writing and save yourself the humiliation of being paid less than you are worth. The only thing worse than that was the terror of dying when your agent still had an unrevised copy of your latest work, and the thought of what that posthumous publication would do to your reputation. Both great men felt that such a fate didn't bear thinking about.

Then the subject was about breasts. Picasso, you know, had written a little play about breasts. Picasso had missed a trick there, the men agreed. Tiresias' old dugs had been better served by T. S. Eliot. No, the real play about breasts would celebrate the other painter, our friend Degas. All those breasts of women in the bath. All those gravity-defying breasts in the bath. Ah, and then there was Renoir. More breasts. Whereas the family doctor was sometimes forced to deal with problematic breasts, the painter saw nakedly brazen breasts. So Renoir was the pre-doctor version. Romance to old Degas' sensuality. *She would remember to write down the phrase 'brazen breasts'.* It was Pewter who was saying that death was, indeed, a tragedy. A tragedy because of the endless fondlable breasts it put beyond reach. And that one must get in there now, now and fondle breasts, endlessly.

The men then admitted to Miss Vanesa that this was sexist talk; and they invited her to punish them. Or to propose another subject for conversation. Either to punish them or propose another subject for conversation.

So no wonder she was pregnant, after all that fondling. She was pregnant for her body had gone funny; her body had stiffened and filled out, like a child's rubber dinosaur at the beach, and was surely drawing attention to itself. It must be a miracle how these two men had raped her while she was half-attending to something. They were so clever, maybe it had happened while they were discussing ethnicity or Africa or the correct pronunciation of Nabokov. Or even when she was serving breakfast, serving them their sardines in virgin olive oil with the half of forget-the-cholesterol avocado. That sort of thing – something by proxy – turned men on, didn't it? And they had lived in cold countries, and lived with frozen women where you had to use devices to get yourself going; and the White Ladies' Ethnic Conquering Army were, it was said, tireless in these matters.

Anyway, they had clearly got her pregnant and Look! Already she was nearing her term – a twelve-hour, a twenty-hour baby. They were so cool about it, these men who had seen it all, that they would acknowledge the resulting child, name it something amusing, and send it off to govern a small country.

IV

When the jackarse came – oh, the big men had gone; the planes tried to be gentle with the sky when the big men flew out showing their feminine side; and she now had a jackarse on her verandah for her pains. Already she preferred the way Pewter Stapleton had sung for his supper. Here, on the verandah he had told the story of the Swedish prime minister and his dancing partner from Norway. The man in question, Olof Palme (*not* Palm Olive. *Note*) was a small, athletic man prone to table tennis, famous for holding his bat the Chinese way, and smashing energetically, in a way that reminded her visitors of a famous Shakespearean actor of the past. Anyway, Olof Palme's dancing partner on this occasion – and in the official photograph – was the then Norwegian prime minister, Gro Brundtland Harlem, a large, tightly packed woman of impeccable socialist credentials, in voluminous skirts. Picture the scene. Neat Mao jacket. Little man. And large socialist Norwegian made larger by endless, twirling skirts; he doing his athletic best not to tread on the skirts: an image that would live on, securely, on the verandah. From that to this jackarse.

She almost caught herself using the logic of the original man in the white suit. (He would be at pains to point out that a shirt and trousers of roughly the same colour did not constitute the white linen suit and helmet, with or without the rifle slung over the shoulder.) Though Pewter had had ideas to help Miss Vanesa locate her ex-lover's provenance. For first, there was our friend Pierre Trudeau in Canada, in all those old Commonwealth prime ministers' photographs. He was OK, was Trudeau; he told jokes, in his white suit, even to the Queen of England; and made her laugh. Had an amazing wife, Margaret. And then the parody of the white-suited others: Tito of Yugoslavia – a square man – looking down at you from the supermarkets of Belgrade. (Not any more, of course.) And now to the psychopath ('I shall return'), late, of Liberia, less said of him the better. White suits addressing the crowd.

But this man on the verandah – a big man so squat in his suit – has come late to the party, has missed the play. He is dressed more appropriately for the sand. His message is good works. Good Works. He is coming to her just after the famous men have gone, knowing she is vulnerable, unsettled by the experience of her guests; she would be in no state to deny him. So sand-resistant. Such short arms.

v

And now she's summing up. She must sort out what to keep and what to jettison from the experience. Was it a case for sadness that *A Moveable Feast* was published after Hemingway's death, put together one weekend by a young boy from Cape and Hemingway's widow, from the great man's notebooks? Should we be saddened that the big fellow missed out on the publication of his most engaging book? In the light of that – and there are many examples of this – shouldn't writers be paid now, while they're alive, for the books they wouldn't live to see into print? Miss Vanesa decided she wasn't important enough to be exercised by these concerns. So she checked through her notes. She looked up the spelling of Houphouët-Boigny who had said something or other to de Gaulle. Or of whom de Gaulle had said something. She looked up the spelling of Michel Houellebecq, a new joker who, though pornographic, should be read. Like an efficient secretary she had recorded something of the sweep of political comment on the verandah, noting the frame of reference from Pliny the Elder to Bush the Younger. And she suddenly panicked and apologized. She panicked and apologized for breaking wind on her verandah; and then she realized there was no one around to apologize to.

And she paused: this wasn't getting her to the new place she had hoped. These notes were theirs, the men's; she was their secretary. So she flicked to the *reflections* that the notes had provoked at the time, hoping to discover her own voice.

NOT-QUITE NOTES

When they had a fight over the glass of wine I thought: how like the men proving who could have the extra glass and defy his doctor. The next day it was raw material: the term 'raw material' had a slightly disturbing taste to it.

So: Pewter pours a glass of wine and drinks it. He then pretends not to have drunk it: could he have poured it down the sink by mistake? (There's no sink on this side of the verandah.) Maybe he tipped it over the railing. (As you do.) He's playing the game now. But the slight anxiety of having drunk the wine without realizing it, is registered. (Getting old. Growing confused. Kaput.) *More mundanely, his doctor – a good-looking woman, young – has asked him to cut down on the red. (He's virtually off the white.) He is loath to acknowledge this biological malfunctioning* corps d'occasion, *for Carrington, he's pleased to say, is further along the line to a wine-free Nothing. So Pewter relents and pours himself only half a glass. Starts again.*

And that's the raw material; that's how it's done. Pewter calmly links the confusion over wine to the loss of primary powers: what was the name, again, of that writer from Sri Lanka, he couldn't remember, and it caused momentary panic on the verandah? An old friend. Lives in Crouch

End. Did I drink that glass of wine or pour it down the sink?

Then there was the session, not noted at the time by Miss Vanesa – the session to convict the nasty, little man from some joke country who pleaded guilty to cutting off the nose and lips of the nineteen-year-old wife of his brother because she wanted a divorce and the religious sect of a country she lives in doesn't allow divorce for abused women without connections. And here on her own verandah, many miles from the scene of the crime, they convicted this 'terrorist against women' and subjected him to appropriate punishment. She would be proud to record when this gallery, this verandah had served this necessary purpose.

Returning to the notes, other jottings she might work up into something:

A secretary of state under Reagan whose name was like Hamburger.

A man in a white suit leaning over the verandah shouting Romesh Romesh Romesh Romesh Romesh to the crowd.

In Barbara Pym's novel, An Academic Question, *someone at a provincial university is doing research on the local West Indian community. The researcher is a comic character called Coco; and the only West Indians to appear in the novel are two university porters (off-stage) reportedly grumbling at having to lift heavy boxes. Apart from them and some people glimpsed at a street party, the only other West Indian spotted is a large 'ethnically dressed' woman on a bus taking up one-and-a-half seats. Having damned the 'little book', Pewter nevertheless says he likes the idea of the large 'ethnically dressed' woman taking up two seats on the bus. He would incorporate her into something he was writing, and he would call her 'Hackney Woman'.*

Miss Vanesa would incorporate this raw material into something *she* was writing. And she would read the Barbara Pym book.

It was Apollinaire, not Picasso, who had written the little play about breasts.

4

Miss Vanesa's Secret

It was in Marks & Spencer's that Pewter thought about Miss Vanesa, again; and that night Michael Carrington phoned from America and talked about Miss Vanesa.

'It's the jacuzzi thing, isn't it?'

'Go on.'

'Or the mysterious lady friend in Stockholm.'

There was a slight pause. Then Michael said: 'The Stockholm lady isn't mysterious; I've met her.'

Over the phone the men were supposed to be recalling the time on the island. Michael was trying not to be smug, Pewter not to be on the defensive. Michael had seen Miss Vanesa more recently than Pewter had and was stressing the fact: he had experienced sessions in the lady's jacuzzi.

This was a transatlantic call – Boston–Sheffield; and Michael decided to ease up on his friend; so he allowed the conversation to slip to a level that was comfortable for Pewter whose image of the woman in question had stuck at being 'Our friend, the sardine woman'.

As Pewter talked Michael had images of Miss Vanesa as an oiled fish swimming in a glistening sea; though he didn't see sea, he saw a big fish swimming in a small pond; not swimming, really; trapped, trapped in a tin. So maybe it was he who was off the mark. Pewter's image of the sardine woman was intended to be funnish, not sinister; Pewter had something of an English sense of humour. Michael recalled for Pewter the morning of the business with the sardines.

They were sitting on Miss Vanesa's verandah, on the island; both men. It was the first time in – what? – fifteen or sixteen years that they found themselves in the region together – the last time being the funeral of Pewter's mother. So, though their names were associated in people's minds, they hadn't really worked that much together. But Miss Vanesa and others in the 'artistic community' were determined to do something about that. Anyway, they had been 'doing' the islands together a couple of years ago and Miss Vanesa had been one of the people playing host – she being a newish 'returnee' anxious to contribute something to the islands' artistic tone.

'I'm not a food fascist,' Miss Vanesa had said, as she served the sardines. It was breakfast time and Miss Vanesa said that sardines were good for diabetics. And all three people at the table assumed that someone other than himself, than herself was being referred to.

'No, I'm not a food fascist,' she said. 'But I can't help noticing the difference. This is Vasco da Gama. In olive oil. With the avocado added. And this is your Princess. Also in olive oil. Extra virgin. What's an extra virgin, I wonder?'

Both men had notions, but didn't feel ready to reveal them to Miss Vanesa, who was still being the gracious host.

'I always prefer the olive oil, don't you? . . . To the . . .'

'Oh yes, much better than . . .'

'Y'know, the tomato or . . .'

'All that . . . Oh . . . barbecue and . . . horrible.'

'Sardines in smoky barbecue sauce. Horrible.'

'Horrible. Even the hot sauce.'

'The hot sauce isn't quite as bad,' Miss Vanesa suggested, 'if you cool it down with the avocado.'

They agreed to that.

'Some people serve them to the pets,' Miss Vanesa said. 'But I think that's a bit cruel. With the hot sauce.'

'Probably no worse than the heroin.'

'I've never had the pleasure,' Miss Vanesa said; and Pewter wondered if he should say that was a quote.

'But the olive oil's cleaner. Simpler.' Michael came to the rescue.

'Dalí used to rub it on his moustache. Oil from the sardine.'

'That old fraud.'

And Miss Vanesa continued: 'Vasco da Gama is Portuguese, as you know.' And without a pause: 'Though having to add the avocado doesn't help the cholesterol.'

The conversation slipped to things Portuguese. Miss Vanesa had spent some time in Lisbon and had the *Lusiads* and Eça da Queirós on her shelf. Pewter had been to Mozambique and regarded himself an expert on that country and Michael, being the successful writer, reckoned he had an interest in everything.

So at the breakfast Pewter told a story of his Great Uncle George in St Caesare who had been to Brazil. He hadn't set out to go to Brazil, he had gone to work on the Panama Canal and somehow ended up – for how long no one knew – in Brazil; and on coming back to the island sported knowledge of a language that everyone assumed to be Spanish, only it turned out to be Portuguese. And Pewter told the story of how he learnt elements of the language from his Great Uncle George by skiving off Sunday school and luring the old man – who lived on the back road to the Methodist church where Sunday school was held – to teach him something of the vocabulary.

Neither Michael nor Miss Vanesa believed the story but they understood that when you lived your entire adult life abroad you more or less constructed these types of stories as part of your heritage, because living abroad stripped you of so much that was yours, and even more of things that might be yours. And both Michael and Miss Vanesa had invented enough stories to sustain them, too.

Pewter was conscious that the Uncle George story wasn't entirely accurate, but he was a guest here, he was being treated well – not least being given equal billing to Michael Carrington, a more successful man – so why shouldn't he be content to, as it were, volunteer to sing for his supper? So he spoke about Uncle George teaching him Portuguese (*Obrigado obrigada*) on his way to Sunday school – something that happened so far in the past he couldn't even be bothered to get the details right. For what he was thinking was about Miss Vanesa's sardine fetish (*spicy, in tomato sauce*); and then of someone else he knew, who had a fetish for yogurt (*plain, all the textures and cultures of plain*); and he couldn't dismiss the feeling that he preferred the fetish for yogurt to the fetish for sardines; but then he thought such comparisons were maybe invidious; so he span out the story of Uncle George in Brazil, more as a way of being a good guest.

Now, on the phone, a year later, both men were talking about Miss Vanesa's other fetish; but pulling back out of consideration for someone who had been a good host to them on the island. Also, they didn't wish to mock their own participation in those scenes at breakfast where they had commended the fresh juice and the fruit, and where Miss Vanesa had displayed considerable finesse in preferring some sardines to others. She knew the danger of being with men like this, who would take what they wanted; in the case of these two it would be *material* they would write up later: she had no intention of ending up as the butt in their *play*.

'But how can a person sit down here going on about these things . . . ?' Miss Vanesa had said lightly, but with a sigh. And she waited for the men to supply the refrain.

Which they did. What with war and terrorism in the world. Aids and child soldiers. Religion religion everywhere. Tyrants in power . . .

So that Miss Vanesa could sum up: '. . . as if there's calm and harmony in this world.'

So naturally they reassured her again that she was not being overly sensitive about her taste in sardines. For if normal people lost their fine sense of taste-discrimination, that could well affect their ability to weigh weighty things going on in the world. Later, they talked a bit about yogurt, a taste that Miss Vanesa had developed abroad – like the mushrooms. But these things caused raised eyebrows here on the island; you had to be careful.

Pewter was surprised that he had introduced the subject of yogurt.

Now, over the phone, the men were 'taking the conversation forward'. About Miss Vanesa's Swedish friends. The people who had installed the jacuzzi downstairs.

'Miss Vanesa's Swedish friend was the *wife* of one of the people who had installed the jacuzzi downstairs.'

'Ah!'

Now Michael was hinting that Miss Vanesa was getting depressed with the puritanism on the island, where even the tourists were beginning to act like retired people. If Pewter wasn't careful Miss Vanesa would soon be descending on his Paris pad, for a bit of light relief.

*

The very next night Pewter saw a programme on swing parties taking place all over Britain. From South London to Bristol to Sheffield to Durham they were revealing a secret life that people like him dreamt of; only it wasn't secret, for here they were on television, these – dare one say it? unprepossessing – unremarkable Labour-Tory-Liberal voters; more elderly than young. So this was the sexual life not imagined by Hollywood: a postman from an unnamed street in, wherever, and a tax collector, and a secretary in the pensions office in Mexborough. Certainly, Beverley Hills and Fellini's *La Dolce Vita* all seemed rather stale, *young*. This wasn't even the sudden madness of Pools or Lottery-winners; these were people who watched *Coronation Street* or whatever on the television, and who took their medication at night.

On the television you saw these 'swingers' preparing for their night out, buying the costumes and dressing up to the approval of their long-term, married partners (for these weren't solitary, sad losers); and later, stripped of the costumes, eight or ten to a bath (the jacuzzi) they got acquainted with the nearest bit of mature flesh before repairing to the bedroom; tiny bedrooms, large beds, bedding on the floor, for these are very ordinary, not middle-class houses – and then talking to camera afterwards about the experience. The wife-swapping women were more adventurous than the men, who all seemed strangely prim and 'straight'. So it must mean – if Miss Vanesa, say, had been involved in this type of activity when she was in these parts – she would have had a man in tow; for the one lone, young man featured (in South London) who wanted to get in on the act, had first to advertise for a partner – and had struck it lucky with a ravishing creature who, though she spoke with a French accent, was assumed to be English.

It depressed Pewter that Miss Vanesa had chosen Michael Carrington to reveal her jacuzzi secrets to on the island. While Pewter had stayed at her house she had contented herself with discussing Caribbean drama and black American literature and her own Portuguese authors. And this while she was supposedly 'swinging' on the island with all sorts – the local librarian, the returnee electrician from Balham and the Methodist preacher with wife and children on another island. Pewter could live with the thought of her preferring that nice woman solicitor who had a 'professional' contempt for men; but not, surely, with being rejected for the rogue Methodist preacher!

Carrington's phone call had been intended to rub in the point; so now Pewter's resentment went way beyond Carrington. And beyond Miss Vanesa to a woman he knew in London, and her children. Whom he was now prepared to charge with abuse.

II

THE STORY OF THE WOMAN IN LONDON, AND HER CHILDREN

He had been thinking of this that morning in Marks & Spencer's. There wasn't any desperate need for him to go shopping, except for tea; he'd run out of proper tea and only had in the house the scented stuff that people were forever giving him. Vanilla flavoured this, Tilleul that. And as he couldn't bring himself to drink that stuff he got the bus into town and from the bookshop drifted into M&S. (He'd bought another couple of books he didn't need, but never mind.)

So there he was in the supermarket with the temperature well down – as if to make your senses keen – there he was pondering the shelves of, what? Pasta: Cannelloni. Penne with Tuscan-style Sausage. Macaroni & Thyme. Tuna Conchiglie. Smoked Salmon Tagliatelle. Asparagus Lasagne, etc. – all at £1.99. (These were the economy, serve-one packets.) He stood there and thought of Miss Vanesa in Paris. But this was Sheffield: in the end he bought eight packets, at random: he'd invite six or seven people to dinner, and have a rave. His special *in*-set. And spend the evening comparing pasta.

*

His secret family lived in London; he had played his part for them, over the years; and now he wanted credit. (For, apart from other things, what would the swinging Miss Vanesa think of this?)

The last visit was not like a last visit, just like any other time; so he must see it as someone else might see it – as, indeed, Carrington would see it.

He'd packed the small bag to show them that he hadn't come to stay. He might stay over, he *would* stay over but not as of right to the prime bed of the house. To prove his welcome he'd be given one of the children's beds, dis-lodging a child to the couch, or to a friend's for the night. That ripple – *no splash, see!* – that ripple of displacement was just about right for all concerned, the mother not hinting that she'd become a tart, the children indulging the mother's fantasy and their own curiosity, and the pro-fessor doing his duty, a duty which made him feel virtuous and uneasy in the right sort of measure – *Ah, a purpose in life!* – without being sucked into a situation from which he couldn't extricate himself. ('Extricate'? The term was too clinical. Rather a situation from which he couldn't, with-out the accusations of shabby behaviour, detach himself.) So he would pack a small bag and proceed to London.

Anne shouldn't have told him what her daughter had said; that was the sort of thing you expected of your teen-age daughter, and you worked out a way of living with it, while you hoped she'd grow out of it. But it actually wasn't helpful to be called a boring old fart by someone to whom you tried (though not very hard) to be a father, because you had an understanding with the mother. But he wouldn't think of that; he was thinking of Henry (pro-nounced the French way) who had turned out to be nor-mal, if depressingly clever: Pewter suspected the boy didn't share his mother's assessment of the professor's abilities. Pewter had to *prepare* himself to communicate with this boy. He didn't need this: he'd really rather sit at home in Sheffield and watch the cricket on television: West Indies were learning to respect themselves on the field once again.

He hadn't bought the children anything. He'd come from the bookshop that morning with Alasdair Gray's massive *The Book of Prefaces* which he'd heard discussed on *Front Row* a week or so before, and he couldn't resist it, even at £35. This is the sort of outlay that made him begin to wonder where his library would end up, and whether he was beginning to purchase splendid tomes with a view to manipulating future students' (and scholars') opinions of him. Naturally, he couldn't deliver a present of that price to Henry; that would be too-obviously an attempt to buy his way in; that would, rightly, earn him the lad's – and his sister's – pity, contempt. So he would savour the book himself, working on the principle now that if he was good to himself, other people might sense his level of expectation and be good to him, too. And if not, well, it didn't do any harm to be good to yourself. So he flicked through the book, even while he kept an eye, an ear on the progress of the match. (Of course England were playing Germany in Belgium tonight, so he was probably one of the few people in the country obsessed with the cricket, and looking forward to spending an evening in a French house in London.)

West Indies got the worst of the umpiring decisions, and yet they were ahead. Gough's foot was over the line when he bowled Campbell. Reon King's stumping was border-line, his foot was on the line, his foot may have been a shade behind the line; so why didn't he get the benefit of the doubt? And the Adams catch. Adams was on 98; last man Walsh in. He smashed a square cut off Gough to square point, and young Flintoff takes a blinder, scoops up (off the ground?) the catch. Endless replays: he seems to drag the ball along the ground before wrapping his fingers round it. *Doubt. Benefit of the doubt.* Why didn't the bats-man – and a batsman on 98 – get the benefit of the doubt? Adams' demeanour was magnificent. Adams didn't even hesitate at the crease. No hanging back in case the third umpire was invited to adjudicate. Adams was the man he'd hold up to Henry as an exemplar. Though the lad wasn't keen on cricket. Then what can you do with other people's children? Henry's father was a musician and a parody – that's the current word, parody – so Pewter could only do what was possible for him in this situation, and maybe talk a little bit of philosophy with the lad who, at least, must be made to accept that Pewter was an *educated* old fart. He opened the book at random, the Alasdair Gray: 1660 DIARY Samuel Pepys LONDON. Years ago, travelling in the Caribbean, he heard someone, a well-connected, highly cultivated businessman–politician, mispronounce Pepys – giving it two syllables. But there was no space in an island society like that to correct such a man. Pewter had thought that maybe his role was to help create that space. Ah, but who wanted to be ostracized, frozen out, to be labelled *English.* 'When Charles 1st's head got struck off all the parliament supporters there applauded as if at a play.' Good, racy, republican prose. He flipped over a chunk of the book. 'The Lollard Bible'. And again, Geoffrey Chaucer and, towards the back, David Hume and then Wordsworth. Surely, this is the book, 600-*plus* pages of text that he'd take with him on the Desert Island. And his luxury? A woman who was not Anne. Anne was not a luxury, Anne was a duty. *Anne had not liked his novel.* Forget about Anne.

At Edgbaston the West Indies captain collected a cheque for £21,000; and the Man of the Match got a jeroboam of champagne. Jeroboam is now a Caribbean word because of the cricket. The Man of the Match was Courtney Walsh. Jeroboam to you, Courtney!

That time the boy had asked him about Plato, and Pewter had discussed *The Symposium* – one of his favourites – with something like authority; only to discover that the lad was having him on; and really what he was interested in was music. He remembered an earlier trap about Mike Tyson. Letting a convicted rapist into the country to fight. Mother thinking he was a man, that's what men do – rape, fight; daughter more concerned that the rapist–boxer was not vegetarian. So in her eyes, Pewter, a meat-eater, might not be a million miles away from Tyson where public scorn is concerned. (So Pewter would have to learn more about music, about jazz, to secure the brother.) So who was he going to talk about *The Symposium* to? Forget about *The Symposium*. *The Book of Prefaces* gave him an idea for a book of his own – putting together his introductions to poetry readings, his setting up of the audience before each poem; but there was no one to discuss this project with . . .

So not to be wrong-footed by this sixteen-year-old: don't *play* the professor, don't encourage the fantasy of a mad woman from France who married a worthless black man in England, and now demands redress from another black man with his own problems. The secret karate lessons will remain secret. *Look at me walking along the street: I'm not just any old black man with white hair, an easy target* psshahaw*!!* So he will play his *human* card tonight, he will talk of, what? The visit to the supermarket that time – the one at Broomhill, at Somerfield – where he steered an unsuspecting mother away from buying a too-hard avocado as a treat for her young daughter. Though he must be careful of seeming to pat himself on the back.

So she wasn't happy with his novel, the mad Frenchwoman; she thought the ironies harsh and unfriendly. (*And you, heir to Voltaire and La Rochefoucauld?*) Don't get into that. Rather *think* music, for conversation with Henry: *Who wrote the lyrics to 'It Never Rains in Southern California'?* (Not jazz, but popular.) The girl, rebellious and unsophisticated, and wanting to pull the professor down a peg, was rightly scornful of his sudden interest in her recycled costume jewellery. So no room, then, on this trip to talk about (Gray) comparing Tyndal's and Coverdale's polemics on the Bible.

But Anne is not a figure of fun. Anne is a white woman with black children: she has been abused in the streets of London and Saint-Ouen (and elsewhere); she hasn't been spat at but she has been emotionally spat at; she has been threatened with sexual violence, by white men, by black men, *and she blames Pewter*. She has been taunted with being *easy*. Or shunned as an embarrassment. So with Pewter she would not be easy. Or seen as an embarrassment. She is amused when others talk about being on the front line. She is not amused, but claims to be amused when others talk about being on the front line.

So he's preparing himself for service in London. When he gets out at West Hampstead and arrives at the house Pewter learns that the children have gone to Glastonbury. So Pewter turns on the television while Anne makes a salad, and they watch Glastonbury together. It is easy to watch Glastonbury because at Euro 2000 France aren't playing until tomorrow – it's Portugal and Turkey this afternoon and someone else tonight. So they tried, unseriously, to see if they could spot the children in the mass of faces in the field. *Isn't Glastonbury one of those names that appears in Shakespeare?*

'You're always quoting Shakespeare,' she says. 'Give it a rest.'

'Sorry,' he says. 'Bad habit. *Mal idée.*'

And now what to do with Miss Vanesa in Paris, tomorrow, next week. For he has invited her; she is to be his guest. From the day after tomorrow.

Last time round, on the island, Miss Vanesa complained that everyone in England had treated her as if she were a man: they had set the bar higher for her; if this were a game of high-jump she would have to scale the heights set for the men while the women were let off with a lower level. And that's because she didn't have children, or a husband; and that was not to be tolerated. It was not tolerated at work because she didn't have children to pick up at a certain time; it was not tolerated at school or college because she didn't have children to be sick at awkward moments and hence force a change in your colleagues' schedules; and, of course, she didn't get the maternity leave: what was the point in being a woman with all the disadvantages of a woman without being able to claim maternity leave? Miss Vanesa had always argued that a woman had a right to maternity leave whether she chose to have a child or not. Instead of that they were now granting the *men* maternity leave (though they called it something else), but Miss Vanesa wasn't a man, so she didn't get paternity leave, either.

This conversation had taken place on the verandah, and Pewter had tried to see Miss Vanesa's point; though he feared she was setting him up. That's where he made his mistake, not reading properly between the lines, not realizing that Miss Vanesa was telling him something else. He imagined the same conversation, on the verandah, this time with Michael Carrington. Michael (no doubt armed with his divorce and new recklessness) would have read between the lines.

'So what mood are you in now, man or woman thing?'

Or, he would lead up to it. Even though thinking of the swing parties in England and Sweden, he wouldn't rush it. He would nod understandingly and brush her arm lightly with the back of his hand. He would ensure that the hand was naked, no rings. He would do it a second time to catch her attention in a special way. He would call her Nisa. Or Nise. He would encourage her in the belief that she was not a man; he would then gently urge her to demonstrate that she was not a man. They would end up downstairs in the jacuzzi. (*Later, with friends?*)

And now it was Pewter's turn to entertain the lady, in Paris.

He was still in Sheffield, at the bus stop, opposite the cathedral. And he felt vaguely wrong about everything; tomorrow, he'd be in Paris, and he wasn't ready. The trip to the supermarket was unnecessary. He'd been to Waterstone's to get a book on Sartre and Camus that someone had mentioned, but it wasn't in stock, so he bought another couple of books, unnecessarily; and he drifted round the corner to M&S for some tea. And fruit. Apart from the tea and a carton of strawberries at half-price, he ended up with some brown bread, olive oil and lamb chops. Why? There was already too much food in the flat, and he'd be away for at least two weeks. But that wasn't his main worry, it was more a question of whether he was losing grip; it was when he plunged his hand in his trouser pocket for the money and came up with a handkerchief instead. No big deal. (*Or, make a big deal of it. See? Magic!*) He usually kept his handkerchief in the right pocket and his money in the left. Why the switch over? Now he couldn't use the handkerchief contaminated with all that money *residue*. He had a brief fantasy of walking down a banking street in Zurich and dabbing his face with a handkerchief coated with gold dust. But it was more than the aesthetic thing. He had felt slightly wrong walking to the bus, and walking from the shop without quite knowing why. The weight of the coins on his right thigh seemed like an alien presence: he was accustomed to pushing lightly against it with the left thigh: was it because he dressed, as they say, on the left? That shifted you somewhat off-centre, necessitating the extra forward push of the left leg, urging against the arbitrariness of coins on the thigh to preserve the balance; for all you had against the corresponding right thigh was a white handkerchief – and the body knows about these things. Was he getting into the quality of sensation that would chime with Miss Vanesa in Paris?

Getting into the frame of mind to entertain Miss Vanesa he thought of his purchases in the supermarket. The olive oil. It was seriously expensive. Greek extra virgin olive oil. £3.49. Nearly two pounds more than he usually paid, at Somerfield. The Spanish virgin olive oil was exactly the same price, though more lightly coloured. And that was it, no great range in olive oil. Except for some half-bottles of 'organic' – at suitable organic prices. So he thought – as he waited for the No. 60 bus to Broomhill, he thought – two drops of Greek virgin olive oil in the jacuzzi should do it. (Thinking of the sardine breakfast on the island he had turned to another shelf in the supermarket. *Honey.* He would put out on the table: New Zealand Clover. He would offer a choice of Wildflower and Orange Blossom and Acacia. Cut Comb in Acacia . . .)

And then the bus came and sabotaged his fantasy.

*

He had invited her in return for the good time had on the island. He had invited her, also, because he thought the lives she had constructed for herself in Lisbon and Sweden needed augmenting. So Paris would be a treat for her.

He had, himself, known the city since the late 1960s and had effectively moved there a couple of years ago, commuting: 'Paris' had been intended as his gift to provincials like Miss Vanesa who had an imagination. Now, with the Carrington update, he feared he had miscalculated again; and it was the sophisticates (like Miss Vanesa) that he was luring to *his* parish. ('There's me, beside Beckett. On the wall of the Dôme.')

So the plan had to be revised. To pass it off as a sightseeing, a tourist thing. The slow build up from the Louvre and the Musée d'Orsay (and maybe the American bookshop nearby); and the trek over to the Marmottan, that was altogether too tame. World-weary discussions in this or that café that others had written about: 'There's me, beside Sam Beckett, on the wall . . .' The magic of the Degas at d'Orsay, yes, or the mystery of the Monets out at the Marmottan. But Montmartre? Do us a favour. Though the brutality of Sacré-Coeur might be reassuring. The bookshops. Shakespeare & Co. to say hello to young Sylvia. Checking out who's reading this Monday night. Or to the Village Bookshop down at Mabillon, that and for the restaurant on the corner where you got the best curried *moules* in Paris.

Then what? (*Miss Vanesa asks him after she has at last succumbed to his entreaties.*) Then what? Would she be interested in the street market on rue Ordiner, round from the flat? The tasteful, wholesome (sensual?) mounds of fresh fruit, the cheeses . . . that showed they were still in Old France? Or would they fake it, language-wise, attempt a French play (*Le Balcon* was playing, last time round, at some theatre in the middle of town, near Notre Dame. Remember to reread the text in English beforehand). An Old French restaurant afterwards, to deplore the fact that French cuisine had gone off, hence this new taste for curried *moules*. By now, he would have incurred Miss

Vanesa's pity. So maybe the music option might be the thing. There was a place he knew in Saint-Ouen – the One Way Bar. His flat was in the eighteenth: this was local. They had a blues band, not jazz (sorry, Henry), and it wasn't too smoky if you went early. French working-class rave-up. Weekends. Five o'clock start on a Sunday. This to show you're not a tourist. Failing that – what? You could get off the 95 at the place de Clichy and try to find Henry Miller's old Café Wepler, the place where Miller picked up that mysterious young woman who needed money way back in the 1930s – all set down in those early pages of *Quiet Days in Clichy* – and where the uncomplicated sex that seemed the order of the day was to be had. The worst you got in those days was the clap. Nys, her name was. Nys.

Well, had to think of the options, for he as yet knew of no private jacuzzis in Paris.

5

RT: On Missing
His Father's Funeral

I

RT wore a white costume now instead of a black one, but that wasn't intended as a crude ethnic statement, he said.

There were three things that irritated about RT (Russell Trajan, to give him his full name. Or Russell Trajan Harris, if you like), and that included his slight French accent and his vague air of condescension, a feature of which was his pose of sending himself up ('I may have married into the Morton clan in Guadeloupe, but that doesn't mean I've joined the legal ruling classes; or have my name on the family plaque on rue Delgrès'). He presumably wasn't part of any ruling class, living in one room in Highgate, in north London, as long as one could remember, eking out some sort of living, doing nonsense.

He also had a limp, consequence of a road accident in Pointe-à-Pitre; and we all knew the story of the accident to the point of disbelieving it. (It was a Sunday morning and he was visiting, less to effect a reconciliation than to agree the amicable distribution of the spoils of marriage. His share, a little house in Basse-Terre – fine by him – the wife [and family] properly lawyering their way into the rest of the property.)

He didn't live there of course, didn't live on the island; from now on the prospect of being a less-than-regular visitor promised. Forgetting that the bus didn't go to Basse-Terre on a Sunday he was stranded with a heavy bag and his case, thinking he couldn't return to what was now an ex-wife's preserve, and hence he had to consider booking himself into a cheap hotel as befitting his new status, and kill the rest of what would be a long Sunday; and head for Basse-Terre in the morning. The enforced idleness would do him no harm.

It was as he was crossing back into the quai Lefèvre from the main road that he looked right instead of left – all those years of living in England – and *bam*. It wasn't accurate to say that he woke up in hospital in Pointe-à-Pitre because he had never really passed out, but, yes, true to some god of irony or destiny, he opened his eyes to the ex-wife looking down serenely at him. (The power of the Morton clan.) He wasn't complaining, just sorting out in his mind whether this messy dénouement to the marriage showed culpability, or a satisfactory weight of closure; or whether it showed, in spectacular fashion, that he had always been an unsuitable match for the Mortons. Of course, what he was really wondering was whether he'd ever walk again. Later, he reflected: this is the price you paid for a little house in Basse-Terre that you weren't to see again for three and a half years, your leg broken in the process.

But we were talking about things about RT that irritated. The fact that he dressed as a priest now probably wasn't one of them, as that was a recent affectation, though it may have been adopted before his father's death. He'd always been into costume, anyway, though he saved us the embarrassment of body-piercings and tattoos. (When he came up to the university to give that talk, the costume certainly upstaged the lecture: his posing as a member of the order of the Fraternité Sacerdotale Saint Pie X intriguing us enough to overlook the incongruity of the talk.)

Oh, yes, one thing that didn't particularly irritate about RT was his tendency to lie about the state of his health.

II

At the university lecture RT told a joke about Antigua that would be expected to resonate with people from the region; and there was only one other person from the region present. (This was his 'Africa' phase, so West Indies was fair game.)

The joke was an elaborate defence of his missing his father's funeral in Montserrat, but all it seemed to do was to confirm that he had missed his father's funeral because he was busy swimming elsewhere in the Caribbean. (That's what his answerphone message had said when I had rung him to discuss details of the talk: 'I choose to assume you're not a burglar. For the next two weeks I shall be away swimming in the Caribbean. Voilà. Thanks.') Puzzling? Maybe not. For a lame man a small act of bravado? But then he wasn't very lame. And swimming would de-emphasize the lameness.

So RT had missed his father's funeral in Montserrat because he had been swimming with his mates in Guadeloupe, and the cover story of Antigua didn't mitigate that fact. Surely, it was not meant to. Later, the woman with the French accent in his flat in Highgate filled in the details: *RT and a couple of people whom he knew down there, casual fishermen down at Basse-Terre, would go swimming at Les Saintes when he was around. It was some sort of game that they played. A boat to the islands and then some sort of mad race from one point to another – Fort Joséphine to Fort Napoléon, or whatever; the things that boys do. Then the jog along the beach.*

After the City lecture I had wondered – during the lecture, really – I was wondering why RT (T for Trajan, Son of Hadrian, Emperor of Rome, AD 53–117, builder of aqueducts, roads, of course, and canals, bridges; conductor of a lengthy exchange of letters on the *affaires* of state with Pliny, the man, not the boy Pliny; subduing all sorts of peoples whose names we forget, building a library) – why RT had not made more of his being named for (as they say) the illustrious ancient? To my knowledge RT never talked Ancient History, and preferred, anyway, to answer to Russell than to Trajan, though RT was how he was generally known. Was his deliberately missing his father's funeral – swimming in the Caribbean, indeed, doing the channel between the islets in Les Saintes – part of a traceable line of filial rejection that had made RT the arrested adolescent he was?

I wasn't that exercised by the question, but an invitation to RT's room in Highgate provided an explanation. It was after a poetry reading at Lauderdale House on the Archway Road that I had occasion to visit his room, and met the explanation.

There I met Gabby. The name rang a bell, and the accent was the clue: she clearly knew him but this wasn't her place. She was familiar with him as a partner of long-standing would be but she treated the room as a visitor might; she had been his partner, yes, but she was no longer his partner; she was Gabby, his Morton lady from Guadeloupe. (RT's way of explaining her was to be expected: 'When we were married Gabby showed me contempt, now she shows me pity. I like it that way.')

RT was dressed as for his lecture, elegant and magnificent in its simplicity. All white, down to his sandals, with a low collar. Slimline cut, describing the body of a swimmer. White socks. Black sandals. The deep cuffs on the sleeves and broad band round the waist had had the members of staff deconstructing it round the lunch table next day. As expected, on my visit to Highgate, he told the Antigua story again.

He had come into Antigua on the day of the funeral, on his way to Montserrat. You couldn't fly through to Montserrat from Guadeloupe, had to get a new ticket, change planes at Antigua. From LIAT to whatever, Winair. So he's at the counter at the airport in Antigua trying to buy a ticket to Montserrat. But they can't accommodate his Mastercard, his Maestro Servicecard. Nice girls, polite, too; but: didn't he have a Visa card? And the hole in the wall – neither of the machines – couldn't help, either. So he has to go to the bank at the other end of the counter and queue for forty minutes – the lone man behind the counter scribbling, scribbling – only to be told that the bank, too, can't deal with his Servicecard. Did he have a Visa card? No. Yes, but not on him. He had used the Maestro card that morning in Guadeloupe. No problem. But now he's told he must go out of the airport and across the road (his bags untended), to the Bank of Antigua on the corner. The building was imposing in a way he didn't quite trust, the air-conditioning too severe, but the message was the same. This time he was directed across town to the Bank of Nova Scotia; he had had to mug somebody in the street to get the money to pay for his flight to Montserrat, but he missed the flight anyway. There was only one detail of this story, he said, that was made up.

What was RT wearing, I wanted to ask – fascinated by his

changing costume over the years – when he went to the bank in Antigua?

But the woman anticipated me. 'The banks are on to them now. And their disguise.' And she hissed, conspiratorially, 'Terrorism.'

'Don't shoot, I said,' RT chipped in. 'Blood on the cloth. Nasty. Never wash out. Excommunicated from the Ordre.'

The ex-wife was more forthright: 'What is it with these men? You send a child to school, he knows where the school is; he doesn't have a problem in getting to school. You send the girl who works round the house to the shops, to the market. You say, Fania, go buy the fish at this place not that other place where the fish not fresh. Test the pears and fruit and thing and don't bring back no foolishness. Whether the salad tired or whatever. And even a girl from the country area can do that after you train her for a little while. Before the supermarket shopping you check to see if you're low on matches, whatever. So what is it with these men? When you drive them to the airport. You put them on the plane and all they have to do is to change planes one time – is only a twenty-minute flight – to change planes one time to go to his father's funeral – and even then he has to go miss the funeral!'

RT had no satisfactory answer to that except to clown.

'Is possible,' he said, 'that the secular orders at the airport were intimidated by my mission.'

'They're all very religious, don't talk foolishness; they'd be queuing up to help a man of the cloth.'

'The cloth,' RT said, in a magisterial way, 'was in its wrapping in the case. To be unveiled for a sterner test than a twenty-minute shuttle in a V2-LFL 19-seater . . . Where the skygod may well have been thinking: "You have not yet written that epic of the crabs and the sand."'

And then over dinner we talked about life in the islands

(and in France), and had the usual minor disagreements over the sameness/differences between the Anglo and Franco outposts in the Caribbean. And the point of RT's dress at the airport was being lost. Instead RT did a well-rehearsed description of the Morton clan gathered at dinner, spouting legal jargon. Naturally, I tried to block it out by easing the conversation back to that time when he missed turning up to his father's funeral.

For surely, in Antigua, they would have accepted his card if he had been dressed as he was now, in his sepulchral white! And his limping would add to the effect. Because even for me there would be a hinterland of experience behind all that. Punishment behind the grace. The body elegantly clothed despite its disfigurement. Yes, I had images of RT pushing himself to the limit, this way, that way – running, boxing, cycling – and after the shower walking (limping) out in a new environment, resplendent in clothes for the perfect body. (Would he be donning a tracksuit, next, and training for the London Marathon?) That, stupidly, made me think of Herr Stumph, a man I used to know in the South of France.

Herr Stumph was a German businessman building a villa in the South of France, somewhere between the Alpes Maritimes and the Var. Now, this villa was a long way from Cannes but the deal was that Herr Stumph should be able to see Cannes harbour from his terrace in this village in the Alpes Maritimes or the Var or wherever. And as the land on which the villa was being built was in a bit of a dip, forest all around, no way could he see Cannes harbour from his terrace. So the solution was to go up a storey so that the businessman could see Cannes harbour from his terrace. But still no luck. What to do? New plans are drawn up in Paris and Berlin. Raise the building, add another floor – effectively converting it from villa to château. No expense spared. But the problem is: Herr Stumph is dealing with a Socialist Building Cooperative. The members, predominantly French, have ideas of what the buildings put up in the region should be like. They don't like châteaux in villa country. Stumph arranges to fly in with his lawyer and his architect. They are genial (Herr Stumph is a big man with one leg and an ill-fitting stump, but he's game); it's lunchtime on the *chantier*; Herr Stumph supplies the wine, and partakes of a glass, though he doesn't have lunch. At the end of which socialist principles rule: the building will go no higher; Herr Stumph will not get to see Cannes harbour from his terrace.

But this is not the point of the story about Herr Stumph that first comes to mind as I observe RT's limp under his beautiful whatever-it-was priestly costume. It was Stumph's limp, that I recalled. There were steps everywhere in the villa. Up from the dining room to the indoor pool, and then down. Up to the first floor, of course, but especially narrow. And then a steep winding construction (designed by Stumph and his architect – or by Stumph and his lawyer) to a sort of concrete 'bird's nest' look-out. Now, the boys on the cooperative put down Herr Stumph's behaviour to good old-fashioned Germanness, some guiltily, others openly associating this attitude with a national trait. I thought of this now as I tried to work out an explanation of RT's behaviour. I wasn't entirely convinced of the analogy, but I couldn't be bothered to pursue it further.

III

But I couldn't give up on RT's way with disguise – or costume, if you like. Was the African phase over? I scanned the walls for clues. All available space in the main room, the tiny kitchen, the passageway, the loo was covered with maps, dominated by a giant plan of the London Underground. Framed. This hit you as you entered the apartment. Apart from two what you might call real pictures, one of the Caribbean, all the other wall-coverings were prints of foreign cities and – clearly – computer-generated pictures of Africa. But large. With the individual countries colour-coded. In this one Africa consisted of only seven countries in primary colours, in that one, nine, and a lot of blank space. I knew why, I had heard his lecture. But there were pictures of Africa where four or five countries were in pink. RT had scorned the suggestion that he was colour-coding Africa according to some notion of Western democracy. No, he was merely registering the civilizing habit in Africa of heads of state retiring, without violence or the need for exile, after their term of office had expired. Of the civilizing centres he named those we all know: Tanzania, Zambia, Senegal, South Africa.

I asked to be reminded of the others.

Of course, he said, the habit had spread in Senegal, when Abdou Diouf, the fellow who followed Senghor, also left when he was voted out of office.

'And the others?'

'Even the kleptomaniac, Siaka Stevens in Sierra Leone stood down voluntarily, in 1985. Of course he was eighty at the time. And he'd hand-picked his successor.'

'I see.'

'And over in Cameroon Ahmadu Ahidjo, again after twenty-two years, decided he'd had enough.'

'Not bad. Twenty-two years.'

I was in the process of saying that I fancied that the Frelimo leadership in Mozambique would stand down if it was voted out of office, when Gabby intervened. Enough of boy-talk, she said. This was all very interesting, no doubt, but could we talk about something else? So I looked around – past the Guadeloupe scene – to the other real picture on show. It was in the bedroom but it could be seen from the passage. The main interest of it was Gabby looking regal as the Queen of France. It was a family photo with RT, Gabby and their young daughter, whose name was something like Thérèse or Ismé; and it was taken, Gabby admitted, in the gardens of Fontainebleau on a sunny day. It was one of those jobs where the cardboard cut-outs are in place with a space for you to insert your head; and RT confessed how good the family still looked as Henry IV (of France), Marie de Medici and (the girl) the young Louis XIII. Dressed simply, but royally.

Gabby was playing her part. 'For some men,' she said, 'the games never stop.'

Lisa, who teaches renaissance at the university, and is our renaissance person, generally, says that the Fraternité Sacerdotale Saint Pie X is legitimate. A massive Catholic organization dedicated to the memory and teachings of Pius X (obvious, really) with branches all over the world. So now I must assume that RT wasn't wearing his kit when he was being given a hard time at the bank in Antigua, and at the airport. If he'd come through all white and virginal, the two nice girls at the counter would have found a way to convert his Maestro Servicecard into money. Or the slow man behind the counter at the bank, endlessly scribbling on the customers' receipts (notes for a post-colonial novel?) would have come up with something better than an apology. Or the ones at the Bank of Antigua. At some point RT would have pulled himself up to his no-limp height, flicked the card and Hey presto: Maestro would be transformed into Visa. (Gabby had revealed, at the house in Highgate, that RT had possessed a Visa card, but had misplaced it.) Or he would have clapped his hands as if to release a bird and Antigua would be instantly joined to Montserrat by fresh volcanic land, and the chauffeur pulled up ready to drive the thirty miles to the funeral. Or RT would just simply begin to chant a favourite bit of St Augustine's *Confessions* in an educated language and . . .

But then he would have got to Montserrat, wouldn't he? In time for the funeral; and that would be another story. (And why, I ask, didn't he choose a less well-known religion to travel by?)

6

'With Regret, Mr Watford . . .'

After the event the delegation arrived at Miss Vanesa's house, two women of a certain aspect and a younger one, Nora Hyphen being the first. She was early and they had crossed on the road when Miss Vanesa had popped out to get something at the shops; and Miss Vanesa had felt a bit guilty that the time had crept up on her and she hadn't got around to reading the Paule Marshall story again. As the two cars swung towards a standstill, the road being gutted, Nora had made Miss Vanesa smile.

'Your road makes me look like a drunk, and I don't drink.' She had said this absolutely without the least flicker of a smile, looking neither right nor left, gripping the wheel and staring intently ahead. Vanesa signalled she'd soon be back.

Miss Vanesa didn't know what amused her more, repetition of the joke she had heard so often before, or the suggestion that Nora Hyphen didn't drink. Her usual defence of that extra glass (or two) of wine, was a source of mild amusement to her friends: 'They don't tell me I have diabetes or high blood pressure yet, so let me drink it while I still can.' Or, in equally deadpan manner: 'I don't start flying the aircraft yet. Don't panic, you're not going to crash. So, cheers!' Of the other women, who hadn't yet arrived at Miss Vanesa's, one was Winifred, an old friend, and the other was a young woman not long on the island: they formed the Committee Against Arwell Barnes.

Arwell Barnes was or was not a figure of fun on the island; his utterances could be impressive and lure you into thinking that he was something of a scholar: after all, he had worked at a university in England. 'After the sack of Rome in 410,' Arwell was known to explain, 'Europeans almost entirely forgot how to read, write and lay bricks. For a thousand years.' And it was the odd detail in his information – the 'laying bricks' in this case – that had even intelligent men like Pewter Stapleton and Michael Carrington claiming that the man was 'interesting'. At the very least it was meant to signal that Arwell had spent 'quality time' in another country, and was now a prominent Returnee. Like an astute politician he was prepared to confirm that his job had been as 'gatekeeper' to the users of the university library, and he left it to others to draw their conclusions as to its importance. The fact that no one, after his words of wisdom, remembered much of what Arwell said was neither here nor there. He'd built a reputation for being informed.

Back on the verandah when the women were discussing something else – Nora was explaining to the others the difference between a debit and a credit card, in terms of the interest you paid for the service – Miss Vanesa thought back to scenes with Arwell, right here where they were sitting, when Arwell's stock of useless information came in handy to fill a gap in the conversation. She didn't mind him, really, his big talk; at least he was striving to improve himself, unlike some others they could name. If he had chanced to come back to the island without a wife, without a woman, at least he didn't bring back some sorry joke-figure, snatched up at random, who thought a few years in the sun with a returnee was compensation for all that bad light and depression and dampness: she was thinking of the sort of wife Paule Marshall's Mr Watford might have had, had he been in England instead of America where things were more colour-coded. But Arwell got things wrong, that's why he had to be watched; the way he jumped the gun with his cards, for instance.

ARWELL BARNES SR.
(*President*)
RETURNEE'S CLUB
LONDON AND CARIBBEAN
Tel: 491 449 7864

'President of a club of one.' That was Nora Hyphen's verdict.

'Can't damn a man for an apostrophe,' Fred said. 'Just because the apostrophe in the wrong place.'

'I thought you was on our side,' the young woman said.

'We have to start talking good English, you know,' Nora said. 'To show we're not the same as Arwell Barnes . . . To show that *we are* not the same as Arwell Barnes.'

'What, with a bit of French and Latin thrown in?'

'We don't have to go that far.'

'Arwell's English not that bad,' the young woman said. Then, looking out over the railing: 'Is that pigeon peas I see you put in there next to the red pepper? Like you having green fingers now, Vanesa; like a real country woman.'

'Vanesa will be feeding us all come the revolution, eh?' Fred teased.

'They're not getting on too bad, badly,' Miss Vanesa conceded.

'The garden's looking nice.' Then Nora returned to the earlier subject under discussion: 'Arwell's English mightn't be that bad; just sometimes he gets caught up in his own cleverness.'

'Sad fact of life,' Miss Vanesa confirmed, 'men getting caught up in their own cleverness.' But she, too, echoed Nora's anxiety about Arwell, now elected president of the Returnees' Club.

Some said that the Returnees' Club was exclusive, but the election of Arwell put the lie to all that. Maybe they should just call it the Inclusive Club and throw membership open to the whole island. Fact is: the club wasn't exclusive enough, not because it admitted people who were not returnees, but because it was open to *all* returnees. Did they really think a brain-doctor, what d'you call a brain-doctor, again?

Daddy and Sweetie Pie . . . Sugardaddy?

A neurosurgeon.

Did the neurosurgeon have more in common with the ex-mini-cab driver in London or the truck loader in Toronto, just because they happened to be returnees?

'Is not a matter of class,' Fred said. 'We talking of experience of the wide world.'

'We *are* talking.'

'What you say, Nora?' (Deliberately.)

'We're talking. Not "we talking".'

'You not in you boardroom now, you know, Nora; you can't sack us because we're . . . idiomatically challenged.'

'Lord, it's getting worse.'

'Boys, boys,' Miss Vanesa called them to order, and getting up, made for the kitchen. 'Maybe we should have a little drink and settle down.'

'I don't drink, as you know,' said Nora Hyphen.

'I don't drink either.'

'Nor me.'

So Miss Vanesa went to get the drinks.

Fred, who was secretary of the club, had sketched out a programme of events, to be discussed with the committee before being put to Arwell. They would keep dominoes out of the club, and all that kind of foolishness; but admit card games.

But not for money.

No, not for money, no; that was common. This ain't Las Vegas.

'Though this *isn't* Las Vegas, it would be nice to have a Frank Sinatra coming to sing.'

'There was a programme on Sinatra the other night, you see it?'

'I never like the way he wear – wears – the headpiece. The toupee.'

'What them man get up to!'

'If it was woman doing that sort of thing, they would have call her every name under the sun.'

'Are we talking about Arwell Barnes or are we talking about Frank Sinatra?'

'If I was a man married to you, Nora, I would fraid fraid, you know!'

The suggestion to get Michael Jackson to come along to the club to explain what he had done to his face didn't lessen the tension, so Miss Vanesa told a story about Arwell Barnes.

It was a story about the ignorance – or maybe it was the wit? – of Arwell, but she didn't get very far into it. She wasn't herself into this foolish business of going around stressing that the people she knew on the island were all medical doctors and lawyers and successful business types – though, she was proud to know that in Nora here, they had a successful business type among them. But people thought they were green; all this talk of someone they knew making a million dollars speculating in America and then coming home to build a big house. Miss Vanesa's only criterion for people who came regularly to her home was that they weren't narrow minded and that they read books.

So what if they beat their women and read books, too?

OK. People who read books and didn't beat their women were welcome.

'Of course some of the women and them out of control,' the young woman said.

'Girl, where you grow up?'

'London. And then I went to live in Birmingham.'

'And you went to university, what you study at university?'

'Media Studies.'

'So you know a lot about films.'

'Come, man, let's not fall out among weselves. Ourselves. Like thieves in the Bible.'

And after a pause, Miss Vanesa said, 'Give him his due, Arwell reads books.'

Did Arwell really read books, Fred wanted to know, or did Arwell just say he read books? Just pretended to read books; and quote from them?

What we needed, said Nora, was to redevelop the art of conversation. In danger of being lost. Each home should have a drawing-room space, for digesting as well as reading.

Digesting sounded like a problem you went to the chemist for.

Had Arwell read the Paule Marshall story? Miss Vanesa wondered, trying to concentrate their minds.

'I don't know if I like that story, you know,' the Media Studies woman said.

'None of us likes that story,' Miss Vanesa said.

'He wooing you with he coconut tree and ground dove.'

'Five hundred coconut trees, not just one!'

'And a big house even though it not finish.'

'Don't get your hopes up: he only wears a doctor's coat,

he's not a doctor. Just a hospital porter all those years in Boston. Of course I'm not prejudiced, I don't mind the job a man does for a living as long as he has manners where women are concerned,' Nora said.

'Arwell would never recognize himself in that story,' Fred said.

None of the men would recognize themselves in that story, Nora was certain. 'What she calls him? In the story. "Nasty, pissy old man."'

'And some of these old men are nasty and pissy, you know,' Fred confirmed.

'I don't know any old man like that,' the Media Studies woman said. 'In fact, I don't think I know any old man, period. Except family. Not in that way, you know.'

'You lucky.'

'I hope that you're not implying that the rest of us know old men like that. Nasty, pissy old men like that.'

'There should be a law against nasty, pissy old men.'

'Certainly, they should ban them from the island.'

'That's a fascist attitude.'

'You and your big words.'

'You know I rather have a what you call a racial prejudice man in my bed than one of them nasty, pissy old men.'

'Jesus God.' And after a pause. 'It's the Last Days,' Nora Hyphen said.

'The Last Days,' Miss Vanesa echoed.

'Even though they old they still mistreat the women,' Fred said.

And there was a slight pause.

'So where does that take us?' Miss Vanesa asked. 'Talking of Arwell.'

'He have to go, man, he have to go.'

'Girl, what have you got against the English language, the language of Shakespeare and . . . Vidia Naipaul? Like you did your Film Studies course somewhere inside Russia?'

'Media Studies.'

'All right, Media Studies.'

Ever the diplomat, Miss Vanesa resumed the little story about Arwell that had been interrupted earlier.

When Miss Vanesa had finished Fred said she believed the story.

Nora said she believed it, too.

The young woman said men were strange; particularly when they got to be older.

The other women thought men were strange, full stop.

Returning to Arwell Barnes, Fred said: 'I think you're right, we should find him a suitable partner . . .'

'Like the Vikram Seth book.'

'. . . Or any presentable woman.'

'So we're in the marriage guidance service, now,' the young woman observed.

'Jane Austen in reverse. Genderwise,' said Nora Hyphen. 'I see.'

II

At the next meeting Fred had some amended texts for approval, one of which was Arwell's card. The three women observed it. (The young Media Studies graduate was not present.)

'OK,' Nora said, 'the apostrophe is the easy part. But it still says Senior here. "ARWELL BARNES SR." What's this mean? What's he senior of? I can understand when the Americans and those sorts of people put Junior after their name. Meaning son. Like Martin Luther King Jr. Showing that they have something of a family tree to their name. You know about family trees, Fred, you've traced yours.'

'I don't even know if I want to go there any more,' Fred started to say. But Nora spoke over her:

'So I can understand that. Or I can understand, you know, the Third. Henry Cotton the Third, or whatever. Like the kings and Popes and . . . those sorts of people. But when Arwell calls himself Senior does it mean he has a son somewhere he's providing with heritage?'

'He have a daughter. If it's a son, maybe it's an outside son.'

'Fred, you're beginning to talk like our departed friend.'

'She not departed, you know, she only leave the committee.'

'I hope she doesn't think we didn't appreciate her input,' Nora said unconvincingly.

'She might come back,' Miss Vanesa said; 'we're a broad church.'

'Muhammad and the mountain,' Nora said.

'Bringing Muhammad to the mountain,' Miss Vanesa confirmed.

'No, man, that's the easy bit. It's when you start bringing the mountain down to Muhammad that's when it gets interesting.' And, changing tack; back to the card: 'And, of course, in the wrong context, Senior could mean senior citizen. It's what they call the Law of Unintended Consequences, you know. Are we hinting that this is a retirement club?'

'The returnees are nearly all retirees, Nora. Except for the few children and –'

'I'm talking of the concept, you know. We want to leave open the possibility that you might wish to return to the island not only when you're old and exhausted, and given your best to some foreign place; but when you're at the peak of your . . . of your, whatever: fitness and . . . mental adventurousness.'

'Pulling power,' Fred said. They ignored this.

Nora continued. 'We have to educate people like Arwell away from their own sense of importance.'

Vanesa usually knew when to step in to prevent a situation developing in the wrong direction. So now she said:

'And I think it should be specific.' She was looking at Arwell's card. 'I think the island should be put on it, should be named; rather than all this London and Caribbean business. And an address. Pinning down the idea to a place. I know that Arwell is from St Caesare. So this isn't his place. But this is where we are.'

'That's right,' Fred agreed.

And the conversation became more concrete and productive.

But Fred had a question. What did Nora mean by Muhammad and the mountain? She didn't understand, she must be particularly slow today.

Oh, that. Nora was only thinking of Arwell's joke; the joke about Arwell that Miss Vanesa had told the other day.

Miss Vanesa liked the story: *the day when someone was visiting, a university lecturer from England whom they knew; Arwell, naturally, must have muscled in on the gathering. And she wasn't even that aware of Arwell till he made the comment. But of course, knowing Arwell, you could see that he would find some way of trying to engage with the lecturer, however stupid. The professor was saying something about lack of communication and the class system still being in place in England, and such like. Anyway, on the occasion in question, at this university in England, everyone was invited in to this lunchtime talk, including the support staff – you know, the secretaries and technicians, and people. And this professor came on and did his stuff. And the talk was way above the head of most of those present, intentionally; because the professor was into his power-trip thing. The usual. And it was at that point that Arwell, who maybe wasn't even invited, Miss Vanesa couldn't remember . . . At that point Arwell piped up and said that if the high talk was taking place in a space above where the audience were gathered – i.e. above their heads – then all you needed was to get the bright*

*people to go up there into that space; and then they could
tell the professor what's what. That was Arwell Barnes.*

'They call it linguistic pragmatism,' Nora Hyphen observed,
leaving the company no wiser.

*

The problem now, it was agreed, was Nora Hyphen. Mrs
Shackley-Bennett living up to her name. Lady Nora asserting her status as a member of the English upper-middle
class. Nora, who would draw attention to herself and (by
association) other returnees and put them all at risk. Of
ridicule.

Nora duly admitted to travelling not with baggage (a
crude term) but with luggage. She would not collude with
those of her parents' generation who had made the journey to Europe and America in the 1950s and were conned
into leaving much of what they possessed behind. And she
was not, of course, talking about physical possessions –
she wasn't one for rewriting history – she wasn't talking
about things you could weigh and measure and count.
Because you couldn't measure and weigh them, people
tended not to put a value on them. In fact, they even
thought you didn't have them. Now on the return journey,
the return trip after fifty years, the same thing. Of course
they now had possessions. If you drove the buses and the
trains, and cleaned the patients in the hospitals and whatnot – worked in the service industry – you picked up new
skills along the way; you weren't like the ignoramuses
who thought that the water just came out of the tap *like
that*, or electricity from the turning on of a switch. Or, for
that matter, that your body waste just disappeared by you
reaching out for a little handle on the cistern of your toilet.
If this was understood, if these things were understood,
people would appreciate the legacy owed to us.

So, yes, they had all built their houses on the island, on the islands. The furniture was modern, the kitchen well stocked and all the usual electrical and computer gadgets accompanied the new returnee. And for what? Everywhere in the region they were encountering problems with the people who had stayed behind. In one place that shall be nameless, returnees were actually being murdered for their fridge and computer. Generally, it hadn't come to that here; though you daren't leave your house empty for long and go off-island in case the rascals invited themselves in and gave you a beating, in a manner of speaking.

So, both in order to respect the time you had spent abroad, and to protect yourself from the rascals at home, you had to prioritize the *invisible* assets: the drawing room of C. L. R. James and Toni Morrison; of Shakespeare and Claude Monet, etc.

Nora's ideas for the club would exclude everyone, not just the Mr Watfords; and Fred was on the point of resigning. Fred, as club secretary, had worked on the correspondence, and had brought some papers over for checking with Vanesa. Nora had been so brutal with Fred's drafts that Fred had no option but to resign. Nora wasn't present at this meeting, of course, it was only Fred and Vanesa. The general letter of rejection to applicants to the club had been prepared, essentially to reject Mr Watford without unnecessary hurt to his feelings; and it had been thrown back into Fred's face by Nora. Fred was a big woman with a father whose name was still respected in the arts and sciences in the academic world, she didn't have to accept this sort of insult from anyone, certainly not in the place that she was now and called her home. Fred showed Vanesa a copy of the original letter of rejection – the black-balling letter – demanding to know why it had received such rough treatment from Nora:

Xxxxxxxxxxxx
Xxxxxxxxx
Xxxxxxx
Xxxxxxxx

xx.x.xxxx

Dear Mr Watford,

The Returnees' Club welcomes all Returnees
back to the island, and we wish you a
pleasant and crime-free retirement. And
you would be very welcome, indeed, to pop
in any time we're open, and make use of
such facilities as we have.

It is with regret, Mr Watford, that we
can't, at the moment, enrol new members to
the Club. The aims and responsibilities
are under review — and we would very soon
be able to clarify the situation. When
this has been sorted out, and we know
exactly where we stand, we'll be able to
discuss things further with you.

Thanks for your patience; and thank you for
thinking of joining the Returnees' Club.

Yours sincerely,

Winifred Belair
Club Secretary

'Back' (second line) was circled in a green pen; the phrase
'sorted out, and we know exactly where we stand' was
underlined, at the end of which was a question mark; and
in the space after the signing-off, Nora had written: 'Not
sure about "crime-free" environment. First of all, it might
not be true, and secondly, to stress it, seems to strike the

wrong note. "Returnees" would presumably, anyway, have a sense of the law & order situation on the island – they must have visited, from time to time – and, anyway, shouldn't the club we have in mind be prioritizing something *cultural* rather than going in for police forecasting? PS: Hope you don't mind my editing.'

Yet there were three pages of single-spaced suggestions of how Fred should proceed with the club; also an analysis of the results of the questionnaire that Nora had put out about a flying doctor service for the returnees. Something to connect them with hospitals and specialists in neighbouring islands.

*

They had all been patient with Nora, whose island was still in the grip of volcano. But the women didn't all go along with her fantasy club; her aching for a drawing room of the good and the great, with C. L. R. James and Derek Walcott in conversation. It might be therapy for her, but the rest of them didn't need therapy. But the women were alerted when a car pulled up, prompting Fred to say something under her breath.

'We have to stay calm,' Miss Vanesa said, also sotto voiced; and then turned to greet the visitor.

'Nora, good to see you; sorry about the road, again.'

'Vanesa. Winifred. I'm glad you're here. Just the people I want to take into my confidence. Look, talking of the returnees, I have an idea. I have an idea, as Michael Caine said to the gang of criminals at the end of that film. You remember? When their truck is balancing over the cliff.'

7

Background to the Rumour that the Women Are Lesbian

*O**n Fred's verandah. Nora Hyphen is on the phone, the mobile. Rock music in the background. Off.*

'. . . and they have to learn to distinguish between the foot and the leg. I'm not saying anything strange. "My foot, my tutor". The man didn't say "My leg, my tutor". Not the same thing, eh? Right. OK . . . OK, let me put it this way. Say, you're a doctor, a medical doctor, one of those y'know, surgeons with a malicious temper, the ones that like to use the knife and the . . . the saw, as in the old . . . Well, I wouldn't put it past some of them. Anyway . . . Well, anyway, you go into this surgery place, this surgery with a problem with the feet; it happens all the time, diabetes and . . . yes. So. And you need a radical solution. It might be that the toes and the foot have to come off. Eh, what's that? No, I'm not being morbid, just sensitive of what you need to do to survive in this modern world and . . . Yes, as I was saying, all that's bad enough. Dancing days over and . . . Well, I do sound as if I'm joking; what I'm saying is this: imagine if the doctor, the surgeon doesn't know the difference between the foot and the leg. And he takes the whole thing off – I'm assuming this joker to be a man – and he takes the whole thing off up to the knee. Now, that's not funny, either. And just because the man can't tell the difference between foot and leg, you understand what I'm saying! . . . Yes, of course. Of course a . . . an out-of-the-ordinary example because I don't want to bring this down too close to home. It's too easy to depress each other with what's happening when it's under your nose.'

At that point another woman, Fred, comes out of the house with a placard; swaying to the music inside. She holds up the placard, silently, to Nora, who, after a few seconds, nods, while she responds to the person on the other end of the phone with uncommitted grunts. Fred suddenly sings 'Foolishness, foolishness, *foolishness*' along with the climax to the song on the radio, or tape; then leans the placard gently against the wall; and goes back into the house.

Nora apologizes to the person on the other end of the phone, and becomes animated again: 'I know, I know; just because you want them to call me names, names that I don't even think are in any of the dictionaries on my shelf. That's how the guilty react. You point out that this is a foot made for walking. It's such a logical thing, evolution-wise: what else are you going to do with this thing at the end of your body, but to use it for balance as you try to stay upright? As you try to shift your position forward. If a snake had proper feet it would want to stand tall rather than be forever wriggling about in the grass and scaring people, wriggling around in the grass like a nasty metaphor in the Bible; you get my meaning?

'But when you point this out to these men they hate you; they call you names, you'd never believe they ever had a mother. And of course they wear shoes most of the time; the angry foot nearly always comes with a shoe, like they used to do with the horses; so it's a foot with added value that's getting you in the ribs, in the stomach . . . In the back. So what I'm saying is: you don't have a shoe on the leg, you have a shoe on the foot. Language is not a stupid thing. And that's your weapon in the home. What I say is, the home is the most dangerous place for a woman to be . . . What? . . . I don't know, child, I don't know; if I knew I'd take it to the patent office and I'd be a rich woman today.

'But I see I'm boring you with all this; you've gone all silent; you're listening to me now out of politeness, calling me names in your head . . . that's if you're listening to me at all. Paula, you there? I know you have on your whatever-coloured glasses, and you're hearing the music we all want to hear, so don't let me spoil your daydream. But I tell you, girl, no man in this world is so dirty and ugly and illiterate that he doesn't think he can use his foot on a woman and get away with it. I have to say in that case I don't have a problem, personally, with the foot coming off. I'm not a Moslem; not even an eye-for-an-eye Christian; I'm not referring to any higher law; I'm just for the law of civilized behaviour. And normal treatment of women, that's all; nothing heavy. But I'm making you uncomfortable, now. So I'll let you go and . . . What? . . . Something wrong? No, child, I'm sitting here enjoying the view – with Fred doing her thing – I'm thanking my luck that there's a man somewhere slaving over a hot stove preparing my dinner for tonight. I'll tell you about it, sometime. And sorry to lecture you again, I know you're just indulging me.' She signs off and switches off the phone.

Fred comes out of the house wearing a T-shirt – a new song on the radio – modelling it for Nora.

Fred's T-shirt reads:

THANK YOU
FOR NOT FINGERING
THE GOODS
WOMEN FROM MANY LANDS

'That's nice,' Nora says, turning her full attention, now, on Fred. 'We'll get this one mass-produced; and distribute it free. Courtesy of Mr Shackley-Bennett.'

'He'll praise you from the grave. For committing him to all these good deeds.'

'He was cremated, you know, he's not in any grave.'

'It's just a figure of speech, Nora.'

'I know it's a figure of speech. But is it the right figure of speech, that's all I'm saying.'

At that moment a vehicle pulls up and a young man – a boy – gets out and greets the women. He opens the back of the vehicle and brings out a box of vegetables, which he is in the process of taking to the verandah, to Fred.

'Ainsley, good to see you,' Nora says. 'You got something for me, too?'

'Yes, Miss Nora, I have it there.'

'Well, you'll best leave it here; put it in the back of the car there, when you're finished. I hope you're not bringing me anything tired and past their sell-by date? Like last time.'

'Is what you select, Miss Nora.'

Ainsley takes Fred's crate of fruit and vegetables to the verandah.

'Bring it inside, Ainsley,' Fred says. 'If it not dripping.'

The boy's attention is caught by Fred's shirt; similar to his, but different. The lettering on his saying:

THANK YOU
FOR SHOPPING
AT
ASTAPHANS

'Do you like the lady's version?' Nora asks, about to make another phone call. Fred straightens up, her tits prominent, embarrassing both the lad and Fred. Fred pays him quickly without further comment and the lad hurries to put Nora's order in her car.

'Thanks, for bringing this,' says Nora, as if nothing has occurred, fishing in her bag. 'You're a good boy, Ainsley. Good looking, too. How's your mother?'

'She there.'

'You have to treasure her, you know; she won't always be there. And you're not getting yourself into any trouble?'

'No, Miss Nora.'

'No drugs, or anything like that?'

'I not into any drugs or anything.'

'Not getting any young girls into trouble?'

'I don't know what you mean, you know.'

'Well, you're on the right track. Thanks for bringing the vegetables.'

As the boy drives away Nora tells Fred that her T-shirt was going to make her the talk of the island. And had she considered going into politics? And then hearing a car, without looking in the direction of the sound, she announces the approach of Vanesa.

'Fred, can I trouble you for a glass of water?'

'Glass of water coming up.' But she stops and checks. 'You mean water, Nora?'

'You know, the thing that comes out of the tap.' She opens her bag and takes out some pills; maybe aspirin.

II

The three women were going to dine with Arwell Barnes, the new president of the Returnees' Club, and they hadn't decided yet how to play it. Interesting, that Fred has changed her T-shirt for a dressy top.

'He's clearly making a statement,' Nora said. 'Taking us to his house; his home. The normal thing would be . . . the normal thing for a single man –'

'A widow.'

'In effect, a single man. The normal thing would be to do this in a public place.'

'We can take care of ourselves.'

'Like a restaurant.'

'Well, he wants to show he's got nothing to hide,' Fred assumed.

'Of course, you've been to his place.'

'I haven't been to his place, Nora. I stop by once or twice when I'm passing to drop off some English papers I finish with. Better than throwing them away. I've never been inside the man's private place.'

'These men are devious,' Nora said.

'They wouldn't be men if they weren't devious,' Vanesa agreed. But continued: 'But I think he'll be on his best behaviour. Out to impress. Showing off his social skills acquired abroad.'

'And after the dinner we settle down to a nice game of dominoes and swearing,' Nora mused.

'And the man scratching his private parts.'

'I don't know why they call it "private parts" as these men seem to do it in public all over the place.' And after a pause Nora asked: 'So, what's our strategy? We can't go into this thing like a bunch of innocents.'

'Are you going like that, showing your cleavage?' Nora asked Vanesa.

'What cleavage?'

'No one's suggesting you're bursting out all over,' Nora agreed. 'It's the modest bosoms that seem to turn them on nowadays.'

'Like the models.'

'Now, you're making me self-conscious.'

'Don't mind me, girl. You're no more self-conscious than Fred here, with her high German collar.'

'What you mean?' Fred asked, fingering her high German collar. 'What you mean, "High German collar"?'

Vanesa explained: 'She means, German with a lot of Catholic ritual thrown in. And then afterwards confession with a nice priest.'

'I mean,' Nora said, patiently, 'I simply mean German ladies of a certain era used to favour that style. A high, delicate collar. With a little lace. Concealing the passion beneath. And you have a nice, long neck, Fred; the men would like to kiss it.'

'Lord, I fraid to be in your company, Nora.'

'What's in your mind that's making you fraid, Fred?'

'And the Germans are largely Protestant, not Catholic.'

'Not in Bavaria. That's in south Germany.'

'We know where Bavaria is, Nora; we're not those people you like to call ignoramuses.'

'We used to have friends in Bavaria. In Würzburg. A nice man at the university. He had two doctorates.'

Fred changed the subject. 'Arwell lived in England all those years. Do you think he'll do charades after dinner? I hope you all well up on your films and your Shakespeare.' And then she started telling a story about Arwell and his security dog.

So they had a plan, the women. It could be built on the story about Arwell's dog, even though that showed less class than if it was a cat. A man living alone with a cat had an eerie feeling to it; it suggested one of those baddies in the old James Bond films, and nobody supposed that Arwell wanted to blow up the world, even though you sensed he was power-crazy. He had tried to interest Fred in the idea of a security dog, one that barked even though it wasn't a real dog; and the women agreed that the man was peculiar.

Fred tried to explain that it was just a security device,

and that if the mechanical dog didn't work then you could always get a real dog with razor teeth.

Why not get a real dog in the first place, Nora wanted to know.

Fred said that this was to show they weren't living in Jamaica and you could still finesse a little with your security. If you got a real dog in Jamaica the rascals would just shoot down the dog before shooting you; and it was bad here but not quite so bad.

It was getting bad in Trinidad, too. And Guyana.

It was always bad in Guyana. Choke 'n' rob.

So, forget about the foolishness about the dog; they must go over the plan for dinner.

And it was dinner, not supper. They had to be careful not to pull rank.

Dinner was more neutral than supper.

So, to concentrate minds: over dinner Nora would talk about the places she had travelled to with Mr Shackley-Bennett. Nothing heavy; no pulling of rank or anything like that; just to show that she had travelled, and travelled in style, and she would expect a man on the island to respect that.

And Fred would talk about her cultural interests. About her father's work in archaeology down in Martinique, and her own Carib fabrics and ceramics; though you had to be careful and not put a price on these things that made you a target – that made you a customer for the mechanical dog. So, that was Fred. Vanesa would talk about her writing and the book club and that sort of thing. OK, Vanesa?

Vanesa wasn't really listening at this point: she was imagining Arwell at work; Arwell cooking and . . . speed-reading at the same time. She saw him with pots bubbling on the hob and maybe four or five books open, none of them cook books; and there he was, spatula in hand, moving from one book to another book, memorizing a few facts here, a date there that might come in handy over dinner. So, Nora repeated the question: would Vanesa talk about the book club?

Yes. But only if the subject came up.

'And then Nora could introduce him to Pilates yoga,' Fred said.

That drew general silence.

And then as they were travelling in the car Nora spoiled it all by saying to Fred: 'I think he's sweet on you, Fred . . . I read all this business of the security dog differently.'

Fred simply did not respond; so Nora was forced to expand. She was driving in her usual way, gripping the steering wheel tightly, looking neither right nor left; and Fred was in the back seat. 'So when you greet him,' Nora cautioned, 'if he wants to hug up, just go stiff and send him a message.'

'Why are you telling me this, Nora? If you were a little child I would ask you to wash out your mouth.'

'It's after the man going stiff that the woman should wash out her mouth.'

'Jesus God. I think the world end and we're already in hell.'

'In that case, hell not so bad,' was Vanesa's rejoinder.

'Though it's when the *man* stiffens up you have a problem,' Fred thought of saying, but didn't.

III: ARWELL

Arwell needed to get back to England. It was urgent; it wasn't a snap decision, but the package he received this morning from London was concentrating his mind: maybe it was occupying rather than concentrating his mind; his better-educated friends would know the difference, but he – he admitted it – he struggled to make ideas bend to his will; but he wasn't going to be defeated by the more-educated class. The package of newspaper cuttings concentrated his mind, for here he was, sitting on his verandah, planning his English campaign rather than thinking of what he would prepare for these people's dinner tonight. Three ladies coming to his home.

Were the killings getting worse since he left? A boy mangled to death with an axe; was an ice-pick what he thought it was? A boy walking out with his girlfriend in Liverpool and he's killed like something in the jungle. It says they came out of the bush and killed him. England reverting to bush. Because the boy is black and the girl, his girlfriend, is white and the killers – who are themselves little better than children – don't like it? Arwell thinks of the things in this world that he doesn't like, and he's never killed a man for it. So you take them away, out of harm's way and you protect their human rights; you must be careful, even, not to call them names; so that when they come out in x years time, they'll be the only people in the country not mentally damaged. Inside, they must be treated with all the normal courtesies: *Would you like the grilled chicken for dinner, sir? Or the fresh trout, not farmed?* When the time comes, Arwell's child, going about her business, in England, if she bumps into them in the street will just walk by as if they haven't got a history. She wouldn't thank her old father for insisting that something broke down here and it's up to someone to fix it. And Arwell wonders what he would pack in his case, in his trunk for the task ahead: he has to think this through, for there'll be no back-up, he's on his own, he can't afford mistakes; he has to bring justice to the bereaved of another murdered boy; he has to provide protection for his daughter who, though not in that particular city, is in obvious danger. The hint of arthritis in his hand doesn't deter him; don't kid yourself he's more simple-minded than those other nuts out there who take action.

*

Maybe it's occupying rather than concentrating his mind, so he turns from that story to another cutting that doesn't engage his interest, and another that he couldn't see the point of. True, he worked in the same place as his friend who sends the cuttings, but his friend is the educated brother; though a man long neutralized by being an educated black man in England. Arwell, free from the country, sees himself as his friend's fighting arm. A very rich man could do this in a direct way. But Arwell and his friend would have to employ finesse.

'Fathers 4 Justice' were jackarses. He's surprised his friend bothered to cut this nonsense out. The Water Wars to come, he can't be bothered with. You need younger brain cells to stay with this one. Racism in football; so what's new there? An Italian story this time. An African in the Italian league. What's new? Interesting, though, the article talking about the change in the nature of racism in football, in Italy, in England, in Romania, in Bulgaria: 'a change from parochial to strategic racism'. He didn't understand this. He would have to read this article again. But not now. He needed a drink, a Tony Martin was in order. But he was entertaining later. Entertaining the ladies, no less. Couldn't afford to greet them with liquor on your breath. Couldn't become unsteady on your feet even before they came: *he would grill the fish. And maybe wrap some potatoes in foil and put them in the fire. And, of course, the salad: women like their salad, which was already made. These women who will talk of books and art and . . . speak the Queen's English – as if they are themselves the Queens of England.* The child-abductors, though, the child-abductors and women-traffickers from Eastern Europe, from Albania, they had to be dealt with. Despite the dangers to his daughter he refused to grow morbid. *The barbecue would be outside, it wouldn't smell up the house. People don't like that. Women don't like that. He knew what he had to do to entertain these women; he was a man of experience.*

*

He's lit the barbecue and put in the potatoes; these superior women would want to put on a show of being on time. The wind is away from the house so no fish smells indoors when they sit down to eat. He's made the salad, the fresh salad, as these women like their salad. *Salad Days.* Never occurred to him to find out what that phrase meant, but preparing the salad he had an inkling. Must look it up. Not now, but must remember to look it up later. What must they have been like during their salad days? . . . The Sikhs stopping that play in Birmingham were out of order. Demonstrating, yes, but breaking windows of the theatre and intimidating the cast, driving the woman, the author, a Sikh herself, into hiding was out of order. Breakdown of law and order. England. Who would have thought it? And who's left to defend old England: who's there to make England safe for the children with him sat out here, 7,000 miles away, wondering whether this fish or that fish is right for the occasion? *As if one barbecued fish tastes that different from another barbecued fish.* Except for herring, perhaps, a taste he still didn't like, the only fish he had as a child. Apart from jacks. Sprats. (Of course they had new names now for jacks, sprats.)

*

The car's coming; put on the fish; put the fish on the grill. *The boy got seventeen years. The one who delivered the blow got twenty-three years. Will be out in the prime of life.* But here're the ladies to brighten the scene; Miss Fred with the nice complexion, who speaks French and whose daddy was something fancy in Martinique, and Miss Vanesa with her writing and her book club, and Madame Nora with her hyphen and her Queen's English.

120

8

Arwell's Speech

Arwell

He's disappointed that the packet of cuttings collected this morning isn't from the Professor; but from another friend in England, a man he used to work with at Mount Pleasant post office. He was relying on the Professor to assist him with this speech that he would have to make. But Arwell wasn't a man to be overly dependent on others. He would prepare his speech, not a big deal.

So, he went back to running things through his mind. He would be positive, he would mend fences and show he was up to the new job. Starting with his daughter. His daughter was restored to being the Queen of France; he would help her to live up to her responsibilities; he would pay for her to go over there and brush up on the language. (She wasn't far, she lived in London.) He was pleased that not many people on the island would get his reference to the Queen of France. So maybe he would explain it in the speech. Maybe as a preamble to the speech, as in the American Constitution. But this wasn't urgent; his daughter had all the time in the world. But for now, the speech: he was disappointed that he hadn't heard from his friend, the Professor, whom he had e-mailed about the speech. But the Professor had given up on him. Arwell didn't want to talk to anyone on the island about the speech; he didn't want them to know how much energy he was prepared to put into it.

So he had called whatisname again, the boy wonder, to be talked through the intricacies of the computer: it was no shame to seek instruction from anybody about things you didn't know.

When the boy they call Mozart came, they went over everything again, from the password to the e-mail. Arwell took the opportunity to change the password: on second thoughts HOVE seemed a better bet than RICE, less easy to decode.

So, after he tapped in HOVE and was shown the ropes one last time it was natural to send the message he had already sent to the Professor:

<u>a.barnes@aol.com</u>

```
Professor. Talking about the lady with the teeth.
Is it the wife of Hove? Confirm.
```

He paid the boy off and decided to take a rest from the machine, which was already giving him a headache (not really a headache, but headache in a manner of speaking). He hadn't given up anything in changing from RICE to HOVE; he still saw the same woman; he saw her getting off the aircraft in her neat, dark suit – and those teeth! Then he saw her at the podium, restrained and correct, denying the rumours without ever raising her voice, as if to confirm her power. Then he saw her behind closed doors, whip in hand, whip coming down like a whiplash, coming down on the bare flesh, coming down on the screaming, pleading unfortunates who were there to do her bidding, and she alone, the lady in her neat, dark suit, slim but with an athlete's power, *iron-strong*, the only one in the room not sweating, bringing down the whip, repeatedly. But he mustn't let this get out of hand. When you looked at the people who fell foul of normal behaviour, when you saw them being interviewed on television, you found that most of them started out with just a little excess here and there, an extra drink before hitting the road, a one-night stand with a friend of the wife, or venturing into the betting shop that first time. No, he was a man in control of himself. Though he would not stifle his imagination to conform with the boundaries of this little island; he had lived abroad, he had had temptations dangled in front of him, and he had not resisted them; but he had resisted some. Many.

So back to the speech: the two ideas, the two *concepts* that he would explore in his speech were 'Barbarism' and 'Community'. Barbarism according to C. L. R. James and Community according to Pewter Stapleton. Only problem is, C. L. R. James was vast and Pewter Stapleton wasn't answering his e-mails or his phone.

Pewter
(Pewter is not at either address his friends have for him, in England or in France.)

Arwell
He will be positive about his daughter. She hasn't chosen well but she has chosen her thing. Her thing, it seems, is Communication Studies. He will say nothing about this as it always causes an argument. Though he will be positive. He now wouldn't want her to be a doctor or a dentist. The things the doctors have to do. At least a Communication Studies person doesn't have to look at the body decomposing, doesn't have to put her finger up the unpleasant parts of a human carcass and think she's insulated because she's wearing a glove: he's had this done to him by a superior man who no doubt goes home to hold his wife's

hand. So Arwell will be positive about his daughter and her choice of career. And her choice of partner; her job at the airport. He will be positive full stop. Now take the Jamaicans.

Arwell didn't go along with this nonsense about Jamaicans. True, Jamaicans were their own worst enemy, swaggering about their 'big island' as if they were Nigerians. But because some people were ignorant you didn't damn the whole race on account of that. So, there were the druggies, those who made women transport the evil stuff in their private parts. Of course these were creatures of a lower order who should be made to live down there with the snake. Just as the racist animals in England and the Asian hoodlums in the East End and wherever; and all that woman-trafficking low animal life from East Europe – shouldn't be allowed the privilege of being housed and fed at Her Majesty's pleasure. At the taxpayer's pleasure, more like. No, real Jamaicans had nothing to do with that.

He thought of his old friend in Hackney; on the High Street. Not that he knew Walters socially, but he went into the shop from time to time when he happened to be passing that way; to get some decent bread and a portion of fried chicken. (Bad for you, all this fried stuff, but what the hell; a man had to have some pleasure in this life, particularly if he's past a certain age, and is likely to die of something else. Anyway, he won't be diverted into that.)

So, from time to time he got talking to Walters, and the first thing he noticed about him was the man's command of English. He wasn't fast-talking like some of those Americans on the TV; in fact, Walters was more than averagely slow. *But the man was correct.* Giving the lie to those folk who said that you had to come from this family or go to that school or vote Conservative to have that sort of command of the language. But it wasn't just Walters' language that appealed to Arwell. After all, language was no guide to anything other than your ability to be fluent with words. It was the man's general composure that impressed.

He had had more than once to explain what he meant by composure. He's not talking of anything physical, even though Walters, standing behind the counter, a seriously black man in a spotless white coat as if he were a trainee doctor on television, as he moved slowly to put the chicken in the microwave, looked like a man who could handle himself. Once they had a little chat about the health implications of the microwave on the chicken, *and this was something Walters had already thought about.* Though the effect of the greasy chicken was probably worse for you than the effect of the microwave. However, when you're a certain age – and both Walters and Arwell were that sort of age – you could afford to take a small risk. So, what was he saying?

Yes. Walters was looking forward to retirement, to selling up and . . . not going home but travelling a bit. Not even travelling in the aimless way that some people do but looking forward to visiting two places. One was Venice and the other was Cuba.

Venice was OK; Walters was never specific about Venice – and it probably didn't matter whether you visited Venice when you were young or when you were older, though it might affect the way you got along with the ladies over there, the Italian women. And Walters got quite philosophical over the question of women. (Imagine a world where there was only one sex and it was male, etc. The fact that that didn't happen almost made you want to believe in God.) But with Cuba it was different, personal. Walters wasn't one of those intellectual types who went in for the *ideology.* Nor did he have a thing about the Spanish language spoken by a woman in a certain intimate setting. His admiration for Cuba was based on personal experience. True, like everyone else he admired the way little Cuba stood up to the big US of A over all those years of threats and bullying and sanctions. But that wasn't the reason he rated Cuba. The reason was his cousin.

Walters' cousin was a woman who had a lot of children: she lived outside Kingston. She wasn't poverty-stricken, she didn't have to come to England like the others. She owned a couple of houses outside the city, and that's where the Cubans came in. In the time of Manley, in the 1970s, when the Cuban doctors and whatnot came in to help the people of Jamaica, his cousin was lucky enough to rent out the two houses to the Cubans, *and she learnt a lot from them*. She wasn't an old woman but she had thirteen children; and the children grew up in the environment of the visiting Cubans, and today *all thirteen children are civil servants*. Now, you didn't have to put two and two together to see that it was the environment of the Cubans that had contributed to making those children come good. No nonsense with drugs, no foolishness with the children coming to England and learning all sorts of slackness and disrespect and blaming racism for their slackness. And the children weren't angels, either. Some of them were rebellious-minded. Independent-minded. The girls, too. So Walters wanted to go to Cuba while Fidel was still alive to say thanks for what the Cubans had done for his cousin.

And Arwell admitted that from time to time he thought of Walters back there in his little shop on the High Street in Hackney, selling his local bread and greasy chicken, and he felt like buying a plane ticket and going straight to England and popping in one last time at the shop just to have a chat with the old man in his doctor's coat. So don't tell him any nonsense about Jamaicans, he wasn't preju-diced.

Pewter

(They say his mail hasn't been collected from the university, where he's not teaching anyway, this semester. So maybe he's in Paris. Or in the West Indies. Or in Mozambique. Or . . . A friend in Ealing said he spoke to Pewter, and that Pewter was in France, and Pewter had said he couldn't watch French television because all the films were dubbed, and the lips and the sound were out of sync, and this was the sort of thing that drove you mad.)

Someone else, close to Pewter, said that his concern at that time was finding the right wall, in a small flat in Paris, on which to hang his expensive medicine cabinet.

Arwell

On researching 'Community' he had occasion to change his mind about Nora Hyphen. Initially, he didn't like her comments about black people in England, but on reflection she was right. Black people in England seemed more racist than black people at home. This wasn't always so, but now this was so. In the early days he had been excited by meeting other West Indians. Africans, even. But something has happened over the decades, with little islandness now reasserting itself. And it's worse with those other people who don't like to be thought black. The Indians and the Chinese. Nora's point that we exhaust ourselves with the fight against white racism so that we don't have any energy left to deal with the racism within what we call the community doesn't seem so wrong now. So whether you liked Nora or not you must take what she says seriously, and try to deal with the racism in your own community.

Pewter

Pewter is in Paris but he's leaving Paris, he's about to head for Eurostar, but his flat is only ten minutes from Gare du Nord, so he has a little time to admire the books now on the shelf, snug as if they've been there for ever. There's a bounce from something he's just read. It's Montherlant's *Malatesta*, a play that falls away at the end, but the start is terrific. The play confirms a feeling he's long held that it's pointless to write books. To give lectures. He's spent the best part of his professional life lecturing and writing. And aeroplanes still crash. Doctors misdiagnose. The deserts in Africa remain desert. Aids. Aids everywhere. So what's the point in coming up with a new reading of *Much Ado . . . ?* In *Malatesta* there's this character at the court of Malatesta. (Malatesta is Lord of Rimini and he's doing battle with the pope; in fact he goes to Rome to kill the pope, but that's not the interesting bit.) So this character is a man of letters in Malatesta's court. Serious scholar. And he's written a book, or a chapter of a book, 'On Revolutions'. This is serious. This is the fifteenth century. And the court assembles to hear the scholar read out his chapter on revolutions. So they are all gathered. He takes out his sheaf of papers and prepares to read. And he reads: 'On Revolutions. Revolutions waste a great deal of time.'

And that's it. The court are standing round waiting for the rest, but that's it. 'Revolutions waste a great deal of time.' And note, he doesn't say, 'Revolutions are a waste of time.' That would be a cheap shot, that would be too *knowing*, that would be vulgar. 'Revolutions waste a great deal of time.' So does writing books. So does giving lectures. (*And he blames the Romans, anyway; for the desertification of Africa, cutting down the cedars in North Africa, long ago.*)

So, he mustn't miss his train.

Arwell
The Americans are clever. They threw up Hollywood to confuse you. We could be as nasty as you like, as blatant as we like and you will still come flocking back to the

movie. We will treat the black people just as we like, humiliate them on screen, and film it to show the world we don't care, *and even make your child go to university in England and praise the miracles of celluloid.* And then we have a government that will pull down its pants and do what it likes in your face and say to you: *You have a problem with this?* And all the time maybe, just maybe, something else is going on underneath, which is the real revolution. *And the name of that revolution is Condoleezza Rice.* Clever.

For he dreams of the lady. They used to say that a black man in his dreams saw the white woman coming down on him. But the woman he sees is Condoleezza Rice. Whip in hand. A Bible and a whip. She will read a passage from the Bible and then she will lash you. First, into the schools. Boy, you not performing. You making your mother shame? *Lash.* She moves from the school, to the playing field. So I see you come in last again in that race, like you playing truant. You are a disgrace to the black children not yet born. *Lash.* She moves to the prisons. A lot of black people in prison in America. So what have we here: a holiday camp for black people? You call this a joke. You think I laughing? You think Uncle Colin over there laughing? *Lash lash lash.* And then she get on the plane. Private plane. This is hush hush business. And she visiting all those poor devils already kidnapped and bound to do her will. And I tell you that woman walk away from all that exercise without even breaking sweat! Forget the white man, the white man always liked that sort of thing. But now every black man wakes up some night screaming for his Condoleezza.

Pewter

He wants, for some reason – it's not urgent – to reread Ibsen's *Enemy of the People*. He's in a flat in Sheffield, a flat that gives the appearance of being dismantled, in disarray; for he no longer lives there. But the bulk of his books are still there. He finds a copy of Ibsen. The translation says: *A Public Enemy*. No, this doesn't have the resonance of *Enemy of the People*. That must affect the rest of the translation. He's in the box room now gazing at the computer screen. He's not reading the one line printed on the screen. He is thinking . . . he is conjuring up two images. One is the human face, unblemished. The other is a bit of landscape, unpolluted. He is not a painter or a photographer; he reads, he writes, he teaches.

After a pause of he doesn't know how long, he focuses again on the screen. Something has changed his mood to a past tense. *He read, he wrote, he taught* is how he now thinks of it. So he is unaware of how much has changed, since he thinks he's in the same place as before. At the end of it all, he writes something – force of habit – he writes: *Les Clochards de Paris*.

Arwell
(Arwell has gone for a swim in the sea.)

Pewter
He's in a flat in England. Sheffield. He has a sense of being in the middle of a conversation. With himself? No, that's too boring. With others who might know him: 'My granddaughter used to say. Or was it my grandmother who used to say . . .' something that I'm now claiming as my own. 'After the killing of the multi-ethnic city – Sarajevo, to you – oh, my friends, your mixed marriages won't save you.' Grand-daughter or grandmother? At this stage of the game why make fine distinctions between the two? Keep the debate within the family. 'What is the point of Pewter Stapleton?' They didn't say quite that, not in his hearing.

A friend said that of a man in the news. A gay man said that of another gay man's young wife. These speculations are erasing, overlaying what Pewter first had in mind to write; but he can't decide which is more accurate.

He is thinking: must go to the shops and buy something; must add to the clutter. He's doing well with the books, sorting, transporting and storing, archiving and ultimately giving away. The aim, to get rid of at least two before replacing them with one, has long been met. The way of getting rid of them not quite elegant; many remain unread. Not quite an intellectual or environmental outrage, perhaps, but a minor defeat of ambition. But he must go to the shops today to buy not books but a case. He would go not to Waterstone's but to John Lewis. Not for a book but for a case, larger than its predecessor (itself larger than the one that went before), a case for the transportation of his pills.

The odd thing, the puzzling thing is that he is not a man in particularly poor health. Yes, there is an eye problem (two sets of pills) and a problem with his sugar levels (one set of pills, and another set of pills in case the sugar in his blood triggers something else in the system). So far so good. All fitting snugly in the medicine bag. Only, he's a traveller. One set of eye drops must be kept refrigerated. A few hours out of the fridge shouldn't matter. But transport is unreliable. EasyJet. Eurostar. Three and a half hours – Sheffield–St Pancras. Then taxi to Waterloo – to Eurostar, an hour waiting around, three hours across the channel and half an hour at the taxi queue outside the Gare du Nord. That's eight hours. How much potency would the Xalatan lose being heated up for eight hours? *Heated up. Shaken. Stirred.* Hence the mini icebox, acquired at John Lewis last time round.

Now, a new challenge. After new tests – and these are precautionary, no apparently pressing need. But if you live in the First World you must have them or you might be forgiven for thinking you were living in some other world. People say – indeed, the government spokespeople say: you must go for these tests, if you are a man of this age, and of a certain race. So after those tests yesterday, the result is – and this, surely, this is the stuff of comedy – *seven* more boxes of precautionary pills. *Can the NHS bear this! He must write something about it.* Precautionary for a month, six weeks. At the end of which the tests could take place. Hopefully, at the end of six weeks that would be the end of it. All this, so that he can finish his book? Is he that desperate to finish a book? It would make more sense for the doctor to have said: 'You have written books enough and wiped your arse and wiped your feet on the books of others, shredding texts like a Top Secret machine in the English Office, savaging them like an animal of a neighbour from hell. Now is the chance to read and read again and reflect. The NHS, which has a purpose higher than merely maintaining you as a bag of food, a stomach for medicine, will sustain you this time to read and reflect, read and reflect, and go out – if not quite civilized – at least a mass of educated protoplasm.' So he will repair to John Lewis's for a medicine case large enough to fit his condition. *Oh, my Damien Hirst of long ago, all is forgiven.*

Arwell
(Arwell is in his darkroom.)

Pewter
For a brief moment, in Sheffield, Pewter thought of Arwell. Maybe it was Arwell, maybe it was Arwell's daughter. He remembered when he visited the island a couple of years ago and was staying with Miss Vanesa, and he ran into Arwell, whose daughter was visiting. They were all having something to eat and it was clear that there was some sort of tension between Arwell and his daughter, to the point

where the daughter fell to correcting her father in public, in company. Nothing heavy, but needling. It's not that she was correcting his accent, just his way of speaking. (As far as Pewter remembered the girl's 'black English' lingo was far less accommodating than Arwell's 'West Indian'); but Arwell was putting on a bit of a performance. At table he was making some sort of point, stressing that the coming of something was inevitable, and he stressed 'in-evitable', making it sound like two words.

'Is that the same as "inevitable", Dad?'

And to give him his due Arwell never flinched, and said, as if it was scripted: 'It's similar.' Only then did he pause to reflect. 'Though "in evitable" is more *emphatic* than "inevitable".' That was a bit of linguistic finesse that impressed everyone (nearly) round the table; and set off a competition of rhymes and half-rhymes leading to words not thought to be in the dictionary. Until, finally, Arwell came up with 'vatic'. Was that a word or not? The daughter thought not. (Was it spelt with a 'v' or a 'ph'?) Refer to the professor. The professor didn't want to get between a man and his daughter. The professor said they should get the dictionary and look it up. They got the dictionary and looked it up. The word existed, spelt with a 'v'. The daughter left the table. The silence was embarrassing. That was the English way, Arwell said lightly. They switched the conversation to West Indies cricket.

(The daughter's boyfriend, sitting at the table, smiled through it all; and said something in a language no one understood. He was a man from Eastern Europe who didn't seem to speak English much and Arwell may have been trying to pull rank on a non-English-speaker. He then went on to explain to the stranger how West Indians had built up England after the war, had run the trains and done the cleaning, kept the factories going and washed up in the restaurants and hotels. And now they ran the risk of being done out of their English inheritance by a new wave of migrants who were coming over from everywhere to cash in on the Health Service and the benefits that those early migrants from these islands had built up; or made possible. The visitor smiled and nodded, not letting on what he understood.)

Recalling this now in Sheffield, Pewter had in mind to send Arwell the two-volumed *Oxford Dictionary* that would otherwise only go into storage because he had more than enough dictionaries already in Paris.

But the thought soon passed; he was already distracted by something else.

Arwell

Still no news from Pewter Stapleton. Out of sight, out of mind. So instead he is in his darkroom developing his snaps.

There is not a single photo of Condoleezza Rice hanging on the walls. (Wonder why her friends call her Condi rather than Condo?) Instead, his snaps are about landscapes, the beauty of the island. You can't tell whether an island is large or small from shots of the landscape. And he takes people, too; he took some snaps last time at Miss Vanesa's literary gathering.

So he was thinking again about Condoleezza Rice, high heels, whip in hand, travelling the torture chambers of the You Know Who, getting confessions out of the enemy. In this one he is the enemy. How brutal would she get before he confessed?

Could he hold out? Would experience of racism in England give him the strength to hold out against the Rice, against the Rice, *Against the Rice*?

Pewter

In Sheffield at his computer, he's writing something he's lost the thread of. But no matter. There was someone else in the house, in the flat, hence the need to show concentration at the screen. He isn't falling apart, he hasn't given up, hasn't lost it.

The person in the house turns out to be a young man; he approaches Pewter's den rather diffidently, a book in his hand. Pewter finishes off his typing before looking up.

'Hi. Howryou doing?'

'Sorry, Professor. Sorry to disturb you . . . I wonder, may I look in here, as well?'

'Yes yes, of course. Of course. Help yourself.' He points to a small bookcase, only three shelves, but with books piled on top. The lad goes towards it, does a quick scan, and forages. Meanwhile Pewter types, rather more fluently than before. There is sudden energy in Pewter's typing. After a while the lad straightens up. Half a dozen books in his hand.

'OK with these?'

Pewter gives a cursory look.

'Good choice. Well done.'

Young man hesitates. 'Well, thanks, Professor, I've taken . . . I've taken five boxes in all.'

'Good. And if you've got any . . . any friends who read, there's still a lot left. I've packed up all the books *I* want. You OK with transport?'

'I could get that within the hour.'

'Good.' He waits, as the boy hesitates.

'. . . I'm thinking . . .'

'Good.'

'This is what Spinoza did to Schuller – Schuller was his doctor, if you . . . When he was dying, Spinoza, that is. When Spinoza was dying – Schuller was just a young man, even though he was Spinoza's doctor – Spinoza gave Schuller a choice of his books . . . Just thought I'd –'

'What're you studying again?'

'English Studies with Philosophy.'

'Good. Good.' And after a pause: 'Only, I'm not dying
. . . I think. At least not immediately.'

'Oh no, I didn't mean –'

'I know you didn't mean. Anyway.' Briskly: 'If you need
any more books. Or perhaps more accurately, if you want
any more books, do come back. Always partial to a student
who reads.'

'Thanks, Professor, thanks again. You'll be in for the
next half-hour?'

'I think so.'

Pewter then typed in a sentence unrelated to the rest of
the text. He was thinking that the boy would take his
books to the second-hand bookshop and not get a good
price, like those poor Africans selling their own into slavery,
long ago. But he would hang tough, as the Americans say;
he would not buy them – the books – back.

The sentence he typed was: 'When Brecht was your age
he was dead seven years.'

Arwell

Change of rhythm. Fred's son is visiting from Martinique –
with wife and child. Photos needed, chop chop. Also, our
Lisa's disappeared. No phone call on Saturday. Breaking
the arrangement. Not answering the phone on Sunday. Has
no number for the man from the other side of the Curtain.
Usually, they traffic women the other way. From East to
West. But now the Curtain's down, the Wall's down, no one
knows which way the traffic's going. But to work. There's a
happy family photo to take. Three damn generations of them.

Pewter

Something catches his attention on the radio. John Simpson and other people in the media. (It crossed his mind
that this lot didn't read Media Studies at university; and
that made him think of Arwell Barnes in the West Indies

who seemed so upset at his daughter reading something like Communication Studies at university. You could read that in two ways. But Pewter was minded to give the returnee Barnes the benefit of the doubt. The usual thing would be to congratulate the girl for having got into university to read *anything*. Stamp Collecting. But could it be that Arwell knew what a university education was? Could it be that Arwell was measuring his daughter's ambitions and achievements against something *outside the community*? Maybe the man was, after all, an ally.)

But this form of speculation wasn't really engaging him; he was half-listening to the radio, the quiz, while working on his '*Clochards*' piece. Something that might, if he got it right, interest the *Paris Review* people. He was fascinated by the *clochards*, how they had seemingly taken permanent possession of the city of Paris (it wasn't August any more), marked it out like a military campaign, the Napoleons of the street. They lounged in pairs now, confident of their territory; the one outside the little supermarket on rue Damrémont now has a companion. So he could leave his things in place and not have his territory seized (or cleaned). Further down the road towards Guy Moquet, on the bench outside the underground shopping centre, a living Two Ronnies. More authentic than the old sketch. On the other side, going towards Jules Joffrin, on rue Ordiner, outside Picard's, the voluble and imposing Gallic presence is joined on his pavement sitting room, sometimes by a side-kick, sometimes by a desperate woman who might be black, might be mad. And again outside the cake shop, the *pâtisserie*, a few doors further down. Three hits in one stretch of street from home to Métro. From Métro to home. Where do they go to the loo? Where – as a well-brought-up child reputedly asked her mother as they walked past a similar scene in London's theatreland – where do they brush their teeth at night?

But Pewter is still half-listening to the quiz programme on the radio. To John Simpson and company. Tame stuff, really. People surprisingly ill informed about recent history. (Is this, too, what you call corruption?) One question has caught Pewter's attention, question of a black man, the first human, apparently, to stand on the North Pole. He had vaguely heard the name Henson before, though he wouldn't have been able to cite a context. Matthew Alexander Henson, the quizmaster says. With Peary. Robert E. Peary, leader of the expedition, who, naturally, got the credit over the African-American. Pewter hadn't heard of Peary, which he had to look up in the *Biographical Dictionary*, to check the spelling. (*Must take* Chambers Biographical Dictionary *to Paris.*) So, maybe a Pyrrhic victory for Peary. Not that Pewter was hugely interested in the American, Henson. He had a book about all that. *World's Great Men of Color.* Hated the American way with titles – with more than titles? Shooting themselves in the foot, as the 'men of color' included Mary Seacole – and he was pretty certain there were one or two other women too. The book, he imagined, was in storage. Wouldn't have taken it to Paris. One of those books, on reflection, he could afford to get rid of; could send it to someone like Arwell Barnes.

Arwell
Punishment. No phone, no answer. Would he now have to go to Poland, or the Ukraine, in search of his daughter? Meanwhile he was in his darkroom trying to find the shadows hovering under this happy family, happy family, happy family. (Suddenly it struck him what a good-looking woman Fred Belair was.)

Pewter
They say Pinter has made a storming speech from his wheel-chair, the Nobel Speech (on television) excoriating the

Americans for destabilizing the world. Not bad for a man who's apparently dying. So that's Pinter. And somewhere in a school in London Dario Fo is putting on a play for peace. Words by a mother who lost a son in Iraq. So the world's in good hands.

So it was back to the *Clochards*. Add to that the smoke, the smoking, the impossibility of having a meal in a restaurant in Paris without the penalty of smoke. Dogshit on the street. *Clochards*. Smoke. Were Hemingway and those fellows blind or just conned?

Then you bust a gut to get to Eurostar and it's late leaving Gare du Nord. You get somehow, later than planned, to Waterloo to St Pancras to the taxi rank at Sheffield. Whose fault? Some multinational: Mr Branson? Midland Mainline? Who cares? You get into a taxi after eleven o'clock at night having travelled seven hours, eight hours. You get in a cab at Sheffield station. (The new taxi rank having been moved several hundred yards away from the station exit, for you to curse your bags.) You get into a cab and it reeks of cigarette smoke. Moslem driver. *What is this*? *Why is my name not Coriolanus*? You are ill, your head aches; you are out of commission for as long as it takes. Don't talk to me.

Arwell
The daughter rings. 'Why don't you chill out, Dad?' she says.

9

A Mixed Marriage

A rwell Barnes was determined to marry Condoleezza Rice because he was eligible and she was single; he was a widower in good trim.

But the woman was a diplomat, frequenter of the gilded palaces of the world – palaces and military bunkers open only to the select; she was accustomed to finesse, not just to a form of words but to words that would smooth the wrinkle – supposing that there was the suggestion of a wrinkle – from her beautiful brow. So, he must rethink his plan, *present* it differently. Or maybe present it *differently*.

So, Arwell was planning to marry Condoleezza Rice because she was still single, at fifty-one, and he was eligible. (She was tantalizingly single, she was not gay; she had had boyfriends, once even, she had been engaged to be married; she had been holding herself for something . . . unexpected.)

She had been engaged to a football player; she got proposals by the dozen; she just hadn't had the right one.

He felt, he *knew* that she was a woman of imagination – even though she was a Republican, but they would sort that out in time, one to one. She had had her foreign proposals but here Arwell was in luck; for not only did he not see himself as foreign, being West Indian; he knew that with Condoleezza's present position she would have to be very careful how to hitch up with a foreigner, particularly one from a country not friendly to the United States, or one suspected by America of being communist. Think of the loss of face (and ratings) in America if she were suddenly to announce her engagement to the love of her life, a man from Syria. Even that earlier princess, Jackie K, never quite recovered her shine after she became Jackie O; and Greece was an OK-ish country on the edge of respectability. So that eliminated suitors from all but four or so places. (He had thought about this; the lady was proud of her methodology in her study of Russia and the old Soviet Union; well, Arwell, too, had his methodology in his study of the lady. *She loved American football; she loved skating and running, jogging, she kept herself trim; above all she loved piano, classical music; played the church organ, too; played with a famous string quartet in Boston; she spoke Russian, Czech and French; she was five foot ten inches in her stockings; she had the ear of the president.* Well now: he could be five foot ten inches with the right equipment; he would resume his morning run, afternoon swim. He would do her justice in the darkroom.)

Of the four places left for a suitor there was the non-aligned Third World, the neutrals, citizens of the USA and citizens of the wider USA. He discounted the non-aligned Third World as the balance of opinion among her advisers (for a decision in her position couldn't be purely private, a bit like the kings and queens in those countries that have them) – the suspicion would be that the non-aligned Third World country would be getting more than it was giving in hitching up, through one of its members, to America's most dazzling star. (Arwell might have reservations about the lady's Republican mates, but that might work in his favour in this instance.)

The neutrals were a threat, of course. A Swiss or a Swede would be a serious challenge; they were understated, those folk, stronger and more determined than they looked – like the lady herself. The Swiss and Swedes made their mark, with their funny accents, in the wider world, in the NGOs, in Africa, in international diplomacy (*Ah!*), at the UN. But, here again those were the things that America didn't care for. (*Wasn't Hans Blix from one of those countries? Didn't they have unusual influence at the UN?*) So that would rule them out of favour with the Rice inner circle. The thought crossed his mind that the England (soon to be ex-England) football manager, Sven whatisname might have been a candidate. He had a high profile, he (mysteriously) seemed to have a way with good-looking, powerful women, and most important of all, he was into football. Arwell only hoped that the difference between English football and the American version was clear enough to rule out the weak-lipped turnip of a Swede. Plus his deteriorating public profile.

That left a man from the USA as a rival; and, also, a man from the wider USA. When you are concerned with the balance of power, as Dr Rice obviously is, and you look around the world at its one hundred and ninety-five countries – including the joke ones – you could argue the point that for the most powerful woman in the world to choose as her sleeping partner a man from that same most powerful country is an act of thoughtlessness. Looking at this thing strategically, it would represent an *imbalance* in the forces of international power. If that happened the rest of the world might as well surrender and stay marginalized.

Unless she were to correct the imbalance within the country itself. Unless she were, if you like, to take affirmative action and marry a poor man, a nobody, a dropout, a druggie, a man on death row, or an illegal immigrant from Mexico. In which case the most powerful woman in

America would be going against her training and background, against her instincts and home life, and her politics. Yes, Condoleezza might be lots of things, she might be a Christian lady from a Christian family, but one thing she isn't is stupid. And in any case, as a staunch Republican she doesn't believe in affirmative action. And this, too, plays into Arwell's hands. (There are some who include Canada as part of America, and Canada could be dangerous – a man from Canada, who sounds like an American but isn't quite: that combination of yeast-like blandness and small-jaw snapping at America's heels that their politicians go in for has its dangers for Arwell. Harmless enough to be endearing to Big Brother? But Arwell ruled out Canada: what would a black woman from Birmingham, Alabama, want with all that snow? *Though it's true, she likes to ski, she likes to skate.*) But Arwell, fingers crossed, represents the one marriageable category left; and that's the wider USA.

A little island in the Caribbean is a lot of things but it is not a nation. Either you're part of the colonizing power, or you're part of other islands in the region, or you're part of the economic and political power that matters; that's why Arwell says of his little island and all the other little islands around: do yourself a favour and join the imperial state. As a little islander he's no threat to America, but he's related by proximity (despite the failed English experience), and he speaks her language. When he gets in close to Condoleezza he will need no interpreter. Not that he comes empty-handed; he would brief her about things America needs to know about the rest of the world that America doesn't yet know about the world.

Arwell thinks he's in with a chance. (He's careful not to mention China, the threat from a billion-plus Chinese, by all accounts two-thirds of them men.) But fortunately the Lady, herself, doesn't seem to show much interest in China. And, remember, she's five foot ten inches tall. The Chinese, though reputedly getting taller, would be struggling to look down on her, beaming, in that wedding photograph.

*

'Do I look hysterical, Fred?' Nora asked, not amused.

'I didn't mean hysterical hysterical, I just meant . . .'

'Some things you take seriously,' Nora said. And after a pause: 'Because they have consequences.'

The committee was meeting in Winifred's house because Fred was just up from Martinique and not paying attention to things on the island in her absence; Nora and Vanesa were there to bring her up to date.

'What is it with the French connection that always . . . that turns your head so?'

'Like you forgetting. I long resign from this job.'

'Then you have to unresign,' Vanesa said.

'Well, if the money is right, I might consider it. You must have budgeted for the role of secretary while I was away. You must be got a new sugar-daddy with more money than sense.'

'Fred don't joke, this is serious.'

'I look as if I laughin'?'

'Fred, why do you go on so, as if you don't know how to talk English? You've had more privilege than anybody I know. Education. Father, a big international professor . . .'

'He still gone and dead.'

'. . . Languages. High society in Martinique. You know Aimé Césaire from way back . . .'

' "*Au bout du petit matin . . . Va-t-en, lui disais-je, gueule de flic, gueule de vache, va-t-en je déteste DETESTE DETESTE les larbins de l'ordre et les hannetons de l'espérance,*" ' Fred declaimed with great passion. And then in her normal voice: ' "What I like 'bout you, Fred, is your pedigree." That's what a married man tell me while he was barbecuing the fish in the garden. With all his assets on display. "So what sort of a degree your wife have?" I ask him. You get it?'

'And then you slept with him.'

'You know, Nora, I can't rightly remember. It was only last week, but you know, other things intervene.'

'We're here to talk about Arwell,' Vanesa said, patiently.

'So what he do now?' Fred asked. 'I knew that jackarse was always going to be trouble.'

'He's writing letters to Condoleezza Rice.'

'What, the woman in America?'

'We've got your attention at last. Love letters.'

'The woman in the government, the secretary of whatever? Defence.'

'State.'

Fred took time to digest this. 'So he wants what must be the busiest woman in America to take time off and come out here to say some foolishness at the Returnees' Club!'

'Fred, you're not listening; we're talking of love letters,' Nora said, impassive.

'How you mean, love letters?'

'Fred, you're a good-looking woman, you must have had plenty. In English and in French.'

'Most of them can't spell. So Arwell is one of them pappyshow men pretending to know everything. Adolescent at heart. So what's new there?'

'His ability to compromise us, that what's new.'

'How so?'

'As president of the club. The one you resign from, remember!' Then patiently, 'You know this foolish talk on the island about the new bourgeoisie. People turning up their nose. They'd love to use Arwell as the big stick to beat us with. It's all right for you, Fred, your social position's secure from way back.'

'They will just think Fred's slumming it, as usual; like having her little bit of rough on the side,' Vanesa said.

'I thank you very much; and I love you, too.' But Fred had to take this seriously. She was trying to work out what was new here. Speaking aloud, more than asking a question, she said: 'So this Arwell man writing letter to a woman he's seen on television. They all get letters like that. Film stars and actors. Footballers. It don't mean nothing.'

'On our headed paper?'

'Particularly if the woman powerful and good-looking.'

'We're not talking normal fan-mail. We're talking marriage proposal.'

'Nora, how you know that?' Fred demanded.

'Like you defending him, Fred, because he used to be sweet on you. I remember your story about the way he pointed his camera at you.'

'*Ça pas me dit quelque chose.*'

'And when he offered you his security dog.'

'When he photograph the children up from Martinique you could have hang the pictures up inside a church.'

'That's not what you said at the time.'

'This sound like a cross-examination, Nora, and you not even drunk yet.'

'You know I don't drink.'

'None of us drink.'

'OK, drinks coming up,' said Vanesa. 'Maybe then we can settle down. Something happens to Fred whenever she . . . goes down to Martinique. I reckon it's some man we don't know about. Fred, what're you drinking?'

'I forget what it have in there. Anything.'

'Nora?'

'Oh, just water. And any little thing to go with it.'

Vanesa expressed helplessness and disappeared into the house; Fred declining to play host. But Fred was more receptive now.

'How d'you know he's writing fresh letters to this woman in America?' she asked Nora. 'Don't tell me Arwell walking round town saying . . . Like a crazy man, saying: "I writing to this woman in America asking she to marry me. Let me show you the letter."'

'You have to get his idiom right,' Nora said, dryly.

'All right, all right. Enough of this damn . . . upper-class slumming slut, cow, Winifred,' Fred said, it seemed without irony.

'It was Mozart,' Vanesa said, bringing out some water and something else in a large bottle.

'That little boy! *Il est trop bavard!*' Then to Vanesa: 'I have glasses in my house, you want to shame me again?' And addressing them both: 'All you call him Boy Genius because he can fix computer and thing. But I never trust that boy. There's something about the boy which make me think. Trouble. Like they say, when you get rape – I'm not saying anybody want to get rape. As you know I don't believe in capital punishment, except for rape. I always say you should kill a brutal man and not get put in gaol for it. But they say, when you get rape, is better to get rape by a man who know what he's doing. The worse thing they say – I'm not talking about instruments and that kind of savage type of animal. And gangs of them with their drugs and . . . The worst thing they say, is to be raped by an underage boy. I go get the glasses. The Tony Martin strong but it still need a glass.'

'Fred, we're not talking about rape,' Nora pointed out, detaining her.

'I'll get them,' Vanesa said.

'And ice in the icebox. The icemaker,' she shouted at Vanesa. And then came back to the question with Nora.

'So what's wrong with a man sending a woman a proposal? I don't understand why you all so upset. The man not married any more, the woman not married; it's a free country.'

'What has he got to offer a woman like that?' Nora said.

'These men living in their fantasy world. And they make the rest of us look foolish. They say he's wearing built-up heels now.'

After a bit, Fred said: 'All you see the letter?'

'Don't be wet. Mozart saw the letter.'

'And blabbed. God, why did I ever come back to this place?'

Nora conceded the point: 'That's something that makes me uneasy, too,' she said. 'The betraying a confidence. The island's small enough as it is. If we can't keep secrets in our own house, we might as well go back to living in some yard full of nosy people.'

'And how do we know the Boy Genius not lying?'

'They always lie,' Nora said. 'Him in particular.'

'So there.'

'The point is Arwell doesn't deny it.'

'He might be playing games with all you.'

'We're not stupid, Fred. Anyway, we don't qualify as the trophy wife. Unless you learning figure-skating on the quiet, down in Martinique.'

'We're old-fashioned, me dear; we still stick to the ballet. And opera.'

Vanesa returned with a tray, glasses and ice. 'Did you say Arwell's doing ballet and opera?'

'We're not the target. We're not the ones sitting round the table at Geneva talking nuclear proliferation and threatening the terrorists. Even Fred doesn't get invited to relax at the White House after a hard day facing down the Russians,' Nora conceded.

'And I take it that's the reason you want Arwell to resign as president of the club. Before the marriage,' Fred said, starting to pour the drinks. 'That, and what with the built-up heels . . . He wearing a gun as well?'

*

Arwell realized that his battle was as much at home as with the protective shield round his intended in Washington. People on a small island with small-island ambition. In a way breaking through the mindset of people here would be as difficult a task as getting past the Lady's minders in the State Department and the CIA. But he was a returnee; some of the returnees came back full of big talk and nonsense; on some islands they were announcing themselves with the big-city crimes they learnt in New York and Chicago. Arwell was just saying to people: Don't think what you see is what you get. The damn size of the island, the geography of the island don't put you out of the race. Any race. People talk about being socially mobile, being upwardly mobile – all these working-class English people patting themselves on the back because they're socially mobile, sending their children to Oxford. So, what he says is this: How about being *laterally* mobile? He knew there was already talk about the music coming from his house: was there something funny about him because he changed his taste in music? He was a returnee, he had ambition, he would take on the whole island if they were stupid enough to frustrate him. They used to badmouth Vanesa in the same way when she started her reading group, now you can hardly meet anyone who doesn't claim to be part of the reading habit. So, if a reading group doesn't have a problem getting most of its books from abroad, why a problem with his music? What's wrong with a bit of Brahms?

II

Pewter Stapleton has miscalculated; he thought by now he would have got the e-mail thing up and running in Paris; but he's still, as it were, between countries; the one day a week in Sheffield, sometimes taking in both Wednesdays, is turning into a week at a time, so he's permanently in the wrong place, and his e-mail isn't sorted. He can access it, of course, from the university library, or from wherever; but not from home. But the e-mail, now, is not the point; the lecture he was stupid enough to agree to giving is the problem, bits of the talk scattered here and there, on three machines. 'The Reader as Bully' is now being overtaken by 'The Text as Unreliable' (*regression regression*). At the very least the lecture is threatening to break up into three separate talks.

And yet it was important to answer that woman at the reading, primed by the chair, to demand that he cut the preamble and get on with the poems. *Preamble?* The chair was a critic, of course. Not unsympathetic, trying to help, *but a literary critic*. Preamble. Hence, the analogy with the house and its buyer, its seller. For buyer and seller collude in this against the builder of the house: the house is a given thing, you view it as being fixed in its place, not movable, like an ashtray. Or a car. Granted. It's at the end of the process of wood and stone and labour – and visual madness. The location of the house is a factor; it will affect the asking price. It might be subsequently modified, the structure, but it will not be moved and re-erected in another place, except for heritage or eccentric reasons. But that doesn't negate the process of thinking about *house*. Hence, the analogy of the house in order to tease out this problem between the writer and the reader.

In the light of that what does it matter that by not organizing the computer you're missing out on certain things. A poetry reading in Lancaster that he is too late to respond to. Other things. Invitation to a Walcott event back in Paris. Just in time, maybe. People getting in touch because of difficulty in getting him on the phone. An e-mail from Arwell Barnes, whom he met in the Caribbean last time. *Two* e-mails from Arwell Barnes. *Three* e-mails from Arwell Barnes. Funny, Arwell Barnes isn't someone he's had e-mail contact with. Of course, the man'd want information; books, maybe. Pewter will deal with that before returning to Paris at the end of the week. Must get down to London to see someone, to visit family. Must get on with writing this lecture. As still (nominally) head of the programme, his job is to make this mixed marriage of creative writer and scholarly academic gel. Match the house-dweller with the house-builder.

Despite himself he opened one of the Arwell Barnes e-mails; it was about Mrs Thatcher. Pewter heaved a sigh of relief that this was something he didn't have to bother about. He spent a few seconds trying to visualize 'heaving' a sigh.

On the train to London he began to note how dreary these journeys had become, no longer disguised by working, reading, marking. Even the newspaper didn't last beyond Derby. So the e-mail – from that man – drifted back. Why was he so fascinated with Thatcher, with her sex-life? What could be more – Pewter couldn't think of the word; in the end he settled for: more of a turn-off? Arwell wanted to know how someone who had propositioned Thatcher in her pomp had gone about it. Was the man thinking of someone specific, or just the notion of propositioning the Lady, Thatcher. He thought vaguely of Gorbachev and Mitterrand, the sort of men that, apparently, fascinated Thatcher – and over whom Thatcher wove something of a spell. (Didn't she famously cut a summit meeting in Paris short because she wanted to see how Mitterrand had had the private rooms of the Elysée redecorated?) But Pewter soon lost interest in this and decided to have a go at reading his book.

It was a long trip to London and, somewhere after Leicester, he found himself thinking about the propositioning of

Thatcher. Alan Clark wrote about Thatcher in his *Diaries*. Thatcher's legs. Thatcher's ankles. But then Clark was something of a caricature. And that nice woman, the philosopher, Baroness whatever – she went on to chair a committee on stem cells, something in that area. Anyway, she recalled when Thatcher, in retirement, paid one of her rare visits to the Lords; and all the old men in attendance, goggle-eyed, the oldest one of them not able to stop himself drooling – he actually drooled, she said – over Thatcher's exposed legs. But that was the sort of anecdote you told at Low Table, over lunch. If only to reassure your male colleagues that there were a few men in this country who were not gay. Arwell wasn't part of that select company. Though the Scottish story might suffice. Here, they are at this party in Scotland one weekend. Everyone dressed up, men in kilts and whatnot. Thatcher wearing her recognizable sailor-outfit. And during this dance this drunken Scottish laird staggers up to Thatcher and starts propositioning her. He praises her dress, her power, her beauty; he goes on in the most graphic way to tell Thatcher what he would like to do to her, man to woman. And the Lady doesn't blanch. She responds in clear, ringing, blue-rinsed tones:

'That is very interesting. Thank you very much. But I don't think you could manage all that at the moment.'

That was one for Low Table.

When, a few days later, he got on to another of the Arwell Barnes e-mails Pewter was surprised at the specificity of the request. The Returnees' Club on the island was in the process of setting up a Reading Room, which would be seen as an extension of the activities of the reading groups that Miss Vanesa had organized so successfully. But whereas Miss Vanesa's groups limited themselves mainly to literature, he, as President of the Club, would want this one to concentrate on International Affairs. In order to bring some focus to the resulting discussions he would suggest that they start with books and materials relating to Russia and the old Soviet Union.

Pewter was surprised by this; he didn't think he had that much material relating to that area; and, in any case the books were all in boxes, some were going into storage, and obviously he wasn't going to unpack for Arwell Barnes's convenience.

But he was relieved that he hadn't got around to sending anything to the fellow, because he'd had a feeling about Arwell from that first meeting at Miss Vanesa's, something he couldn't place. Without thinking too much about it he would have sent off, maybe, books relating to black people and their achievements. Mandela. Something about Mozambique perhaps. African-Americans who had done their thing. Books by Toni Morrison. August Wilson's plays.

Now, he knew not to take the Arwells of this world for granted, either.

*

Of course you have to protect yourself, Arwell thought; you had to protect something as valuable as that. With so many jealous people around. Even though you have the resources. History tells you that all the resources in the world won't help you when it matters. If the Roman Empire fell all empires could fall. And therefore you have to protect yourself; so he understood why the Lady had to change her name. And even though the SS *Altair Voyager* didn't have anything like the resonance and ring of SS *Condoleezza Rice*, nothing like the sexiness of the first wearer of the name, you had to understand – even though you struggled to see the SS *Altair Voyager* as the oil-proud 136,000 dead-weight Mistress of the Seas; but it was necessary; he understood, *he understood*.

Then he panicked. *He couldn't discover the number of her crew.* He had tried; even the little boy had come and tried on the internet; and the number of crew was a state secret. For a ship of that magnitude, a warship, in effect, albeit carrying oil, you needed hardy men to control her. Let's say a lower number of fifty; they still had to carry out their functions in her, *sailing* in her, eating and *sleeping* in her: *was this necessary?* And what if the figure was twice fifty. *Four times* fifty?

And when he somehow stretched every point of credibility and argued against his own logic – he didn't pray, he didn't do prayers; he would take the Lady to her church, of course, but he would wait outside; he'd go away and come back to collect her – he did everything short of praying and was on the point of accepting *the crew* with the Lady: there were cases of man and wife lying side by side in the same bed for years and not having sex. Just as he was about to come round to the conclusion that this was possible without stain on the Lady's character, without harm to the Lady's honour, he realized that the crews *changed*. So he wasn't talking of fifty or four hundred, he was talking of waves of fifty or four hundred all making themselves comfortable in his bride's quarters that he would not have the pleasure to visit, prior to the wedding.

*

'We may have been over-hasty,' Nora admitted. 'They say he's back to his old self, Arwell. Talking about cricket. Not any more about American football.'

'And he's turned off the music,' Vanesa said. 'Turned off the Strauss.'

'Brahms.'

'Nice for the swimming pool,' Fred said, without apparent irony.

'The man was an *agent provocateur*,' Nora said.

'How come?'

'Leading us on to criticize a black woman. A woman born in segregated America who's made something of herself. These men are too devious.'

'She certainly deserves brownie points,' Vanesa agreed, 'to have come through Birmingham, Alabama intact.'

'They pronounce it Birming*ham*,' Nora corrected.

'Whatever. It's the segregated thing that matters.'

'Though the parents were middle class, the father was a parson; so they probably didn't face the worst.'

'You can't escape a thing like that whatever class you be,' Fred insisted.

'And it's not the father being a parson that made them middle class,' Nora said. 'The mother's family were middle class; she was a musician. Unfortunately, she died young. All the women in the family played music. The church choir, everything. Her grandmother, even.'

'They sent her to ballet classes . . .'

'Like Coretta King.'

'What?'

'Coretta Scott King. She played music too; she was a musician. She had a hard life with the Reverend,' Fred said.

'So, we're talking about Condoleezza Rice; when she was a toddler she started ballet. And skating and foreign languages. A bit like you, Fred.'

'Me never went to no skating.'

'And the Russian came later. But piano was the thing. She could have been a concert pianist. She could have played Carnegie Hall.'

'And we're talking classical music, you know. Not just Gospel and thing. We're talking Mozart and Liszt and . . . Brahms.'

'Brahms.'

'She was lucky that she had a daddy who was a black man in America who respect himself. Or with all the brains she wouldn't have ended up as Provost of Stanford University.'

'Like the Williams sisters and Tiger Woods.'

'Except her daddy was probably kinder than the Williams man.'

'More like Tiger Woods' daddy. Tiger Woods' daddy used to use psychology.'

'So why with all that and all she achieve, we think she should throw herself away on this pappyshow of a mixed marriage?'

'You're right, we mustn't get sidetracked into criticizing the woman for nothing.'

'And Mozart's daddy, too,' Fred said, after a pause.

The other two turned to her, bemused. Fred explained: 'Mozart's daddy, Leopold. He exploited the two children.'

'Oh. Right.'

*

It's his rendezvous with colleagues at Low Table, for lunch, their old meeting-ground, first time back in six weeks. They caught up on things, Christmas, the marking, Paris – Pewter talked of the excellence of the English-language bookshops all over the city, not just Shakespeare & Co. and the American Village Voice bookstore down in the sixth, but WH Smith and Galignani's on rue de Rivoli, and yet another one round the side on rue Saint-Paul. And then, in almost an afterthought, he asked what people knew about Condoleezza Rice. (He had been prompted into this by something in Arwell Barnes's last e-mail.) Pewter instinctively turned to Peter, from history.

'Condoleezza Rice? George Bush's Foreign Policy Brain?'

'You know, apart from all the stuff of being right wing and . . . this old obsession with Russia.'

'That's right. Well, let's see. What else?' Peter was thinking.

'Ariel Sharon said he couldn't concentrate on politics when she visited him, because he couldn't keep his eyes off her legs.' That was someone else.

'God, imagine a man like that thinking of women's legs.'

'Imagine a man like that *not* thinking about women's legs.' Pewter's question was on the point of being lost. Someone else at table was talking about 'Rendering'.

At the other end of the table someone was telling a story. 'When the first Bush, Bush the Elder, took Condoleezza Rice to meet the Russians, Gorbachev didn't know what to make of her. Bush introduced her – this was in '89 towards the end of the Soviet Union. They were meeting on this boat in Malta harbour. Big summit. Bush. James Baker. Brent Scowcroft who was the National Security Advisor. Condoleezza is the Soviet expert. And Bush says to Gorbachev: "This is the little Lady who tells me everything I know about the Soviet Union." And Gorbachev looks startled, and his birthmark goes red, goes white; and he says to Condoleezza Rice. "I hope you know a lot."'

And now Peter is ready. 'Well, she was with Chevron,' he said.

'Enron?'

'United States of Enron.'

'No, not Enron,' Peter cut through the nonsense. 'Chevron. That's another . . . multinational. She was a director there for years. Of course, she had lots of directorships between government jobs. Chevron is into oil operations in twenty-five countries. Including Kazakhstan.'

'Ah, Kazakhstan.' That was someone else at table. 'The famous 935-mile oil pipeline.'

In the end Pewter came away with quite a bit of information to go on. He went back to the library and checked out the book list from Arwell. Apart from commentaries on the British and American Constitutions (with a copy of

Walter Bagehot's *The English Constitution*, specified), there were titles by Kissinger and Fukuyama, a book by Walter Lippmann (*The Cold War: A Study in U.S. Foreign Policy*), published in 1947! And then:

The Soviet Union and the Czechoslovak Army, 1948–1983: Uncertain Allegiance (Condoleezza Rice, Princeton University Press, 1984)

The Gorbachev Era (Alexander Dallin and Condoleezza Rice, Stanford Alumni Association, 1986)

Germany United and Europe Transformed: A Study in Statecraft (Philip D. Zelikow and Condoleezza Rice, Harvard University Press, 1995)

He didn't quite know what to make of this.

*

Fred came out on the verandah. 'Somebody dead?'

'Depending on how you can take a surprise?' Nora was standing at her car, the door open. 'Come on, Fred, it's too hot to be standing out in the sun; you said five minutes.'

'What all you so mysterious about, now? A man land on the island?'

'Something more interesting than a man,' Nora said.

'I'm going along just to keep Nora company,' Vanesa said.

'So you man and wife now; you married.' And after a pause: 'I still waiting for a clue.'

'They're unloading the goods at the jetty.'

'So? . . . I still waiting.'

'A piano for our president.'

'Piano for Arwell?' And then after another pause: 'Well, why not? How you going play Brahms the way the lady plays her Brahms if you don't have piano in your house where you can practise, practise?'

10

Enter Madame Constanze

A Story in Six Scenes

SCENE FOUR

They are watching a video, all four of them, in FRED's *large drawing room – she still calls it that.* FRED *and* VANESA *on the big couch with* MOZART *squashed in the middle, and* NORA *in a chair, well apart. The cat,* RILEY, *is on the floor, eyes open. On a side table there's an empty soup bowl and spoon. Two napkins still in their rings, a third one crumpled, used. From time to time* FRED *checks* MOZART *to make sure he isn't drifting off. He is drifting off, no point in shaming him by invoking his name. She sighs and stops the film. At which point* MOZART *wakes up, suffused again by the women's scent, and eases himself away from* FRED's *skirts, careful not to crush her dress. But then he can't let himself lean too closely to* MISS VANESA, *and be familiar.* FRED *gets up.*

'We might as well call it a day,' *she says.* 'All you not taking this seriously.'

There is a suggestion of a cough from NORA, *in the chair.* VANESA's *shoulders heave slightly as if she is controlling a cough, a laugh.*

FRED *gives them a look which isn't difficult to interpret.*

This is a glimpse of a scene to which we will return.

FRED *and the* FLYING DOCTOR *are in* FRED*'s garden. He is seated, relaxed, with a cold drink in front of him.* FRED *is gardening, in eye-catching gloves and hat.*

FLYING DOCTOR: A woman gardening . . . A woman in her garden. I think of you as a natural woman, Miss Fred. In her garden.

FRED: Well, I fool them that time when they were looking for the axe-murderer. And I got off. You know what this is (*a weed; a plant*)? Eglantine, blue vetch, wild mignonette? Slap on the wrist, Fred. Wrong part of country. Wrong country. Stick to the Latin names, I always say. *Then* you have a garden.

FLYING DOCTOR (*sniffing the air*): Can't beat the natural environment. No sir.

FRED: They say the whole world polluted.

FLYING DOCTOR: In this environment. (*He makes an expansive gesture.*) Sitting here like this it's tempting to forget the pollution in the world.

FRED: Like living in denial.

FLYING DOCTOR (*laughs*): You have to . . . A man can't wear his professional hat all the time.

FRED: Why do they call it that?

FLYING DOCTOR: Eh? What?

FRED: Professional hat. With all the things a man does wear when he dress himself up, why you call it a hat?

FLYING DOCTOR (*laughs*): I'm glad you're not a patient, Miss Fred. A patient like you would send me back to my books.

FRED: Failed again. There was I hoping to put you out of

business. (*And as if there was no change of mood:*) Talking of patients . . .

FLYING DOCTOR: Ah!

FRED: I know you can't talk about Arwell, directly.

FLYING DOCTOR: As you know . . .

FRED: Professional thing. And all that. But in a general way, in a general sort of way, is the prognosis good or bad?

FLYING DOCTOR: Prognosis. Ah!

FRED: Me went to school, you know. I studied science. I know a lot of nouns.

FLYING DOCTOR: Ah. I assure you, Miss Fred.

FRED: Forget the 'Miss'.

FLYING DOCTOR: Fred . . . Winifred.

FRED: Fred will do. You say Arwell not mad. (*Then, as if deciding a change of tactic, a change of idiom:*) You say Arwell's not mad. That Arwell's sane. Sane as any man on this island. I agree with you, too.

FLYING DOCTOR: Now, as you say, I can't discuss . . .

FRED: Forget about Arwell, then. Let's think about somebody else. Somebody who might be a bit like Arwell. But isn't Arwell. And you're dealing with his problem, too. And you have a long chat with him on the verandah, not on the couch . . .

> FLYING DOCTOR *scoffs politely at the notion of a couch.*

. . . And after this long chat you come away with the feeling that the man is not mad. (*Snips at the head of a plant in the garden.*) It's interesting to be let in on the secret.

FLYING DOCTOR: Well, as you say, we can't talk about this particular person.

FRED: We're not talking about this particular person now. (*Snip snip.*)

FLYING DOCTOR: I think the man's as sane as . . . I mean – I would say the hypothetical man. Could be described as sane as . . .

FRED: And the rest of us mad.

FLYING DOCTOR: The rest of us (*thinks for a bit*) are sane in our different ways. Or mad in our different ways. It's not a word I like to use, mad. Sane. Words like that. It'd be a brave man to call someone mad in this world. And other people not mad. Or vice versa. That's why the word creates a difficulty.

FRED: You don't think all these presidents and prime ministers are madmen?

FLYING DOCTOR: Oh, I don't want . . . I wouldn't want to stray into . . .

FRED: Maybe that's not your area.

FLYING DOCTOR: I have a problem, as I say, with that sort of language.

FRED: OK, coming back to Arwell. To this man who might be like Arwell.

FLYING DOCTOR: You ask a man. You give a man an option of three names, say. One name is . . . Let's see. One name is Philip P. Upperthorpe. One is Winston Kamuzu Mainwareing. The third name is Arwell Barnes. And you say to him: which of these three names – forget everything but the name. You say, which of these three names are you most comfortable with?

FRED: And he says Arwell Barnes.

FLYING DOCTOR: And he says . . . And *if* he says, *if* he says 'Arwell Barnes' – and his name happens to be Arwell Barnes – this hypothetical man . . .

FRED: *I* would choose Arwell Barnes, meself. If I was a man.

FLYING DOCTOR: Of course, we're assuming you're a man.

FRED (*looking down at her dress*): So I see the disguise not working.

FLYING DOCTOR: What?

FRED: I forget, you're not supposed to make joke with doctors. Particularly when it's to do with the head-thing. My daddy always warned me that my jokes would land me in a heap of trouble.

FLYING DOCTOR: Oh, I like a woman . . .

FRED: Either that or with a millionaire with a rum distillery down in Martinique and an apartment in Paris. *Dixième arrondissement, s'il vous plait.* Married to a big man and his little dog in a nice part of Paris. (*pause*) Or maybe a wife in a clapboard house in America. The puritan part. Forced to wear modest clothes. And, as you can see, I still here. (*almost with no change*) So Arwell likes the open air.

FLYING DOCTOR (*pause. More comfortable*): . . . Speaking . . . generally . . . Given a choice between the private sphere and the public sphere – when you choose the public – given that you're in some ways, fragile – when you choose the public – that's a positive thing, a hopeful sign.

FRED: Like travelling in the landscape rather than raping the environment in your car.

FLYING DOCTOR (*startled*): What? . . . I'm not sure . . .

FRED: I was thinking of *Zen and the Art of Motorcycle Maintenance*. (*then relenting*) I think of the open air of men getting together and making speeches and . . . maybe indoors as women having conversation. But I'm sure that's not politically correct.

FLYING DOCTOR (*able to patronize her for the first time*): No no no, dear. What I mean is: rather than sit in your darkened room, hushed voices, and all that. Like a patient. Be outside. Listen to the birds and . . .

FRED: Bees.

FLYING DOCTOR: Well, whatever happen to be out there. All that. Doesn't mean you have to shout. You can talk about the . . . footfall of the cat as it . . . pads away from you. You can note that when the cat knocks over something, accidentally, it doesn't know how to put it right . . . Whether it broods is something I don't want to get into.

FRED: I never thought of all that. Of Riley going through all that worry; that's why some of them say I mad or stupid. Even though I can still recite the Tudor and Stuart Kings of England. And I know how to spell Stuart.

FLYING DOCTOR: Oh, Miss Fred, you're the . . .

FRED: Fred. (*showing him another plant*) And this is the *Helianthus* adapted to our climate. (*in the same tone of voice*) And Edward Jenner was the African who invented the smallpox vaccine in 1798.

FLYING DOCTOR *gets up baffled.*

SCENE TWO

Another house. On the verandah. NORA, FRED *and* VANESA. *Proper drinks on the table.*

NORA (*to* FRED): So what else did he say?

FRED *doesn't respond. Pause.* VANESA *fills in with a story she has presumably been telling.*

VANESA: . . . And I tell you, they make you shame. I simply said: Is there another Stoke? When she said Stoke-on-Trent.

And she says Stoke Newington. I'm in Manchester, remember. Up north; I want to go to Stoke. That's what I ask for. Stoke. And when she says Stoke-on-Trent, I just thought she was trying to be helpful. So I said: You know, you've got a point; is there another Stoke? I'm trying to get to Keele. And she says: There's Stoke Newington . . .

NORA: They don't know about geography; they're not taught in the schools.

VANESA: She says there's Stoke Newington. And I take it in the spirit that I think it's offered. I say: I'm going to Keele. North Staffordshire. And she looks on the computer and after a while says there's no station at North Staffordshire. She even pronounces Staffordshire in her own funny way. And I say I know there's no station at North Staffordshire, that's why I'm going to Stoke in order to get to Keele University. And then she says – she chupps and says: Why you tellin' me bout North Slaffordshire, den? All rough and rude and pretup. With people in the queue I feel so shame, so ashamed. Everywhere you go these days you have these bitches giving black people a bad name.

Pause.

NORA (*calmly*): I try to avoid England these days, in truth. I can't take it any more. (*back to* FRED) Fred, we have to save you, you know, from this conman. This Fly-by-night Doctorman.

FRED: You know they used to have a Flying Doctor in Australia. In the fifties.

VANESA: I remember *The Flying Doctor*. They used to have it on the radio in England when I was a girl. Sunday afternoons.

NORA: That's all very nice. The Trivial Pursuits information. But we're interested in flying doctors nearer home. So he says listening to the cat walking is sane. What else?

FRED: Why you all so interested in this Flying Doctor man? I thought this was all about Arwell.

NORA: But you say you're not going to talk about Arwell. That's privileged information. I'm the last person to pry.

FRED: He said things about his dead wife in confidence, that's all.

NORA: And who are we to . . . intrude on . . . that kind of . . . privacy?

FRED: Anyway, he didn't mean it that way. The doctor. You misunderstand the thing about the cat. Some people are eccentric and not mad. They might not even be eccentric. It have a man in India who go around planting trees. And his family and everyone want him to get married instead of planting trees. And he's very happy planting trees and not doing anybody any harm. All over Calcutta. *(then, briskly; no change of tone)* Then, we did a quiz. *(challenging them)* What's the difference between Perry Como and Pere Stroika?

A long pause.

NORA: One is a singer.

An equally challenging pause.

FRED: Which one?

NORA: Jesus God in Heaven. *(getting up; slight pause)* Men used to call this thing in women the change. Men used to say women get that way when certain things go wrong in their body. Fred, you have a family name to live up to. People are beginning to talk.

FRED: So it mean you not going to marry me any more, Nora. *(and then as if quoting)* If the world is not how we would like it to be and everybody knows that it isn't. *Hélas.* If the world is threatening and irrational and misogynistic and things are – what they say? – out of joint . . .

NORA: Yes, yes, Fred. All right.

FRED: And the lunatics let out of the asylum. (*stops abruptly*) Sorry I said that.

Pauses, expecting to be reprimanded by the others; but they remain silent. In the end she says, simply:

There's still children's hospitals. You think that sad? I look at my little grandchild and I bawl. Imagine them places in the world where they don't even have hospitals for the children. (*flustered*) You're right, I talking foolishness again.

She subsides slowly, sobs on NORA's *shoulder.*

SCENE THREE

NORA *and* VANESA. *In another house. Middle of the afternoon. Inside. No drinks in sight. An air of conspiracy, voices low.*

NORA: The appeals to logic make sense but they don't ring true. Not for Fred. Who's a lateral thinker. No one bats an eyelid when Fred calls her cat Riley, though it's a female. Because the cat has the life of Riley. That's the Belair wit.

VANESA: She's right, though, about Mozart. Why call a boy Mozart, who can't play the piano?

NORA: Linguistic licence.

VANESA: Yes, but if you're good at computers why not call you Bill Gates or . . . you know, Richard Branson, or someone.

NORA: Richard Branson's not into computers. As far as I know.

VANESA: You know what I mean.

NORA: But if we're talking logic – small people's logic – then we must be logical. It wouldn't make any better sense to call this boy – because he's into computers – to call him Richard Branson than to call him Mozart. Bill Gates, on the other hand, I can understand.

VANESA: All right, Nora; it was just an example.

NORA: Bill Gates is still a young, good-looking man . . .

VANESA: Fred says she likes that Alan Sugar.

NORA: What, a man with all that rabbit fur on his face? Anyway, I prefer to come back to this business – if we're talking about madness – to this business of the cat and the cat's footsteps.

VANESA: 'They make a noise like feathers.'

NORA: What?

VANESA: Sorry. Unless they putting shoes on the cats in the upper-class homes of Fred's friends. Either it's a Shakespearean conceit or it's madness.

NORA: I worry about something, though. I ask you: the difference between Perry Como and Perestroika.

VANESA: That's bad. Fred's got to be careful, you know; there's people on this island who would find that sort of thing peculiar.

SCENE FOUR

They are watching a video, all four of them, in FRED's *large drawing room – she still calls it that.* FRED *and* VANESA *on the big couch with* MOZART *squashed in the middle, and* NORA *in a chair, well apart. The cat,* RILEY, *is on the floor, eyes open. On a side table there's an empty soup bowl and spoon. Two napkins still in their rings, a third one, crumpled, used. From time to time* FRED *checks* MOZART *to make sure he isn't drifting off. He is drifting off, no point in shaming him by invoking his name. She sighs and stops the film. At which point* MOZART *wakes up, suffused again by the women's scent, and eases himself away from* FRED*'s skirts, careful not to crush her dress. But then he can't let himself lean too closely to* MISS VANESA, *and be familiar.* FRED *gets up.*

'We might as well call it a day,' she says. 'All you not taking this seriously.'

There is no suggestion of a cough from NORA, *in the chair.* VANESA*'s shoulders don't heave slightly as if she is controlling a cough, a laugh.*

FRED *doesn't give them a meaningful look.*

MOZART (*guilty*): We miss the mask man, Miss Fred?

FRED: You and your mask man. (*to others*) Anyone like to taste the soup now?

They all decline; NORA *checks her watch.*

Is all right; I don't have any grind-up crappo in the soup. You see it do me any harm? Let me give a little to Riley now it cool down and you can see.

She goes to pick up the cat, who screams and bolts: she is frozen in the bending position.

This is my house. I know where you hiding. Remember where these rascals decide to play dead in the opera? Taking the poison. And the doctor bring them to life with book learning.

And in a weird version of the aria she launches into Despina's role in Act One of Così *fan tutte:*

'Vor–rei dir, e cor non ho e cor non ho bal–bet–tan–do il lab–bro va.'

RILEY *comes tamely back, and allows* FRED *to pick her up and fondle her.*

MOZART (*frightened and confused*): I sorry, I have to go to the latrine.

FRED: Is all right, Mozart, we'll give you a drive home to you grandmother. Go get your shoes from the gallery. And use the toilet in the laundry room.

MOZART *escapes, relieved.*

At least he got something right. Mozart snored.

NORA: Maybe the other one snored in tune. (*and then to* FRED) I hope you're not going out dressed like that.

As FRED *tries to make up her mind how to respond to* NORA, NORA *softens.*

You would have thought the bad language would have kept him awake.

VANESA: They've gone way past bad language in this place, girl; the young people. (*too brightly*) Bad language is nothing to them.

NORA: Nevertheless, they blab and they blab and they . . . make things up. And we're always the sufferer. Because we're a certain age.

VANESA: And we're women.

NORA: We're a certain age and we're women. And we've lived abroad. (*She sighs a little theatrically.*) We're living in interesting times, as the Chinese say. You're not saying anything, Fred.

VANESA: The things we do for you, Fred.

NORA: Fred, what're you thinking? . . . The boy's waiting outside, Fred. Vanesa and I will drive him home to his grandmother, and thank her for letting the boy come to the rehearsal. And . . . (*pointedly*) we'll leave you to change and have a rest. (*then, more conciliatorily*) That's a really nice dress, Fred. You must give me the address of your tailor down there in Martinique. Your seamstress. Not that I can afford Paris prices.

FRED: Did anybody feed Riley while I was away?

NORA: Fred, you know that Riley's well taken care of. We're talking about Mozart.

FRED: Maybe we should call him Bing. That way it would be easier to teach him to sing.

Fade.

SCENE FIVE

MOZART *is reporting back to his friends. He is eagerly interrupted from time to time.*

BOY 1: . . . Under the frock?

GIRL: Is dress they call it, not frock.

BOY 1: Same thing.

MOZART: You listenin' or what?

BOY 2: Tell us about the little men holding up the frock. The Lilli–

MOZART: Is not just the Lilliputins. Some of them not so little. Is big man it have sometime crouching down under the frock.

BOY 2: So they seein' everything and . . .

MOZART: Is part of the style, boy. In Vienna and them places. So that you can't tell the real shape of the women.

BOY 1: So if the woman deform you not going know.

MOZART: Is what they call high society and cosmopolitan.

GIRL: So how big is this dress?

MOZART: It have up to a thousand people making the dress, and if they get something wrong it don't work. The needle prick you finger and you dead.

173

BOY 1: And what happen when she take off she dress?

MOZART: That's another thing, boy. You have to sing another sort of song.

BOY 1: And she take off she dress that time?

MOZART: No man, you got to do this thing right or the crazy man not go get better. You go turn him into dog. Is part of the magic, the obeah they makin'.

BOY 2: And you eating food in that place, Mozart?

MOZART: I protected, you know. Genius Boy. But I just have a snack, not food food. A snack and maybe a cold drink. The women they have their customized napkins already prepare. Is part of the . . .

GIRL: What's that? Customize napkin?

MOZART: I don't have to explain everything, you know.

BOY 1: Go on, Mozart. So Arwell there in the same room with them?

MOZART: No man, Arwell don't even know it going on.

BOY 2: *That* is what I call magic.

BOY 1: And the other woman them take off they clothes?

MOZART: None of the woman take off she clothes.

BOY 1: So you don't see no panty or titty or nothing?

MOZART: Boy we talking important thing like music and opera and *Requiem*. And canasta and symphony.

GIRL: Symphony.

MOZART: And divertimenti, boy, *divertimenti*.

BOY 2: *Divertimenti*.

GIRL: They do canasta as well?

BOY 2: They does have that with obeah.

MOZART: Everything, man. If you're a boy genius nothing go touch you. That's why they call me Mozart. Boy Genius.

BOY 1: And you still don't see no titty.

MOZART: How you know I don't see any titty?

BOY 2: He see titty, you know. Come on, Mozart. Tell we. Which one, which one a the women show you she titty? We not going tell no one.

MOZART (*pause*): It goin' cost you.

BOY 1: How much, how much? (*Starts fishing in his pocket.*)

MOZART (*slowly*): I have a lot of expenses, you know, boys. (*He nods to the* GIRL, *including her.*) . . . In an earlier life a man would have a patron. If you know what a patron is. A big archbishop with a foreign name and a big house and palace in Salzburg and Vienna. Organizing the music and playing for royalty. People think they know what royalty is.

GIRL: King and queen.

MOZART: A man need money for all that. And don't forget the travelling, you know. The expenses of travelling and the change of clothes. And having to keep the wife and the pickney. At that time a man is living in palaces with servant and women wearing velvet. (*pause*) So what you got in your pocket?

They hand over money. MOZART *waits. He wants more money. They hand over more money. They wait.*

BOY 1: Come on, Mozart: what these women do when they all together?

MOZART: I not suppose to talk about this, you know.

BOY 2: Mozart, remember when we lick you down that time?

MOZART: I goin' put jumbie pon you. (*quickly*) OK. OK.

BOY 1: Tell us what they do?

MOZART: You ever hear about . . . (*He pauses, starts again.*) You know about napkin rings?

BOY 1: Yes.

GIRL: What's napkin?

BOY 2: Napkin is thing you wipe your mouth with, man; when you eatin' expensive thing.

BOY 1: OK. Tell we, Mozart.

MOZART: Well . . . Imagine them – the women – sitting round together. In this special dining room. People in robes hanging from the wall. And she go to a secret drawer. And she take out these napkin rings. *Customized* napkin rings. The napkins wrap up secret inside the rings. And she hand them to the other women. And one of the women kiss the napkin. You can't make a mistake, you know. Or you goin' turn somebody into hog or snake.

GIRL: Or lizard.

MOZART: Or lizard.

BOY 1: They say it have a woman up in the north which is a woman that turn into a lizard; and she over three hundred years old.

BOY 2: And what they do with these customer napkin?

BOY 1: Where they putting the nappy ring?

Fade.

SCENE SIX

FRED, *in ordinary clothes, is on the phone.*

FRED: Maybe because we're old-fashioned over here. (*What we hear is the Eartha Kitt song: 'I'm just an old-fashioned girl . . .*') And maybe we don't think it's important to be so logical all the time. My father was a doctor but he never operated on anybody. He knew a lot about medicine but he didn't qualify as a medical doctor. But my father was still a doctor. My daddy used to say if you study Molière as a child it teach you a lot about revolution; because the maids are not real maids. (*with no apparent shift*) The idea of getting into the spirit of Mozart . . .

She listens.

. . . Yes, I'm sure you're a real doctor with degrees and . . . a miracle worker and . . . But the idea of creating a Mozart environment to help poor Arwell was never going to be easy, as Nora said. We just make ourselves pappyshow . . . I listening. I hear you. But now is the woman I feel sorry for. The woman who lose all those babies in infancy and still get criticize by everybody: maybe you would have helped her. That's why . . . Yes, that's why . . . well, I prefer to stick to my gardening; and if I make a mistake in the garden nobody dead . . . Well, you are the big doctor. And look at me here, brazen as you like, talking to you with not a stitch on my body. I even shame to admit it. So I have to put down the phone now, and make myself decent.

She hangs up the phone; she is completely dressed.
Fade.

Three

I I

Ms Codrington

FOR LAWRENCE SCOTT

'So you're not staying?' Fred had sensed it.

Oh, why did everyone want to put her on the spot? She had moved house; she had moved house so many times, she wasn't a stranger here, you know, she didn't have to prove her loyalty. So, she'll see.

It felt better, though, without the 'e': Codrington was altogether more trim than the old Coderington, as if you had lost a bit of weight and were feeling better for it; that extra 'e' that you'd been carrying around in your middle obviously weighed something, however light it seemed on the tongue: she now associated it with nothing more than a trinket that the father had picked up in his scavenging way – something thrown out by someone because it was useless or decorative; so she, too, could get by without it. Already, she felt freer to be rid of it, lighter: she would assess her life anew now, and see if it made a difference.

And the beauty of it is that this came about by accident; or, if not by accident, by someone else's devising. When they returned to the island after having had to abandon it because of the volcano, naturally everything had to be rebuilt, restored; not just the houses and churches and public buildings, but the roads and all the services; the infrastructure; and with water flowing in the pipes again the rains came, as if to say that it was going to be all right; and with the rains the birds, and the insects that you didn't mind so much now. And it wasn't till the road signs were put up that they noticed the change of spelling, the 'e' had been left out of the village formerly known as Coderington: in the scheme of things quite a small mistake. (OK, pity it had to be her name.)

But it's a funny thing how people in these parts never want to admit their mistakes: it's not that they think they're right, not that they're wrong and strong, as the saying goes, it's just that they're ashamed. So the tendency is to pretend that the mistake is deliberate, is something well thought out. And so it was the case with the village that bore her name. And Codrington and Coderington sounded much the same, anyway. Though she wouldn't deny she was of a generation brought up to believe that things, even a useless thing like an appendix, had their uses, though you couldn't always explain what they were for, because wouldn't life be less rich in its narrative, wouldn't the world be altogether poorer if we didn't have the possibility of a god of uselessness, a goddess of the unnecessary? *I have come in your dream to kiss that useless 'e': what have you done with it?*

The arguments for recognizing a change in circumstance were familiar: one may be coming back to the island, but not with the same old mindset; this was in some ways, in important ways, a fresh start, a new beginning. (How many more new beginnings, dear God!) One had to be positive and believe that this was not a continuation of the old routine – which had, in any case, led to disaster more than once – a routine only to be played out this time in reduced circumstances.

Vanesa didn't have a problem with making sacrifices because she, too, wanted the thing to work for those who came back; so she didn't know if it was wise to focus on a detail like this, to dignify a sign-painter, to hang hope on a spelling mistake. It was just a question of not being indifferent to it, not saying she was insulated against chance, or bigger than the village. And the new spelling was, anyway, nearer to the way other people spelt the name: it was like walking out of the fantasy of one man and joining a community of the like-minded. She liked that direction of movement; it was different from those women who gave up their names when they got married to men.

So Vanesa became an unlikely defender of the change that was hard to detect in a word and would soon not be noticed at all. (Her friend had had an operation and looked the same afterwards but said she never felt the same: Vanesa wasn't going to be taken in by appearances.) In order to keep this light, though, in order to strike the right note, she preferred to say: Look around you; people are always renewing themselves after these disasters. (You didn't even need a disaster for that to happen: people just had to go abroad and after a few years they would come back with a changed name and upgraded family tree – all those thirteenth and fourteenth cousins of the good and the great now becoming near rather than distant family.) But to come back to the hurricanes and volcanoes: you would have memory of someone living off the beaten track, in a ghaut, say, somewhere where it didn't have a road in or out, only a dirt track that you could hardly cross when it rained. Come the hurricane, come the volcano, with all this general movement and confusion, and the same people would reappear, this time on high ground, above the main road on the other side, a road with wheeled traffic – looking down now on the old place of recent history.

Well, hurricanes and volcanoes were traumatic experiences but they offered you opportunities, too. She couldn't decide whether to make her change of name a significant thing, or to let it pass as a non-event. There might be a way to find out.

So Vanesa sat down to surveying her work, most of it unpublished. It was true she was always too much of a woman for them, for those who wanted her to be less. And she had always refused to reduce herself to fit their image of her. But let's say – and this was just speculation, she wasn't committing herself to anything – just say she could take the hint of the man with the village-sign and tighten up here and there on something, squeeze out the unnecessary letter, if you like; but retain the shape and the sound – Vanesa Coderington; Vanesa of Codrington: you didn't have to live in a place that bore your name. It was down to the speaker now, not the listener, to know the difference. And was she putting herself forward as some sort of speaker? Talking of speakers her old friend, who should be nameless, who came to stay last time – and it is her privilege to decide whether to admit his name so soon on this recovering island – her old friend, singing for his supper, had given a lecture on the Theory of Names.

There were names, he said, that put you in line for literary glory, and names that consigned you to the ranks of the 'also ran'. The key was having a two-syllable name not a three-syllable name. And, to be fair, the friend consigned his own three-syllables to the also rans. Two-syllable-blessed and you were Chaucer and Milton and Dickens and Balzac and Baudelaire. Even those huge-sounding names like Wordsworth and Shakespeare still had only two syllables. Of course – he pointed out – there were exceptions; but for every Cervantes and Rabelais there was the praetorian guard of Dante and Flaubert and Chekhov and Faulkner and Walcott and Rushdie. Again, for every Turgenev outside the gates there was Tolstoy and Pushkin and co. on the ramparts. Her friend had developed this idea into a literary word game which he was going to market. The wild cards were the one- and the four-syllable people, the Irish and maybe the Japanese, or the Indians. But Vanesa couldn't remember how that went. She would concentrate on her own more-modest game. (Though Vanesa couldn't help smiling as she recalled the argument at the end of the lecture over the number of syllables in Baudelaire.)

But how were other people managing the return? Her family of friends had come to take her to lunch – the shape of women getting together outside a crisis, safely transferred; they brought with them the web of conversation that survived the move. (She'd miss this.) And they found a place for lunch, as if someone was preparing for their comfort all along. Today lunch was at Miss Odilie's, which was the nearer of two eating places on the edge of what used to be the town. Miss Odilie served a wicked lentil soup. But this wasn't emergency lunch. There were other things on offer as well, fish and chicken dishes, but the home-made lentil soup was special. There was lentil soup flavoured with a bit of ham knuckle; and then there was plain lentil soup for the vegetarians. Seasoned. Miss Odilie had replaced other establishments, of course, and Vanesa hoped someone would make sure those were not forgotten. After lunch the talk was how good it was to have Miss Odilie; Miss Odilie's was almost better than what was there before. Yes, it was better than what went before.

And so to work.

So: you took out the 'e' and other letters came together closing up the space, leaving no gap. You took out the 'e' and the slight otherness of the name disappeared, and reunited you with a new family; you took out the 'e' and the man who put it in in the first place retreated that little bit further into the background; you took out the 'e' and you were still upright and not missing, not even listing like a little ship in distress; so now you can look around you and survey the rest of the work and see what else can be taken out without hurt or harm to yourself: you are learning from the service you have performed for others; you are learning from the table-talk of celebrated friends who occasionally come to visit. You took out the 'e' to prevent more sprawl in the world; you took the 'e' out and made yourself easier to carry. You took out the 'e' and felt good about it, exhausted but good, as if you'd just emerged from an afternoon swim, or had a morning's run on the exercise bike, to make you worthy of the day.

And no, she wasn't going to push this to the point where it became an obsession; this wasn't going to be the sole focus of her energy. And no, she wasn't one of those people who wanted to be other than she was; she was a three-syllable writer (Morrison, Corinthians ... Hrotsvitha); she was content to be that. It was her more muscle-toned twin sister now, looking over her shoulder, who was urging her on, pointing out . . . that if you took out the 'e' . . .

12

Vanesa and
the Elsham Road Set

Pewter wouldn't immediately have associated Vanesa – Miss Vanesa, as she's now become known – with the Elsham Road set in London in the late sixties and early seventies, so he was the wrong person to approach about it: if this review in the *Guardian* hadn't mentioned her he wasn't particularly surprised; but the book may have done. The book was about John Elsom's theatre company in London, Theatre 69, which operated in Shepherd's Bush in the sixties and seventies. It was written by Lester Philcox, an American academic in England. Did Vanesa think that Pewter would be embarrassed because he had got a mention in the review – and, no doubt, some degree of recognition in the book – and she hadn't? Vanesa was prominent – if, indeed, she had been prominent in the group – in the year that Pewter had been away from all that, out of England touring the Caribbean; and on coming back had decamped to the continent – his first extended spell there. So doings in London, back then, seemed a long way away. Though now he was intrigued; he'd certainly order a copy of the book. Philcox was very knowledgeable about off-Broadway theatre as well as fringe theatre in London; and his articles in the *TLS* and the *London Review of Books* were usually well worth reading. Having scanned the review that Miss Vanesa sent, Pewter put it aside with her letter and started dealing with other correspondence.

Pewter was in his favourite café on rue Damrémont, which was the best he could do in terms of keeping his breakfast local. It wasn't absolutely what he had had in mind when he moved into the area, but then this wasn't the twenties or the thirties of the last century. And *le dixhuitième* wasn't as well provided for as others in this respect (it wasn't just the cigarette smoke that threatened to defeat him, it was the feeling of arriving at the scene after the main action); but he couldn't be bothered to go further up the hill to Montmartre. To have to take the metro to go to your local café and deal with your post and maybe do a bit of writing – that was like organizing a trip, it spoilt the whole ease of the thing. It didn't matter that it was only a couple of metro stops to Abbesses, it would still smack of setting out for the office. So he wouldn't pine for a better café, he would get on with his Paris life.

Though, he was intrigued by Miss Vanesa's letter, bringing back a period of his past he'd half forgotten. Yes, she had joined the group in London just as he was leaving it. He remembered her one night at the house in Shepherd's Bush being somewhat uneasy in the company, among people who had known one another a long time; and he recalled feeling slightly guilty about not going out of his way to put her at ease.

They did talk, later, about her joining the group, and about her possible role in the new play. They talked, generally, as far as he remembered, about the parts a black woman (or man) might play without being typecast (she was the first black actress to join the group; Pewter was one of the writers, he never appeared on stage); and they all knew the work of groups like Wall Theatre Co. in South London, pioneering 'blind casting': Wall had just had a huge success at the Roundhouse. Pewter and Vanesa must have talked, too, of other examples of this, notably at the City Lit. (where Elsom and Pewter taught a class), where a funny guy, whose name Pewter always forgot, was doing something similar with Molière (legitimately so, not, y'know, loaded, in casting black actors as the Miser or the Scoundrel or the Impostor). Miss Vanesa was very strongly of the opinion that theatre in Britain shouldn't go down the 'American road', where a black actress was expected to play a maid in a wealthy household because, in reality in the society, wealthy households employed black maids. That's why she was all for the 'non-naturalistic' approach that the Shepherd's Bush group seemed to favour.

But that was all of thirty years ago. More. Thirty-five. The thing that flashed through Pewter's mind now was Miss Vanesa having a Chinese meal with them at the house, and making a fuss of being vegetarian; while the talk round the table was, as so often, about recent productions: did Peter Brook's efforts at the Aldwych now make it impossible to put on another de Sade-type play? That sort of thing. But Pewter needed to get on; he put Miss Vanesa's letter aside.

Miss Vanesa was at home asleep, x thousand miles away; it was the middle of the night. But when she had sent off the letter and *Guardian* cutting to Pewter a few days previously she had had total recall of those early meetings with him and the group in Shepherd's Bush, in 1969–70.

She had been to the house before, seen a play there, one of their group productions, and quite liked the non-naturalistic freedom it offered the director and the actors. That's when she thought she might join the group, and left her name and address on a paper they passed round. (Though that seemed partly a device to recruit members for the Liberal Party.)

She soon thought she had perhaps made a mistake; after

the way she was treated the night they persuaded her to stay to dinner. (Pewter lived somewhere upstairs in the same house; they were all part of one big family.)

It was the childishness of the men she couldn't get over. They were sitting round this little table, this round, white table at one end of the room (the grand piano was at the other end, near the front entrance) and these men, men who had been to Cambridge and London and whatnot universities, were sitting around talking of women whipping men with their long hair. (Now, she didn't have long hair, and she thought it was insensitive of them – and of Pewter in particular – to be going on about women whipping men with their hair, in her presence.) And then she realized why it wasn't a big thing with Pewter, because his girlfriend then appeared, and joined the table; and she had long, whipping, blonde hair.

Talk round the table then shifted to a Brigid Brophy play, a murder mystery where the victim was cut up into tiny pieces and fed down the waste-disposal unit. (The lady of the house – she was the musician – had come in and gone to the kitchen and briefly turned on the waste-disposal unit, which made a horrible, crunching noise; and that's what started the discussion about the Brigid Brophy play.) It was a ludicrous scenario, and the men round the table thought up practical ways in which the thing could be done – with chainsaws and whatnot; till someone protested that they were about to eat.

And she didn't know why she said she was vegetarian when she wasn't; but Pewter's girlfriend, who was American, *was* vegetarian; so Vanesa had to endure a few more awkward moments talking of wheat germ and – *toasted* wheat germ and all sorts of stuff that had come in from Sweden or somewhere that vegetarians in the know were having for breakfast instead of bacon and, whatever, sausages.

Though they got on well enough now, Vanesa didn't

think she had ever forgiven Pewter Stapleton for those early embarrassments when she was treated as an outsider.

*

Pewter ordered another hot chocolate and put aside his other papers and returned to Miss Vanesa's letter and the *Guardian* cutting. They didn't say much about him except that he was one of the writers (a couple of better-known writers were also mentioned), but they talked of 'ground-breaking' experiments in the group and – something he'd forgotten – their innovative use of music. Yes, John's wife, Sally Mays, was a musician and their resident quartet, the Mouth of Hermes, was often corralled into doing the music for the plays. Well, Vanesa wasn't a musician either; so she'd be up against others for a mention there; though John would undoubtedly have acknowledged her role, in talking to Philcox. John was a very generous critic; he'd written three or four excellent books on theatre, and always gave full recognition to the bit players, often magnifying their contribution. So Pewter was sure that the lack of a mention of Miss Vanesa in the review couldn't be down to John's doing.

And Vanesa would certainly have been worth writing about. Pewter was thinking hard, now. There she was that night when they had the Chinese takeaway. Earlier, they had been discussing a new project to do with the group, knocking around the old ideas. After the success of *Tim, I'm in danger of losing my respect for you* (yes, one of those titles), John, the *Dramaturg*, thought they might pursue another group project, not least because someone from BBC Radio had liked *Tim* . . . and had been making encouraging noises of targeting three or four companies with a view to broadcasting a series of group plays – not just the finished play but the *process* of putting it together. So the old favourites were being dusted off.

John more or less accepted that he wouldn't win people over to doing the de Sade play he had in mind (competing with Peter Brook at the Aldwych, bad idea), and suggested, instead, that they have a go at a Victorian courtesan. *The Memoirs of Harriette Wilson* was another pet project: but the *Memoirs* were hard to come by; there was only one copy in the London Library, and that had to be passed around. Then there was the argument, by someone in the group, to go topical with a play about Enoch Powell. Pewter's own project was *Coriolanus*, which was dismissed as 'Shakespeare', and 'academic', compounded by the fact that Pewter was writing a thesis on it at Birkbeck, on the various stage versions of *Coriolanus* down the ages, not only Brecht and now Günter Grass with his *The Plebeians Rehearse the Uprising*, but . . .

About Enoch Powell, well, the 'rivers of blood' speech would be nice for an actor – Tom, say – to declaim, but there was the old dilemma of being a publicity agent, unwittingly, for the unsavoury fellow, however carefully you contextualized the piece.

So opinion was moving back behind the *Harriette Wilson* idea: Harriette Wilson, the young courtesan who had been mistress to the Duke of Wellington and blackmailed her former lovers with exposure, unless they were prepared to buy themselves *out* of her *Memoirs*; the book was written in some style, by a mature Harriette, from the cool distance of Paris. The shock was when John suddenly turned to Vanesa and said that she would make a perfect Harriette. (He had already lined up a Harriette, the enigmatic Emma, whom no one really knew; except that she was a well-spoken young woman from an acting family, and that it was a bit of luck that she was interested in working with the group.)

So, they were sitting round the little white table in the corner of the big room downstairs, about to tuck into their Chinese takeaway, when Pewter noted that Vanesa, whom they didn't know, had unexpectedly accepted John's offer to stay and have a bite. She didn't say much then, but she spoke to Pewter later.

First, she wanted to talk to him about John, the man in charge. Pewter confirmed that John may sometimes be a bit paternalistic, that he was a prominent member of the Liberal Party, and his new thing was to attract the immigrant vote away from Labour; not a very politically popular move in the present climate. But also, he stressed that John, being a Cambridge man, had a tradition of intellectual curiosity to maintain, and would probably slip in, during rehearsals, references to the orders of chivalry in pre-revolutionary France, or a simile relating something in the play to the contribution, say, that Leonard Woolf had made to the Bloomsbury set.

What Vanesa wanted to ask, then, was whether John was legit in suggesting that she play Harriette Wilson, famed courtesan of Victorian society, mistress to the Iron Duke.

Pewter knew that Vanesa wasn't wild about the idea of playing a courtesan. And that she was also worried about playing the white-skinned Harriette (particularly, with another Harriette in the wings), so he tried to build up the character (beyond race? Above moralizing?) stressing how well written the *Memoirs* were – he had read only a small section, before passing the book on – that the lady was witty and made references to Shakespeare; and littered her text with French phrases. The point was that whoever wrote the dialogue for the Harriette play had so much to go on that the lady could never be undermined by prejudice about her profession. Nor could the actress playing her with such linguistic verve be put on the defensive. And, remember, this was a woman who had written letters to Lord Byron charging him for not liking her enough, true. *But* also writing to him in scolding terms, for cheapening himself by penning popular satires. (Privately, Pewter didn't think the play would happen.)

Enough of Miss Vanesa. Now, Pewter was thinking of that little round white table next to the bay window on Holland Road – the other side from Elsham Road – and the good times, good conversations had round that table. The drama, the excitement. The day, one morning when they were sitting around reading the paper, and they heard the screech of brakes in the street outside; and very soon there was a knock on the door, and this slightly shaken young woman with a Lancashire accent was ushered in: she had been in the accident but not really hurt, and this was the nearest convenient house; and the young woman was a singer and her name was Priscilla White; and after coffee and light counselling she resumed her journey (either to or from the BBC at White City); and this said Priscilla White, who recovered her composure at their table in Shepherd's Bush, turned out to be the nation's singing and talk-show favourite, Cilla Black, later of *Blind Date*. Well, the *Guardian* review didn't mention that, either; so not *everything* that happened at No. 39 was on view.

Though mention of the music was interesting. The Mouth of Hermes (Hermes, you remember, being the messenger of the gods) was something that Pewter, like others, took credit for retrospectively, though it was hard going at the time. It was good to wake up in the morning to the tinkering of the real piano, two floors down, before the rest of the quartet arrived and turned music into something else – atonal, was the word for it – thumping and grinding and scraping out something, ritually abusing their instruments, while they prepared for the 'recitals' of John Cage and Stockhausen and Ichiyanagi and Morton Feldman – at venues deep into the country that friends and lovers had to attend.

When Miss Vanesa came to think about it – and by now Pewter would have got her letter; so she was thinking about it – her resentment against Pewter Stapleton, not Philcox or John Elsom or the *Guardian*, resurfaced. Her resentment against Pewter was his posture of being at ease when he should not have been at ease, it was his assumption of being part of the in-set: was it because they had all gone to those universities and he – he, Pewter – had a girlfriend who had long, whipping hair, so that *she* could play the part of Charlotte Corday and he could be the Marquis de Sade, she whipping him into gratification, he, bare-torsoed, willing her on to humiliate him further? Why did a man think he could *buy* himself into this kind of social security (with the education, with the blonde girlfriend) that a woman certainly couldn't? Wouldn't.

Even when she spoke to him about the thing that bothered her he had affected not to understand. John had brought up the question of the African in Greenland. Apparently, there was this African – he said from Nigeria but it turned out to be from Ivory Coast – who had always had fantasies about Greenland, about going there; and finally, somehow, he got himself to Greenland, and married someone from Greenland, and had a family and lived happily ever after. Vanesa was uncertain whether this was a novel or autobiography; there was a book about it. And John had posed it to her as something they might dramatize. (Would she, then, be asked to play the flaxen-haired woman from Greenland?) And Pewter absolutely failed to pick up on what she was trying to say. What made him so secure: was it the university, or the girlfriend who would whip him with her long hair as he played de Sade? Whip his bare torso into submission and ecstasy as he played the Marquis in his asylum. Vanesa felt she had as much to fear from Mr Pewter Stapleton as from the yobs in the street who shouted garbage at her sometimes. She thought of Pewter now, having conquered one world in London, now blandly thinking that he could conquer another in Paris. (Was he still with that Charlotte Corday of long ago, or with another, half her age, whipping him with her hair, in French?)

He had offered to read the *Memoirs* properly when he got back from the Caribbean, and to map out some speeches for Harriette. But, of course he never got round to it. The play never happened.

*

Pewter had half-thought of revisiting those times; because he remembered them as the good times, not so much because of the quality of the plays (they never made it on to the radio, incidentally), but because of the company, of X, his then partner, of course, long returned to America; and of the experience of living with all those weird and wonderful 'atonal' musicians in that house in Elsham Road.

The memory of working upstairs in the morning to the sound of Sally's piano floating up, doing things together with the family downstairs from time to time, even the obligation to support the Mouth of Hermes (what sex was Hermes? He can't remember what they decided) was something close to nostalgia.

But now that Pewter was living in another country he couldn't really get his mind round the things that were bothering Miss Vanesa. Already the morning had gone, and he'd done nothing.

And yet: there was a play there, wasn't there? Of the Harriette Wilson *Memoirs*. He knew that someone had brought out a new edition, so there must be interest. And the review of the Philcox book was sympathetic. If Pewter knew then what he knew now . . . He'd read the books, hadn't he? On Napoleon, of course. And the Iron Duke. The Paul Johnson, the Gallo *and* the Andrew Roberts two-hander. Napoleon and Wellington. Maybe – why not? – maybe now was the time to do the Harriette Wilson play!

Ah – this was ridiculous – he couldn't have another hot chocolate. He needed to go to the loo. And what's the time? He'd been here all morning – might as well order some lunch. He'd occupied their tables long enough. Yes, he'll start with a glass of wine. No, *un quart*, and have a look at the menu. First, the loo. He had a flash of Miss Vanesa, awake. Miss Vanesa up and on her verandah, in her white dressing gown. Or in some other dressing gown. With a drink. An early morning drink. Miss Vanesa's letters weren't as good as Harriette Wilson's. Pity. Letting the side down. Why didn't Miss Vanesa write to him as if he were Byron or Wellington or – Lord Craven, another of her lovers? Of course he'd never been Miss Vanesa's lover, that's why. Too late now, to be Miss Vanesa's lover. But Miss Vanesa should be setting the pace, the style, the tone of letter-writing on her island. So he'll respond to her in *style*. He'll write her one of those letters hinting at a whole . . . hinterland of experience to draw from, to make her raise her game. He will write to her from *Paris*.

13

A Woman from Montserrat

Day three and the unspoken agreement, the settlement between host and guest was in danger of unravelling. At the post office that afternoon the woman behind the counter spoke to him in English, and later, Nora, his house guest, spoke to him in French: yes, of course, they were in Paris; but this wasn't, really, the script. He had ended up paying way over the odds for the 'Printed Matter' to London and New York – a confusion of language? So Pewter decided to take a deep breath, and start again.

Nora had surprised him in little ways before, which was, really, why he had extended the invitation, second time round. It was an afterthought; it was a decision made almost to correct his first impressions. Initially, at a friend's party in the Caribbean, Nora had come across like any other superior woman Pewter had met in the islands, particularly the recent returnees, doing her stuff. (He was a visitor, they were being kind to him; he would play his part by being non-judgemental.) When he met Nora at Miss Vanesa's garden party in Dominica, and overheard her reassuring Vanesa about her impending guests, that was all too familiar.

Nora was saying to Vanesa not to worry, that of course people were going to show up; because if you provided enough food and drink, you could be assured of a good turnout. Even if you died they would come, whether they knew you or not. Because of the food that was laid on. That's what she had learnt about black people in England: why would they be different here, in the islands, etc.? Yet, you couldn't rush to judgement where Nora Shackley-Bennett was concerned, even though she was said to have prospered under both Conservative and Labour governments in England: she was a woman who had run her own successful business enterprise there; she had pedigree. And, indeed, she dressed like someone who had been a chief executive, in the 1980s.

Pewter had invited her to France – first to the South, to Montauroux, where he had a place, and now to Paris. At the airport, in Nice, she had commented on the number of people in wheelchairs, and had surprised Pewter with questions about the viability of manufacture and distribution of wheelchairs in a region with a lot of older people with money, and younger ones in wheelchairs from skiing accidents; she wondered who controlled the business. Somehow you expected that sort of speculation not from a mature woman, visiting, but from a young person, a nephew, say, just out of university, thinking of ways to make money. But then, you remembered that this woman had run her own business in London employing, by all accounts, dozens and dozens of people.

Of course, Nora had played up to her role of guest and her image of 'businesswoman' by casually turning to the business pages of the *Guardian* or the *Telegraph* or whatever English paper Pewter occasionally brought in from the village. In Paris, later, she maintained something of the act, though not now with the newspapers.

Maybe it's useful to say at this point that there was no romantic involvement between Nora and Pewter Stapleton;

and that that, in an odd way, made it less tricky to relax into their roles. Nora was a traveller, Pewter was a traveller; they shared many things in common (they voted New Labour, despite everything). They had both lived in England for most of their adult lives, though without meeting each other there; and both were now considered to have made a success of their time in that country. Indeed, Nora wore a little badge on her favourite jacket, signifying recognition by the state for her services to industry: she was someone Pewter felt he *needed* to get along with. He was originally from the neighbouring island of St Caesare; and to sustain the old friendly antagonism between the two colonial outposts a few miles apart was like reverting to an outdated script. So they stressed the many things they had in common.

Nora said she felt comfortable staying with Pewter because he left her alone (a general rather than a sexual reference, he was relieved to hear). Unlike some friends she stayed with when she was travelling, she didn't feel the 'stress factor' with Pewter. In London, which was her home from home, even when you were staying in your own place, it gave you an odd sensation to find that everything in the house was in the wrong place; but then you no longer lived there: people who lived there had the right to, as it were, rearrange the furniture, to hang new pictures in place of your pictures. When you stayed with family and friends, you couldn't somehow escape that sense of being pressured; you know the feeling when you're with people who are at work all day and somehow they feel guilty that they can't take you around and show you the sights of London – as if she was new to London. Either that, or they put you under a different sort of pressure, by taking time off work to see to you. Or, if they were retired, by putting themselves entirely at your disposal, as if you were a new immigrant from Eastern Europe, or somewhere;

someone who didn't know how the underground system worked. At times like that Nora said it was beneath her to point out to them that she had first seen St Paul's in the 1950s. And the Houses of Parliament and the Changing of the Guards and the Tower, and all that. Harrods: she hadn't just come off the Eurostar from Azerbaijan. (Nora's prejudices were 'up front'; you took her, you took her prejudices, she'd let you know. She didn't trim her opinions according to the latest company.)

So, here they were in Paris; day three. Pewter had shown her the sights of *le dixhuitième*. Montmartre. Sacré-Coeur; the good restaurants along the rue Ordiner, etc. But she soon reminded him she was no easy tourist. They had been walking along the rue Ordiner round the corner from Pewter's flat, on a day when they had the street market. A Saturday morning. Pewter was explaining that in the three years since he had moved into the area he thought the street had gone 'down-market', slightly, from the pristine display – almost filmic in their primary colours – the mounds and rows of fruit and vegetables, ad infinitum. These were still on show, of course. The cheeses. Fresh fish, all sorts, cooked meats (though he didn't buy cooked stuff from the stalls, he hastened to assure Nora; a sentiment with which he knew she would concur). Anyway, despite all that there now seemed to be a mixture of something else. Tat. Old clothes and stuff. Second hand. If not second hand, cheap. The sort of thing you used to associate with the East End of London in the 1950s. Or the rough end of Portobello Road.

And it was that morning, as they were walking along the rue Ordiner on the way to Pewter's favourite bread shop – special *pain campagne* at that shop, special fruit for the blender round the corner – it was then that they paused at the stall of a black man, an African, selling nonsense.

They were unlikely to buy anything there, but Nora decided to engage the man in conversation. Pewter suspected this was done partly for his benefit. Nora managed some questions in passable French, and the man answered at length, hoping for a sale. The answers didn't quite match the questions; but that may have been on account of Nora's 'flat' accent; or it may have been due to the man's anxiousness to sell something.

So she picked up on the conversation with Pewter as they walked along the road towards his special bread shop; he, refusing to feel guilty about being already set in his ways, preferring one bread shop to another – not counting the endless opportunities along the 'supermarket of the street', to buy anything you needed. Nora was asking him about Leclerc, the supermarket chain. Pewter was confused, partly because of Nora's pronunciation. Then he remembered that she had encountered Leclerc in the South of France when she had visited him in Montauroux. The point was: she wanted to know if Leclerc had started out like Marks & Spencer in England had, on pavement stalls in the East End of London. The French equivalent. Or whether this type of business mobility was more difficult to achieve in France. Pewter had no idea. Nora was the one who knew about business, who read the business sections of the newspaper; she was being disingenuous. She was making a point about the African on the rue Ordiner, selling tat; and they both knew he had no chance of becoming another Leclerc. Or, for that matter, of forming another Marks & Spencer partnership. These were the little ways in which Nora kept up the pressure on Pewter.

Of course he would deny that Nora's presence kept him on edge. The things they disagreed on, like the way the Paris Métro was run – so many passengers being allowed to ride without tickets – were less important than the things, the complaints, that these self-confessed 'old-timers' – shared. They were dismayed by the ethnic zoning of London, by the de-professionalizing of the country, starting with its university system; by the dependency culture. The usual. They both acknowledged that having had to thrive for years, as someone had described it, in a neglected garden, alongside noxious weeds, was something that tested your resilience and ability to avoid contamination. (Here they were talking about racism, but Nora preferred plain speech; so they spoke plainly.) Pewter told of a colleague at his old university who taught eighteenth-century something, but also taught a course on the English essay, forever flagging up Hazlitt and Emerson and company and bewailing the fact that the students didn't have the literary background to pick up classical references in Francis Bacon. The colleague, a pleasant man, indeed, gracious, acknowledged and claimed to admire Pewter's writing facility across several *genres*, as well as his success in organizing his courses; yet whenever said man initiated a snatched conversation with Pewter, in the corridor, say, or in the kitchen over coffee, it was usually about cricket – admittedly, a passion they both shared . . . Nora, for her part, had run up against admiring people at semi-official functions who thought that she had been honoured by the British state not because of her success in business, but because – and here she casually indicated her magnificent torso – because of her build: they assumed that she must have been some sort of an athlete. (There was a flash through Pewter's mind of Nora throwing the javelin, in competition, but he quickly suppressed it.) Without living in denial, both agreed that to refuse to be embittered by all this was also part of their hard-won human rights statement. They had enough there to keep them in agreement over however many visits.

So why, Pewter wondered, couldn't he feel entirely comfortable in Nora's company? He found himself, almost neurotically, avoiding those 'old men's habits' you read about: he made sure he didn't spend too much time in the bathroom; he pointedly stuck to a work rather than to a leisure schedule, spending more time at his computer than he needed to: he felt he had to give the impression of being grounded in Paris and not of a refugee, a tourist. When, a few weeks before Nora's visit, Pewter's ex-partner had popped over from London for a few days, and sex could be assumed to be on the agenda, there was no problem in Pewter's playing the habitué, lauding the Paris vogue for curried *moules* (his favourite was a little place in the sixth next to the American bookshop; but you could get it at the end of his street, opposite the Métro). And he would flag the culinary delights of Japan and Morocco and Portugal and Italy, right here on the doorstep. But, with Nora, he played that down; with Nora he feared that a bachelor, going on about food in this way, might bring him too close to the image he had of old man Pons, in the Balzac book. Cousin Pons was only *sixty*, but being old and ugly and a bachelor was giving, in his case, getting sensuous pleasure from eating a bad name. And Pewter was beginning to resent Nora for this.

They had their truces over dinner, Pewter's home-made dinner, to show Nora that he was at home and had a routine, and she was welcome to share it; and at such times they talked about uncontroversial subjects, like the underachievement of Caribbean people – or more generally, black people. Both in England and at home. Nora brought up the example of the Asians. Take the Uganda Asians as an example. Came over to England with nothing. In 1971. Thrown out by Idi Amin. Ended up in Canada and Australia as well. But mainly in England. Refugees. Locked up in camps all over the countryside. Dispersed, partly by public demand. The lowest of the low in the pecking order. And then what? Did they demand handouts for ever and ever, amen? Did they go around bleating about racism in Britain? Thirty years later, thirty-five years later these same people who came with nothing *but an attitude to succeed*, and who put their skills to work, and educated their children and taught them discipline – these were now among the most prosperous people *as a group* in England – leaving aside the criminals and the property developers. They got into manufacturing at a time when manufacturing was collapsing in the country, and made a success of it; they were into IT; they had got into the professions, leaving behind the people from the Caribbean, who had been here for ever, whose parents had fought for the freedom of this country *in two World Wars*; and had been content to eat brown sugar at home, brown sugar and brown rice at home in the West Indies so that people in England could have white sugar and white rice, as a relief from the bombing. And all for what? So that their children and grandchildren could end up as menials or as laughing stocks or worse – criminalized – in a society of all sorts of newcomers who had never shown any loyalty to the country?

Even though Nora may have overstated the case, Pewter didn't fundamentally disagree. But did he sense that Nora somehow associated him with those non-Asians who had squandered their time in England? He would have – in a roundabout way – to shore up his position there.

II

Nora dressed so carefully and was so fastidious that he would never ask her to clean his flat. There was a game that he played with an earlier visitor, a woman who was also fastidious; but with whom he had a different sense of *play*. He had admitted to this friend that, in the night when he got up, or in the morning before his shower, he usually drifted about the flat naked, to make his cup of tea, whatever – in fact, sometimes virtually all day, when it was hot. Before drifting out to a café or whatever. She, as he knew, would find that normal. But there was more. He had a habit – as she knew – of coming and going. A week or two away, mainly in England, at a time. And part of his system – his neurosis, if you like – was to have the flat spotless on his return. So on the day of departure, or the night before, if he was leaving early in the morning, having hoovered the place, having wiped all the kitchen surfaces and cabinets and sorted the fridge, he would then wash the three non-carpeted floors in the flat – loo, bathroom and kitchen. *Still fairly normal, if a little excessive*, was the guest's un-emphatic gesture. *Ah, but there's more.* He carried out this action – for he left the shower till last, naturally: *he carried out this action naked.*

And now that he had re-quickened the interest of his favourite guest, they updated an old game to fit host and guest: how could guest repay host in a manner that was *aesthetically* fitting? How could guest maintain the *tone* of how things were done in the new setting? And without spelling it out, they knew, for they used to be on the same wavelength, once. So yes, before he popped out to the shops, or wherever, he would say how long he would expect to be out; and she would have that time in the flat to treat it as if she were not the guest. But he mustn't be held *rigidly* to time; should he pop back sooner – should he forget something and return for it, sort of thing, and embarrass her in *not* being the guest! The day he returned from the laundrette to find the kitchen floor cleaned, mopped, gleaming, he noted her satisfied expression and he chided himself for the delay. OK, there were two other floors to go before her return to England; and two days to go.

This was not a game he felt he could play with Nora.

Nora dressed and spoke carefully. The temptation, early on, was to send it up. And when you visited Montserrat, after its destruction by volcano, what struck you was the style and dress that everyone maintained. Carefully laundered, men and women seemed to be demonstrating, for anyone who cared to notice, how to survive a natural disaster, in *style*. So different, so very different from the prideless New Orleans folk after *their* recent mishap.

Visitors to Montserrat were prone to pass comment: did the young woman fashion-model who served as attendant on the functioning petrol station on the edge of town really know what the job entailed? What if she accidentally dribbled a bit of petrol on her designer skirt? So, seeing Nora, who gave a distinct impression of power-dressing – of one of those Thatcher-women of the 1980s – one wondered if Nora, too, wasn't deliberately dressing *against* the logic of her situation – her situation now being a representative of an environmentally stricken Montserrat. So you stayed the urge to mock; and declined to criticize her too-careful English, an English, in normal circumstances, associated with well-brought-up people who were not English. But couldn't that be a comment on the rest of the clan – Pewter included – who long resided in Motherless England, and studied and wrote and taught its tongue to so little effect? Was Pewter part of that system of fakery or parody that Nora was so ready to denounce? She illustrated this at dinner one night over Pewter's curried seafood and special (bought at Picard) rice: there was, she said, a Professor of Hospital Management, who had recently visited the island, putting on airs. A man, originally from a neighbouring island, but long resident in the UK, come back to pull rank. Of course, she conceded, hospitals *needed* to be managed. But why call the person who contributed to hospital management a *professor*? Where was the academic *logic* in that? Again there was a man who came back, also from England, calling himself Professor of Mentoring and Coaching. Did that make sense? What was mentoring and coaching? Did coaching have something to do with football? In fact, she didn't have a problem with the great football coaches being called professors, people like the intellectual Frenchman at Arsenal. Or the pretty boy at Chelsea, who put her in mind of those fresh boys who strutted their stuff on the beach. But where did this Mentoring and Coaching man fit into the pecking order of professorships? And then there was the jackarse who called himself Professor of Materials and Devices. Had the world gone mad? Or was she too unsophisticated to understand its new design? These were the things, Nora said, that made you think that old-fashioned religion wasn't so strange, after all.

This was Pewter's chance to point out that things might be even worse than Nora had feared; for there was, for instance – he had to hold up his hand – there was a species of academic/non-academic, residing in the universities, now wearing the label of Professor of Creative Writing.

Nora was generous. Creative writing was, in a sense, a literary skill; something recognized in the academy; she had long wished that more business people could write clearly and attractively: they could do with a course in creative writing. By the same token she had no problem with other new fashions that had come into the academy – the Professor of Occupational Therapy, for instance. That could be justified. As with the Professor of Creative Writing. Teaching creative writing, she said, must in some way add to the sum of human happiness.

What, Pewter asked himself, had he ever done to this woman to deserve this?

III

He had the answer. He would wear his academic hat and appeal to a higher authority. Perhaps it was true that a St

Caesarian and a Montserratian had first to secure themselves in their own territorial space before they could risk
relating to each other, with their defences down, so to speak;
or with the outside world. When Ms Emiline Charles – the
higher authority – had put forward this view, there had
been, not howls because no one but the islanders cared that
much, but ripples of disapproval. This was at a conference
at Leeds some time ago. Charles was a writer, originally
from St Caesare, but long resident in Africa, in Senegal,
and after the early success of her stories (*Savacou & the Cow
Myths of the Lesser Antilles* and her retelling of her African
myths, *Les contes d'Amadou Koumba*) she was required
reading, by the initiated.

At the conference in Leeds, emboldened by Charles's
paper, Pewter had told a story. (He didn't give a paper on
that occasion but he chaired one of the panels in the
afternoon, and that's where he told the story. An anecdote,
really.) He had been travelling to France, on his way to
Montauroux. Summer. Early evening. He wasn't being
met at Nice airport, so he was thinking of making his way
to Grasse by public transport, then maybe to Cabris or
Fayance, and then taxi. Anyway, at passport control at
Nice, the bored official in his little glass box was about to
hand back the passport when he checked himself and
looked at Pewter again, and glanced back at the passport:
'Where ees St Caesare?' he asked, puzzled, perhaps that
the Caribbean version was spelt differently from the French.
As that was after the volcano when the island was evacu-
ated, Pewter was momentarily stuck for an answer: *this
was suddenly a philosophical question.* There had been
lively debate at the time of whether an island constituted
its geography or its people, who might be living elsewhere.
The St Caesarians, the Montserratians – through their
natural disasters – had become part of the list of un-
anchored peoples associated with Palestinians and Kurds

and Basques, etc. Charles's paper was entitled 'A Stable Context for the Creation of Fiction on the Islands of Montserrat and St Caesare'; her contention being: first, you stabilize the islands for credible fiction, then you employ that imaginative structure for making it credible for other types of habitation. Charles was 'French'; she dismissed objections to her thesis as examples of Anglo-Saxon thinking. (It must be said in defence of Charles that a big section of her paper had to do with the 'psychology of becoming' [Montserrat and St Caesare were both colonies, one a colony, the other a political condominium]; and Charles's contention was that the people of both communities must be kept together, or brought back to their island *together*, or resettled *together* in their own named space so that they could experience the 'intellectual and emotional maturity' of self-determination, before they were freed from 'psychic-doubt', which made the idea of a community impossible. Only then would people, and their islands, achieve, as it were, the 'solidity of fiction'.)

But Pewter had second thoughts: he didn't think he had the strength to tussle with Nora over this one. She was here for a break; *he* needed a break; why not do the normal thing and enjoy Paris? He would encourage her to take one of those Paris Walks, organized by someone he knew. He couldn't, of course, go with her on an English-speaking Walk without losing credibility, but he'd recommend them. Very early on he had gone on one in the Marais area (round Saint-Paul) and was encouraged to reread Mme de Sévigné as a result. And he had – he was ashamed to say – done the tour of Hemingway's Paris (including the courtyard where Joyce finished *Ulysses*, somewhere in the fifth or sixth, not, as he had thought, in Montparnasse). But for now he would recommend the tour of Montmartre to Nora. That was his area; he fancied he knew as much about it as the guide would.

What of the rights of the guest? Surely, part of the cruelty of living in a country which refused to allow you to call it your own was that you could never securely play the host. For properly playing host is a long-armed gesture, beyond the individual embrace; it has an expansiveness not checked by calculation; it extends beyond the boundaries of the household, the domain: if the host is constrained by the larger society, the gesture might not be false, but the welcome is partial.

Pewter could talk to Nora about that; but of course she knew. Nora had created a context in England where she had to play host. She had married an Englishman, called Mr Shackley-Bennett, a man of some means; but her business success was her own. She managed a firm that cleaned offices. They did it efficiently, during the night while others slept. She had had a dedicated, well-paid, literate workforce – five teams of them, making huge areas of London a more pleasant place to work in next morning. She chose people to work for her who had the right attitude to work. She had no time for those who looked on service as demeaning, or as a way of filling in dead time; she liked to talk about Irishmen and West Indians she saw working on building sites all over London in the sixties. By the eighties she could identify twelve Irishmen, running their own building firms, men who traced their apprenticeship back to the building sites. She couldn't find a single West Indian who had made that leap.

Nor was her business made up of cheap female labour. Her first employee was a middle-class woman from St Kitts who had been cleaning other people's houses; and Nora employed her and doubled her salary and registered her for National Insurance. This wasn't an all-woman thing, either; hers was a team of men and women, who had to respect one another to stay in the team; both her son and her stepson were an important part of the team, for some years. Their apprenticeship then made her more relaxed now at the prospect of having them inherit. She didn't think children should be allowed to take their parents for granted.

They talked aesthetics, Pewter and Nora. They talked, yes, about pictures, and about Pewter's latest extravagant purchase – something of which Nora thoroughly app-roved. They talked about teeth. Both had had problems with teeth, and both refused to submit to the indignity of putting teeth in a glass last thing at night. (Pride. And refusing to give up on the possibility of a partnered life.) So they had implants. And – here's the trick that amused them – Pewter, living in France with supposedly the best health service in the world, still had a dentist in England; Nora, living three hours' flight from the USA, still travelled more than twice that distance to *her* dentist in London.

They drank to that.

On her last day in Paris Nora paid Pewter a tribute: she bought him a present, a couple of paper lampshades that he needed, and she paid him a tribute. He had been a sensitive host, she said. She was half-expecting him to smother her with concern for having gone back to live on an island where the volcano was still active, as if her sole concern in life now was with volcanic ash, not with the world at large. So it was good to sit and talk about the coming Water Wars in this or that part of the world; and to learn, say, why *Coriolanus* was an essential text for Africa. And she thanked him, especially, for not giving her a seminar on Ms Emiline Charles – whom she had read and disagreed with, if what the lady was saying was that she, Nora, was less real than somebody in a book. She knew, of course, that Pewter had written about the islands, their tendency towards religious fundamentalism, and their intolerance to those with sexual preferences not apparently sanctioned by the Bible. And, yes, these things – and others – were a problem. But when you are in Paris for a few days, were you going to spoil the good time to be had in Paris by trying to solve problems that would outlive your time in Paris? Instead, they had done something that she appreciated: they had ventured out and enjoyed the city, and had given the impression of liking each other's company; and Nora thanked him. He had been a good host.

14

Cabris, Alpes Maritimes
A Memoir (1972–75)

I

Then we recalled the building *coopérative,* and my en-counters with René Mengingy on the *chantier,* and at the *réunion,* all those years ago. I was visiting my architect friend, Ralph, in Seillans; we were talking of old times, as you do; and he mentioned casually that Luigi had died. Luigi, in my eyes, was a protective presence, an ally on the *chantier;* news of his death weighed the meal down some-what.

Luigi was something of a dandy; even on the building site he didn't dress down. (When, within days of my joining the *Coopérative Ouvrière du Bâtiment,* we downed tools one morning and were bundled into two cars and driven to some strategic point where we could catch sight of the Tour de France stars whizzing past, Luigi was the only one of us who didn't need to change his clothes to be pre-sentable for the occasion.) He was the least doctrinaire of the Parti Communiste boys, and had a string of enviable girlfriends. No, my friend confirmed; he never married.

In order to give the impression that you take these things in your stride, the death of a colleague, a fellow worker on the site long ago, and someone you hadn't been in contact with for – what? – thirty years, we gave some thought to other members of the *coopérative* – all of whom you wished well, in good health, and alive. Then there was René. You wished him all the right things, of course; but yet you did it out of a sense of, if not quite duty, something near to a minimum of shared biological concern that men of our age tend to exhibit; then we went on to discuss, with less hesitancy, other colleagues of the time.

My first encounter with René was just faintly odd: he asked if I was Jewish.

It was my first morning on the site, on the *chantier*, somewhere near to Grasse, on what turned out to be Herr Stumph's house. The introductions weren't yet over and René looked up from what he was doing and said:

'*Juif? Juif?*'

'He's asking if you're Jewish,' Ralph said.

Taken aback; not conscious of having been asked this before, I thought of a way of saying no in acceptable French, as being judged a primitive in the language spilled over into other vulgar assumptions.

We were at a place called Auribeau, a green-field site presently to be turned into a villa for the German banker, Herr Stumph, who was said to have one leg, and to walk with a limp, and whose desire was to be able to see Cannes harbour from his terrace.

But I had to answer René. Was I Jewish?

'*Mais non,*' I said, trying to sound more French than English, giving a new French force to the *non*. '*Pas du tout.*'

Not understanding the fusillade of language that greeted this I relied on my friend, Ralph, to fill in my details. He countered on my behalf and confirmed that I had studied philosophy at the University of Wales, and that I was a writer. René spat, but I think that's because he was at the

216

end of chewing something; not on account of my philosophy, or my being a writer.

Pays de Galles seemed more acceptable than England; and René nodded a truce.

As to being a writer Julian, the *carreleur*, a jovial man, his low centre of gravity reassuring, shouted from a little distance. 'Aragon!'

To which I was able to say. '*Mais oui. J'aime beaucoup Louis Aragon.*'

Aragon was famous for being the people's poet; he had performed in the cafés of Paris; his poems had been set to music. He had something of a folk following, not quite like Edith Piaf, but not unlike Piaf. In momentary confusion I wasn't sure if I was thinking of Aragon or of Jacques Prévert.

But that – with one other query to Ralph: *So you speak to him in English?* – quickly satisfied their interest in me; and having shaken hands all round, I registered what seemed to be a preponderance of Italian names; not only Luigi, but Vincente (Luigi's brother), Valerio (André's brother) and, perhaps, Jeannot. Very soon, I was set to work, along with René and stiff-backed Joseph, to mix the sand and cement with shovels rather than feeding the lot into the cement mixer, which stood idle.

I tried not to let my disappointment show. It wasn't so much the less than bracing entry into the *Coopérative Ouvrière du Bâtiment* that niggled – I had been voted in as a member in my absence, while still in England, on Ralph's recommendation – it was the expectation that I was joining a team geared to *restoration*; turning ruins into habitable dwellings, disused olive mills into villas for the rich and glamorous, granted, but at the same time engaging in an activity that was *restorative*; and here I was, first time out, despoiling wholesome land: the cement mixing, the trekking between piles of brick, sand, cement; iron (for reinforcing the concrete pillars and supports) and wood (for shuttering) – all so that a German banker could see Cannes harbour from his terrace.

One felt vaguely unsympathetic towards Herr Stumph, but tried not to show it; indeed, to steer clear of the feeling so as not to fall into the anti-German trap. Why would he limp? I asked myself, a rich man able to get the best-fitted leg in Germany; this sounded like a film-caricature. Also, Ralph had told me that René – who was short and square – had been taken off to Germany as a child, during the war, and had been somewhat starved there; and had developed powerful anti-German feelings as a result. I wasn't sure how much of that story I believed.

Anyway, it was a long session, that first morning, to coffee-break.

There was a get-together every Friday evening, a *réunion*, a sort of bonding session – as often there were two teams working on different projects during the week, so you didn't have day-to-day contact with all the members. Also, the painters would move into the building after the building team had moved out, so they didn't necessarily meet. The practical purpose of the *réunion* was to review the last week's work and to set targets, and allocate personnel, for the week ahead.

At the *réunion* that first Friday evening the discussion – *in French, in Midi-accented French, in Franco-Italian* – the discussion was of Eric Marsh's house. Marsh was an Englishman who was Vice President of Johnson's Baby Powder and had interests in Hong Kong. I hadn't worked on his house, said to be somewhere in the vicinity of Grasse – Valbonne, as it turned out – but had met him socially, at Ralph's, then in Spéracèdes; and he seemed jovial and down to earth. At the *réunion* Roy, who was director of the *coopérative*, was making the point that there was a fine line to be drawn between conservation and preserving the untenable; for when he had been showing Marsh round the completed building earlier in the week they had discovered mushrooms growing on one of the carefully preserved, newly plastered walls.

What did Marsh say?

'*Il rien a dit.*'

I could renew my interest in this job, I thought.

Two years later a new encounter with René seemed overdue. His proposal to vote me out of the co-op nearly won the day, but for the diplomatic manoeuvrings of Luigi and a couple of others, to delay the vote by a week so that members could think it over and not act hastily. It was a week for calculating the balance of allies on both sides. I could count on Ralph and maybe André, my neighbour in Cabris. I could count on Roy (and maybe Jackie, Roy's partner) from the Les Moulières 'commune' in Spéracèdes – the spiritual home of the *coopérative* – where we had lived for the first few months. But when it came to the vote could I count on Luigi, who was, after all, a member of Parti Communiste, and could not break rank from his colleagues – one of whom was his more cerebral, taciturn brother, Vincente?

So, over drinks in Georges' bar in Spéracèdes – where Georges had recently blown his brains out for no reason that we knew – Ralph and I (with Lindsay, my partner, and Ralph's wife, Béatrice) calculated the possible pro-vote line-up next week.

Apart from Ralph and good-hearted Roy, there was André. He was easy-going; he had a gypsy background and was very fashion-conscious (indeed, he dressed his very young son in designer clothes). But could we rely on André? We'd been to their house, a couple of streets away from ours; and when Lindsay and I spoke to each other in

English (Lindsay was American), André's wife assumed we were speaking German; and said she understood a few words. But the thing that endeared him to me was his habit, out of the blue, of doing the Ali shuffle in the street. (He was to do it a year later when I ran into him outside the boulangerie the morning after the Rumble in the Jungle when Ali imposed his will on George Foreman in Mobutu's Zaire.)

André's brother, Valerio, was less readable: he always seemed somewhat detached from the proceedings of the co-op and, one felt, had set his mind on better things. A bit like Roy and Colin at Les Moulières. Colin was Roy's highly qualified younger brother, a medical man who, you felt, was slumming it a bit with the co-op before getting on with his real career. (They were half-brothers, the same Irish father, different mothers, Roy, I think, having a Russian mother.) Roy had been instrumental in the setting up of the co-op, and was a conciliator. Who else among the pro-vote? There were twenty-four members – though some were independent artisans, like Jean-François, who did the decorative ironwork, and whose hobby was rally-driving. They didn't always come to the *réunions*. Let's say eighteen of them turned up to the *réunion*. I wouldn't be there, of course: I had three votes; and maybe Julian's. *I needed another five for a tie.* René had Joseph (who abused his dog), Colin and . . . particularly our Spanish stone-cutter, Ricardo, to start with. Colin, maybe, was neutral. So Jackie would have to be worked on. Who else? The problem was with the Parti Communiste members, including Luigi: they believed in solidarity. They called it solidarity, we called it something else. We were unimpressed at their unwillingness to break rank – the Gang of Seven – even on the smallest matter. When, towards the end of Pompidou's reign, there were lots of strikes by the *petits commerçants* against the Fifth Republic, and workers (like ourselves) were invited to come out in sympathy, the communists always debated the point. We would have a quick show of hands on the site whether to come out or not, but the members of Parti Communiste would always insist on time to think it over, and report their conclusions to us next day. And they would; and the decisions were always unanimous. The notion that a group of workers (in a socialist cooperative) couldn't decide, individually, whether they wanted to join shopkeepers and others protesting against Pompidou's policies seemed to us, to me, pathetic. René was a member of Parti Communiste. So I knew I wouldn't get the Parti Communiste vote.

The following week I was voted out of the *coopérative*.

II

Friday was writing day in the Cabris household. Part of the flexibility of the *coopérative* was my being able to work four days a week and still be deemed full time. And in truth there was more reading done on the Friday than writing, which tended to happen in between other engagements.

The extra lie-in helped to set up the day. It was pleasant to be woken up every morning to the whiff of Madame Cavali's croissants (and the heat of Monsieur Cavali's oven) – the only thing that separated our living quarters from the *alimentation* being the dining-room wall; and good to know you didn't have immediately to leap out of bed and get ready for the *chantier*. It almost put me in mind of those nights we had spent at a friend's place in Paris, in Montparnasse, where you could lie in bed and hear all the night sounds, the street sounds of people who seemed never to go to bed, a continental, not an Anglophone image.

So, on those Fridays in Cabris, Lindsay and I would go to the park with books, notebooks and a blanket; and spend the morning or the early afternoon trying to be the 'writer' in France, hoping that we hadn't got there 'too late' in the story. Lindsay educated me, among other things, to the psychological deficiencies of Normal Mailer, when we read *The Prisoner of Sex* together, Mailer having a go at a young Kate Millet for daring to suggest that men were chauvinist.

(The first few months, at Spéracèdes, where we lived, sharing Ralph's cabin, or in a room in one of the other old buildings, talk at supper was still of *les évènements de mai*, and the return of the children to land that their parents had abandoned. There, at Les Moulières, we achieved modest self-sufficiency, growing potatoes and courgettes on the terraces, and making wine from our mini-vineyard. Across the way at our friends', the Wisers, we talked American politics, mainly Nixon and literature. My 'restorer's' pretensions were brought down a peg fairly early on when we went to dinner with a Canadian friend in Spéracèdes. He moved in rather more elevated circles than we did, and the talk of 'restoration' at table seemed fairly intimidating. I came away feeling that knowing nothing of the names thrown about with such familiarity, not having heard of Percier and Fontaine, favourite architects and restorers to Napoleon, we were, at COB, very poor cousins indeed, in this business of giving France a face-lift.)

I was writing poems and stories and trying to get them published, but was absorbed at the time at trying to learn French, and fascinated, too, by a book by an American who had lived in the area. *Village in the Vaucluse* was a blow-by-blow account of people in that village, sharp character-sketches, their village functions described, ending up with a very satisfying portrait of a community. (The Vaucluse was a place where Beckett had lived for some time, during the war.) I thought I might do the same for Spéracèdes. Either Spéracèdes, and the Les Moulières compound, which had been our first address (our mail was

still delivered at Pierrot's *alimentation* in the village) –
either that, or I'd present a similar portrait of Cabris up
the hill, starting with, well, Madame Cavali. I'd already
written a poem and a story about Pierrot, a friendly, pear-
shaped man, who had once been a communist, and had
been mayor of Spéracèdes. He was related to the folk at
Les Moulières, and was a generous host. Pierrot had wonderfully neat dancing-feet, and excelled at the annual Les
Moulières New Year dance, when all the young women
associated with the place came to visit.

Not only was our mail delivery in Spéracèdes, so was
our library. Bill and Michelle Wiser had been our neighbours there. Bill was a writer from Cincinnati and Michelle was Belgian, and a painter; and Bill's stock of books –
mainly American novels – constituted our reading matter.
We tended to bypass the classics, as I remember, and
explored the likes of Bernard Malamud and Jerzy Kosin-
ski and Updike (not then a classic) and American short
stories, stocked in his garage overflow. On Ralph's terrace
the talk was about building, of course; and the books
explored tended more to be about art and design, with
much reference to his favourite architect, Frank Lloyd
Wright. But Ralph was Irish: we discussed Joyce, Beckett.
(Ralph regaled us with stories of the time when Brendan
Behan paid a visit.)

Lunch, also, in a sense, came from Spéracèdes. It didn't
necessarily originate at Les Moulières except perhaps for a
couple of bottles of wine from the *cave*. But on the walk
up from Spéracèdes to Cabris with (or more usually, without) the day's post we could look forward to lunch. So
even if there was nothing in the post but a rejection slip,
the bottle of wine from the Les Moulières *cave* – whatever
the quality – would be supplemented by wild asparagus.
Walking the back way up the hill – maybe a couple of
kilometres – we would go through the woods, and pick

our lunch. (The mushrooms were too dangerous; you went mushroom picking with experts, occasionally people from the *coopérative*, and then you'd go to the chemist afterwards to check that nothing you brought home was poisonous: the chemists had panels on the door with pictures of various types of mushroom, so that you'd know what to avoid. In my notebooks at the time there is an abandoned play, a suggestion for a play, really, where someone commits the perfect murder. Using mushrooms.)

There was no denying that as writers we were poor cousins to other writers we could name. Without yet acquiring the language it was foolish for us to visit the nearby *La Messuguière*, a house that had once belonged to Gide, just a few hundred yards out of the village towards St Cézaire and Le Tignet. It was a retreat, and there were literary events held there; but for that you needed sophisticated French. We had a distinguished neighbour, the poet Yves Bonnefoy, but we couldn't fully appreciate the work, even when it was translated into English. And our friend Bill Wiser from Spéracèdes had by now gone off to America as writer-in-residence at Drake University in Des Moines, on the other side of Chicago. Bill had got the residency on the strength of his first novel, *K*, and on another book set in France. So, for us, as well as reading there was a lot of *writing* to do.

Meanwhile, Lindsay had started a literary magazine, *The Factory*, the first issue carrying poetry, prose and an interview with Howard Sergeant, the editor of the English poetry magazine, *Outposts*. But there were problems with getting it properly typed and photocopied; and we were told, due to Hachette's hold on the market, impossible to distribute in France.

The pay-off was dinner at one of Cabris' seven restaurants, though we couldn't afford to go more than once a week – maybe twice, if you counted Le Mini Grille, at lunchtime, which offered a cheap *salade niçoise*, with lots of inoffensive rosé, gratefully chilled in summer. But the ambition was to save up and give ourselves a treat, a proper night out, at one or other of La Chèvre d'Or, Le Petit Prince, whatever.

*

We were determined to make some headway with French. There were the *Assimil* exercises every night and *Hugo in 3 Months – French* that, for me, supplemented having to deal with the language all day, which included helpful phrases like MORT AUX ARABES scrawled on the bus shelter in Grasse. (Ralph had a story that a Mayor of Cannes, Font-Michele, justified the relative lack of municipal public transport on the basis that it would only be used by the Arabs.)

In the interest of making ourselves familiar with the language we tried to pay attention to detail. Were we right to call our organization *Coopérative Ouvrière du Bâtiment* instead of *Coopérative Ouvrières du Bâtiment*? because it now contained a woman? When André shamed us, at his house, into asking for *cuisse* instead of *jambe* for our chicken portion that was well-noted. And to remember that, on the *chantier*, I had *copains* not *collègues*. Also, we played canasta, with recipes in French printed on the back of the cards. (*Hélas*. The barriers seemed insurmountable. How to distinguish, in conversation, between Molière's *L'Avare* and La Var, the neighbouring *département*, which we visited, and sometimes picked up its newspaper of that name? How to say Anouilh [the writer] to anyone's satisfaction?)

The last big event I recall at our house in Cabris was a drink with a couple of friends from the village – Lupio and a woman we knew; plus Michelle – a drink the day after Giscard's victory over Mitterrand in the presidential elections. '*C'est triste*,' etc. Sadness, emphasized by the narrowness of Giscard's win – 50% to 49%. Though Lupio's main point seemed to be that Giscard, the Atlanticist, had compounded his win by speaking to the foreign press after his victory, *in English*. The woman friend confirmed that Mitterrand was a 'poet' and Giscard was an accountant, and the French had chosen the accountant over the poet – a bit like the English would, no?

So, what was the reason for my being on the point of ejection from the *coopérative*?

The short answer is that I was an 'intellectual' and I had called a fellow worker a 'parasite'.

The second charge was harder to refute than the first.

III

I'm revisiting the area with Lindsay and her new husband, he paying a visit for the first time. In Cabris we run into André's mother, Paula, and André's son. The son must be thirty, so André would be in his mid-fifties now. The mother I'd met from time to time, over the years; she doesn't look appreciably older than before. We have a viable chat; then visit the old haunts, the little church wedged between the shops, about twenty seats – rows of little chairs – for the congregation. We check on the prices on the menus outside the restaurants (no longer FF23 a meal) and on the door-knocker of Mammie Richard's old house. And, finally, drift – past *our* old house, on the corner of the rue de l'Hôpital, Madame Cavali long gone, the *alimentation* now lived in – to the look-out with Peymeinade spread out miles below: building, building everywhere, the blue oblongs of pool not really making it better. We call in on Michelle Wiser, from Spéracèdes days, for some time now living just outside Cabris, husband and children elsewhere; we have our private reunion and celebrate her new (late) success as a painter. (There, the story of

Mammie Richard comes up again: she has finally died, at well over a hundred. When we knew her in the seventies – she must have been about eighty, then – she was still riding on the back of her son Lupio's motorbike. The knocker on her door in the village was a brass penis.)

And then to Spéracèdes: we decline the back road – the old route to asparagus – for no particular reason other than that was a long time ago. In Spéracèdes who's around that we know? Ralph and Béatrice are, of course, in Seillans, in the Var. There's a new generation now at Les Moulières. Children, maybe grandchildren, of our friends.

Who else? Ah, yes, David and Laura at whose house we had that weird party in – was it 1974? David was Canadian, Laura French. (Béatrice's sister.) A house-warming, with Hell's Angels riding up from Nice (Nice or Cannes) for the occasion. The plan was for one of them to ride straight into the pool. That didn't happen, of course. Though the opening was fun, with Curtis, an American novelist (putative novelist) entertaining us with his quick-change act.

Pasolini had been promised, he didn't show; David had been something of a film maker. David died, of course. So be charitable to the dead. He took us to the film festival. Cannes. In 1974. Wouldn't let us sit through any of the films. We felt we had to match our tastes to his. Why complain? The man's dead.

'And what of Laura?' my ex-partner asks.

(Laura of the splendid dinner parties, the house the finest in the village: David did a superb job on it; a house, incidentally, on which I worked . . .)

'What of Laura?' Lindsay asks.

It's one of those moments when you're confused about who knows what and who's really in touch with whom. How did she not know that Laura, too, had died?

So the story has to be told.

*

Later, in a restaurant – for food's a sort of, if not healer, something of a restorer – she tries to raise everyone's spirits by telling the story of my ejection from the *coopérative* all those years ago. The story is beginning to sound more heroic than I remember it. (She wasn't there, at the *réunion*, on the evening.)

True, there were two charges against me, brought by René, one was of being an 'intellectual', as I said, which was odd coming from a Frenchman; the other, more serious, was for the sin of calling a fellow worker a parasite.

Of being an 'intellectual', I did a certain amount of reading on the site. It was perhaps something of a counter to not being able to keep up with the conversation that flowed at lunchtime, conversation about – variously about the rights and wrongs of National Service, about Solzhenitsyn and his treatment by the Soviet Union. Or was it about the Soviet Union and its treatment by Solzhenitsyn? About whether Georges Marchais (leader of the Communist Party) should give way to Mitterrand (leader of the Socialists) in the coming presidential elections – as Pompidou was clearly dying. (Ralph confirmed later that René's point about National Service was that he didn't want the sons of the ruling classes to go into the army and be taught to shoot; he wanted that privilege to be conferred only on the sons of the workers. A crank? Or an example of Cartesian thinking?)

So my 'study' on the *chantier* during the two-hour lunch break half-amused *mes copains*, my sitting under an olive tree, or perhaps in the shade of the building, with book and dictionary, and stumbling through Pagnol's *La Femme du Boulanger* or Montherlant's *Le Maître de Santiago*, could hardly be described as being 'intellectual'. (Much later, I was to be embarrassed by Montherlant. To me, then, he was just a contemporary French writer – he died that first year, in 1972 – whom I'd first encountered in the

'Theatre of the Absurd' days a decade earlier. I was aware that he was in the news in France, perhaps not realizing that he had just died. I had found his idealization of the male somewhat quaint, but his staginess liberating. I knew then nothing about his unappealing personality, his Nazi sympathies, his sexual quirks: would members of my *socialist* cooperative, seeing me read Montherlant in my lunch hour, days at a time, think my reading matter strange? This was a French building site; the men there knew about Racine and Aragon. Julian's son was a conductor with a symphony orchestra somewhere in the middle of France. They were not culturally deprived.)

But to the other charge, my calling a fellow worker a parasite.

I wanted to be allowed to plaster a wall, to help decide on the camber of the wood on the roof; not to be forever stuck with René on the cement mixer, to be forever second carpenter, praised for cleaning and washing up tools and containers at the end of the day. For, after all, other jobs rotated. And that included the directorship of the co-op. Granted that the *carreleur* was specialized – and preserved for Julian: with other tasks the object was to prevent hierarchies of labour *gelling*. So Luigi, who was a mason on one site, was *chef de chantier* on another. So when were René and I going to be put on to the plastering?

The mistake was in not realizing that René had no intention of giving up his support role. Indeed, he was proud of it, of being the cement-mixer man.

It was at that point, late in the evening one Friday night, at the *réunion*, that I said something to the effect that someone who had so little ambition shouldn't be boasting about it; that that sort of mentality was not helpful to the *coopérative*, to the idea, the spirit of the *coopérative*; that that person was, in fact, acting like a parasite.

The next few moments were ugly.

15

A Bad Day in Paris, 2006

I

Apart from anything else it might come down to the football, rooting for a French victory in the World Cup, or if not quite that – for they didn't look that impressive the other night against China, though they won – so if not victory in the finals in Germany at least hoping they'd avoid humiliation against Switzerland and South Korea and whoever else in the preliminary rounds. That would not be the best environment for Pewter to conduct matters with his bank in Cannes, with a severe Madame Beauvais, dressed a little like a latter-day Madame de Sévigné, nostalgic for the old Paris. He hadn't heard from her for some time: was she still dressing . . . ? *This, Madame, is the new address in Paris: please send up-to-date photo.* He left his new phone number on her machine. She would say that football is 'stupid' (*But that opening ceremony in Germany this afternoon, very mathematical and precise, eh? Elaborate patterns, the movements controlled. A little like Bach. No?*), and that, anyway, she herself was not nationalistic. And she would be very businesslike – pert and prettily so; trendy glasses – as if the football had never happened, while she tried to determine what he had been doing to rein in his expenses; so he would have to account for himself.

He had given up unnecessary travel abroad, particularly to England – and that would please her: he would stress the cooling of relations over there as he missed first the art exhibition of a friend, and an inaugural lecture of another and the farewell do of an old colleague, someone with whom he had worked for – what? – fifteen years. Madame Beauvais would be solicitous in the way you are at the end of the match to your defeated opponents, slumped on the field. But of course he knew that would not be enough. What else?

He had had his stories rejected by the Americans. Good, that was good. The Americans are stupid people, as you know. If they are not stupid they are nationalistic, not like the French. If they reject your stories your stories must have some merit. Pity you don't write them in French, but then French is not an easy language for foreigners, not like English, which is good, of course, for the foreigners; and good, too, for commerce and shopkeeping. Even for banking. She, herself, as he knew, spoke the language for work. And for this admission Pewter would praise her broadmindedness. So far so good.

But Madame Beauvais isn't a pushover. She would want to see evidence of belt-tightening on his part, not be fobbed off by his being on the right side of the argument. (The old joke of having to pay taxes in three countries is not amusing to a Frenchwoman who has seen her country having to give up so many countries, in her lifetime.) So, he has done the expected *volte face* on the buying of books; but then, you can't have everything.

And why, he asked himself, looking at the morning papers, was he patting himself on the back to be out of England and away from the saga of Wayne Rooney's metatarsal, a word that even regulars in the pub now toss about like small change? Why avoid all that only to pick up *Le*

Parisien with the headline CISSÉ, LE DRAME, with a picture of the big lad writhing on the ground clutching his leg in agony? (A glance at *Aujourd'hui* shows a similar scene.) And suddenly Pewter has a new anxiety; it has something to do with the composition of the French national team, with the considerable number of black players entrusted to raise the hopes and spirit of the nation. Would calls, at the moment largely benign and ironic, to convert chants of *Les Bleus* to *Les Noirs* begin to change in tone, begin to be, as they say, *minable*? But he didn't want to think further about that just now.

But you can't control the phone, once you've rashly decided to pay the bill.

'Allo?'

(He'd been expecting a call; he had phoned the bank in Cannes earlier, left a message.)

'Ah, Madame Beauvais.'

'Ees Monsieur Stapleton?'

'*Bien sur, Madame Beauvais. Comment allez–vous?*'

'*Moi, ça va. Merci. Alors, Monsieur Stapleton – ?*'

'*Est-ce-que Madame Beauvais? Ou Mademoiselle Azoulay?*'

'*Nous vous aimerions –*'

'*Ah, un rendezvous. Attendez. Je vais sercher le diary.*'

'*Je ne comprend pas. Je voudrais le code.*'

'*Ah! Pour le banque. Le compte.*'

'*Mais non, Monsieur. Pour la porte.*'

'*La porte. Ici! Vous êtes à la porte? En bas?*'

'*Mais non. Pour demain. Il y a un paquet pour vous. Il est arrivé cette matin, mais vous étiez sorti.*'

'*Ah. Comprende.*'

We are dealing with the post here, not the bank. More humiliation. (Would it were the medicine cabinet that was being delivered.)

Questions he won't now ask himself: was it cowardly to try to fix the meeting with the bank for *before* France's second-round matches in the tournament? Such questions are pointless in the face of these daily humiliations.

II

When Nora visited some time ago she put an idea in his head and he had been, stupidly, playing with it for some time. As a result he had ended up monitoring the Sri Lankans round about. At the time his main computer, the desktop, was still in England; and he was making do with the laptop, and hadn't got around to sorting out the e-mail and printing, so he tended to go to the internet café round the corner. He found himself going to a Sri Lankan café even though there were six or more to choose from within a couple of minutes' walk of the flat, three of them Sri Lankan. It was Nora, visiting, who had predicted that the Sri Lankans would take over the trade in five years. Three years.

Now, this fitted in a pattern larger than the Sri Lankans. Early on Pewter had set out systematically to rediscover Paris, a city he vaguely knew since the sixties, though his friends, then, his contacts, lived in the south, in Montparnasse. This time round he started out with the bookshops, English-language bookshops, the art galleries and the restaurants. He even went on a few City Walks round places like the Marais and Montmartre and the Isle de la Cité and Notre Dame. After that it was paying attention to the utilities – after Darty for the fridge and Picard for the contents of the fridge and that first table from Conforama (impossible to put together), the move slightly up-market to Habitat. *But to the services: quicker to cut you off over here for non-payment!* And could you deny that queues at French post offices are longer than those in England? Though England's catching up. And what's the verdict on whether the shopkeepers here made vulgar assumptions about you, in assuming your interest in the cheaper ranges on offer? (He remembered Nora making a point of buying some fish-heads at a street stall round the corner, and daring the assistant to think that money was a factor in her decision. Pewter, after that, occasionally bought fish-heads at the same place, with a certain air of defiance.) Now, with all that behind him, he was checking out the internet scene.

The Sri Lankan cafés were down-market. They performed the services that others neglected, open for your convenience, either before eight in the morning or after nine at night. And they were cheap. Family-run businesses, very different in tone and style from the 'French' establishments employing staff who worked office-hours (shut on Saturday, some of them, if not on Monday; and for lunch). Initially, Pewter was loath to hang out in the cramped surroundings, the plastic chairs covered in cheap fabric; the clientèle down-at-heel, often coming in just to make phone calls. But they were cheap; and friendly. (The nice woman, wife/mother on Damrémont, controlling things at the front of the shop, always with a smile, seemed not to mind being wedged in her glass booth of an office, dealing with the flow.) The more spacious, brightly lit alternatives attracted a different assemblage of Parisians; they cost more and, according to Nora, wouldn't be around in five years' time. Overheads. Social Security payments to staff. And she rehearsed for Pewter the story of the tiger economies of the eighties. Pewter tried to picture the woman in the booth, and her 'sister' on the rue Ordiner, as Sri Lankan tigers; but forgetting the unfortunate political resonance, they seemed the opposite of anything tigerish. (The Africans in ethnic dress – phoning home? – made a stronger statement, putting him in mind of London of the fifties, when Africa offered promise rather than disappointment. Recalling, then, the young African student in Westbourne Park selling encyclopaedias from his room, you could imagine him ending up opening a little bookshop on Ladbroke Grove. Or on Chesterton Road. Or at least, becoming a powerhouse of knowledge in the way of that character in the Clifford Odets play, the one who educates himself by reading through the encyclopaedia starting with the letter A – and working his way through to C.)

So the point was more than pride. The Sri Lankans were starting out in Paris; their starting-out position was recognizable, familiar; in a generation, in a decade – in five years? – theirs would be the cafés attracting the smart set, the money. (Interesting, by the way, that they didn't put their names on the buildings, no Bandaranaike or Kumaratunga or Jayasuriya, just the initials, XYZ Telecom, etc. Trying to keep a low profile in a foreign place? Shame at starting out at the low end of the market?) But Pewter wasn't starting out; he had already started out in another country, in two other countries.

After access, the saying goes, comes consolidation. So he must show that he was *consolidating*: when he arrived in Paris to a new empty but inviting flat – perfect space for the medicine cabinet; this wall? that wall? – he had brought over two suitcases of books from England (before he bought a bed), and he had written a Memoir of his First Hundred books in the flat, as a resident of the city. That was not the way of the newcomer, of the refugee. The *clochards* on the streets read no books that he could see, though he declined to pass judgement on the *clochards*, remembering his cousin, Horace. So he had arrived to a different *style.* He imagined – confident of how he had baptized his newly painted shelves – he imagined running into Madame Beauvais as he emerged from a brightly lit, well-appointed (French) internet café on rue Damrémont or rue Ordiner, his body-language demonstrating that he was not squatting, just waiting for his own technology to arrive. And she responding in kind, to an acquaintance who was not *new*. Surely, she'd appreciate the old resistance to selling the family silver, just to reduce the size of your bank loan.

So he would talk to Beauvais as someone in possession of assets. *You, too, would wish to acquire a Damien Hirst. Not the cow, obviously. Or the shark. But the medicine cabinet, twenty-six only in the world. Granted, it is English, Madame, and not to your taste. So, let's talk about something else.* They would have gone beyond the platitudes of comparing Impressionists at the d'Orsay and Monets at the Marmottan and, whatever, at the Louvre. They would not sink into gossip of whether Chirac's *grand projet* for 'ethnic art' down at Quai Branly would end up bearing his name should he manage to escape gaol after the presidency. Pewter would block and parry Beauvais' theatrical jabs at his argument; though he would allow her to defend the home-grown product, conceding that French design has held up, despite the assault from America and the patent-thieving Chinese, almost the same people, the Americans and the Chinese, though they try to confuse you with their manufactured ideological differences; as if any two kings of France had the same ideology. They would agree that certain cosmetic containers, available to all, managed to maintain their distinctive, French shape (like a successful football team); egg-boxes in the supermarket, for instance, having that certain *flair* of design that the Anglo-Saxon versions lacked. As with the framboises?

Les framboises?
   La petite boîte pour les framboises.

Ah. Les framboises!
Le petit truc pour les framboises.
Ah . . . D'accord.'

Naturally, after the success of this joust Pewter would invite Madame Beauvais to his place in her part of the woods, his hideaway in the Var, behind the village of Montauroux.

(She would, by then, have conceded that he was not new; and that he had baggage. For he was part of that pioneer generation that had included people whose contributions had never properly been acknowledged, never written up. He is thinking of a friend in Highgate, who was ever juggling with the history. He is thinking of his cousin Horace who died, who started his own church, his own religion; and went on a Peace Mission to many countries, and reportedly came home and preached his sermons at the roadside, in Latin. All that.)

So Beauvais' invitation to the house must be done in some style. She'd be met in the village by a couple designed for that purpose. Their names are Pierre and Denese Roustan. They will meet Beauvais outside the Mairie and accompany her to the rendezvous where Pewter will be waiting.

(Now, he is writing to Beauvais to tell her what to expect.)

On arrival at the cross-roads, note the signposts to the private road (road maintained by Roustan); then up to the edge of the property, the post box. Then swing along the low terrace – once earmarked for tennis courts – the property on the right sheltered by a high hedge of cypress, the *oliviers* and oak well tended (though the pines, the pines have suffered). Then up to the house where Pewter greets her at the pool and points out the dwarf palm at the edge, the shallow end, an idea pinched from a friend he used to know in the Alpes Maritimes, a Canadian, thirty years ago. *The pool.* Over-designed by Muhammad and Pewter, some say. Observe how it takes the shape of the pond where the old guy, the farmer, original owner, used to bring his cows to water, maintaining respect for what was there before. Beauvais likes that – the pool, though designed by Muhammad and Pewter and an Irishman, gains her approval.

There are other guests; a couple of Americans from Maine revelling in the sunshine; the Riviera hasn't lost its magic for them. Also, visiting, are a couple from Scotland, mother and son; and a woman friend from Sheffield. (It is a big place, two structures, the pool strategically placed between them, fenced now, following the new French law, something that Beauvais approves of, that foreigners, however favoured, must bow to the will of France.) And now, inside, under the canopy – this is the side entrance: the figs, the vine, the long table for dining outside – through to the open-plan kitchen. Alcoves set back into the terrace; original. The *cave* with bare rock exposed behind. Nice. *A glass of wine?* And here you could see the real mix of *rustique* and modern, the rock at the edge of the dining and sitting area, chiselled flat for a table. This bit of white-washed wall, original farmhouse; fireplace designed by Muhammad, modified against the earlier smoking. *And now would she like to see the rest of the house?*

Up the stairs. Mind your head. Design fault. A house of many architects; the way it was done in those days. Here, on the left, is the master bedroom, with the *en suite* – an extra service, if you're so inclined, press that button, and a retainer will come through the arch with your wine on a tray. *A joke, a joke.* The balcony facing south. On the other side the north-facing bedroom. With balcony. Sun and shade as you require. In between, the small bedroom, with a high ceiling, sloping, but spacious because of the ceiling. Books scattered on the shelves. French classics among them.

And now to business. *This must not seem like a seduction.*

So he tells this story of a woman in England; she is attractive and clever, and has made it to university; she is unhappy about the condition of England, particularly its racial mix; she doesn't call herself a racist, she resists the label. Her friends, the boys, are sometimes rough on black-skinned, brown-skinned people they meet unprotected, in the northern cities where they live; and on the women who side with the enemy. She, herself, doesn't approve of the physical stuff, but she has written about her friends as a suitable subject for study. At the university she is writing a thesis on the English woman. The English Woman, to be exact. She defines English in a traditional way. She recalls all those fellow spirits of an earlier age who travelled abroad, unchaperoned (except by the unconquerable aura of being English) to Egypt, to Africa, before coming home safely. And she says, that is what she wants in England now, for the Englishwoman. Deference. She wants it on the trains, she wants it in the restaurants, she wants it on the street, from anyone who looks foreign, the black- and brown-skinned to start with; then who knows?

So why is she interesting? Oh yes, she seeks out the black-skinned, the dark-skinned male to dine out with in public, so that she can exact deference. At the university she insists that her tutor, her supervisor be black so that she can punish him in, oh, so many little ways. What does Beauvais make of this little English story?

The English, as everyone knows, are mad. In France we have not gone in for this stupid idea of multiculturalism. And then she says:

But Mr Stapleton, why have you brought me here? I thought you were going to show me your painting.

Oh. But Madame. The Damien Hirst hasn't yet been delivered. It is a difficult medicine cabinet to get through Customs.

So why did you bring me here?

Oh; just to show you, Madame Beauvais, where the murder takes place.

Who kills whom? she asks in French.

His mother would not approve of this, of a murder in the family, either as perpetrator or as victim (particularly if a woman is involved); so instead he has to accept defeat and say to Beauvais: here is my plan of action; here is the rescue package. I've acquired a new partner, an IT firm in Paris. Great future. Sri Lankan. In the eighteenth. Here's our card. VSK Telecom & Stapleton. Rue Damrémont. If that doesn't suffice, how about this one? VSN Telecom & Stapleton (*nudge nudge wink wink, a way of giving legitimacy to the Sri Lankans, what?*). What do you say?

*

Madame Beauvais rings to inform him that she is no longer dealing with his account; it has been transferred to main office; the man in charge now is Monsieur Xxxx Xxxxxx. Pewter doesn't get the name first time; could she repeat it?

So he might have to talk football now. He doesn't even have a French team, a French club that he supports. The match between France and Switzerland last night didn't bode well: a dull nil–nil draw. What future now for Zidane, Captain of France? Zidane everywhere on the television, in the papers, the face on the cover of this week's *Télé magazine* ('*Pour son dernier défi*'). Will the balding head be crowned (Zidane I)? Fingers crossed for France v South Korea, and France v Togo. Or will it be *A bas les Noirs*, and riots in the street? And what if the new man at the bank is hostile to contemporary art? Pewter might have to come up with a plan to reduce that bank loan, after all.

Meanwhile, he has written something that he is proud

of. This is the best thing ever. But the printer is playing up. So he goes to the café; he goes over the road to the Sri Lankan café with his diskette; and he picks up a virus. Back home, there's no back-up. Vanished. He doesn't, of course, believe in conspiracy theories.

But it's a bad day in Paris.

16

Home

Pewter was standing outside the house in Kilburn, and although it wasn't cold, it was uncomfortable. He'd been moved on a couple of times, a few yards this way, then the other way – the power of the face appearing at the edge of the curtain. But it was dark now, people were said to be anxious in their homes, so he could understand why they didn't want a stranger hovering on the pavement opposite; they didn't turn on the lights in the room and that made him guilty on their behalf. But these were only the neighbours, he was no threat to them. If accosted he would say: 'There's been a shooting in the family; on top of that another member has gone down with . . . something not very pleasant. But you'll be all right. Don't worry.' But he didn't have to account to them, anyway. So he added that little bit of stubbornness to whatever it was that had drawn him back here, and worked through his unease and stayed put – from time to time moving just a few yards this way and, eventually, back again, as you would if you were waiting for an acquaintance who was late home.

If challenged he'd say: This is my old house, that's my old school up the road; but why should he be challenged? Other things kept flooding back; the boy at school thought to be stupid who affected patience to disguise his stupidity, and got lucky one night because of his stupidity: the boy was enamoured of this woman, an older woman, certainly in her twenties, who lived just round the back here; and he stood outside her house for hours into the night to show he knew how it was done, and she explained to him and then gave up, explained to him that his place was at home doing his homework for she had a grown-up man who loved her, a man not only grown-up but jealous. In the end, so as not to have an incident on her doorstep, the woman came back to the front door and dragged him in and was good to him because he was so young and cold; and though stupid, he understood the risk she had taken, and promised not to return to make life difficult. Ah, the days!

But these distractions didn't work now. Behind all this Pewter could sense the weight of someone being carried out on a stretcher, or of someone screaming when the neighbours were asleep. Or – why was it so hard to come to this? – someone being thrown out of the house by a partner. So maybe it was better after all to hang on to that image from schooldays, of the young boy, getting lucky. So he shifted a few yards along the pavement, even though no face appeared at the edge of the curtain.

Once, they had attempted to move him on – the police – outside this very house: two overgrown young boys who couldn't have been long out of the Hendon Police College. (Girls at school were said to fancy the boys in uniform.) Pewter had been hanging around with a friend from Jamaica they used to call Balham, and Mark, who also went to the Polytechnic School, where they were doing their A Levels. They hadn't really been moved on by the police. The uniformed boys came up the road walking slowly as if they were real policemen, and consulted each other when they saw the lads on the steps, and hesitated and then stopped. Then one of the police boy-men asked what the lads were doing, whether they knew someone living in the house. And that was a mistake. Balham, who had been sitting, stood up to show that he was their size. That was a mistake, giving the boys an opening to take on the opposition – A Level Stars v Police College – in real subjects like History and Economics and Logic *and* the ability to mimic middle-class accents of their schoolmates from West Hampstead and Ruislip. And Pewter said nothing and waited for his friends to deal with this. It was Mark who volunteered and decided to be calm and condescending, and to point out, speaking slowly with enunciation you could feel the edge of, that they had come to visit Pewter, who lived in this house, which was owned by his mother, a fastidious lady from St Caesare, who would be reassured that her street was being kept safe by the boys in blue. And when the police showed their confusion and went on their way Balham mapped out a 'Napoleonic' manoeuvre to entrap them when they returned with reinforcements, as they had to do, because it was in their training manual. But tonight Pewter made up his mind simply to say, when challenged: 'I used to live in this house, officer.'

He used to do his homework upstairs; he'd painted the ceiling of his room, while others gave a hand hanging the wallpaper; and then hung his famous picture frame on the wall – no picture, just the frame – which caused comment at the time. Now, if challenged, he'd say: 'I was curious to see how the room is decorated.' Something like that. In the room at the back which he couldn't see from the street, the one next to the box room, he looked out on to a bare wall where the vine had died; and friends visiting used to talk of the lack of view. (With Bob Dylan on the gramophone who needed a view!) He did his growing up in that room, went away to university and came back to reclaim it, and did his research in that room, and thought it quaint of friends to pity him for the bare wall at the back and the lack of view. (According to . . . someone he's not allowed to name because she's no longer in his life, and she won't trust him with her name – according to her these things couldn't be brushed aside; it was macho not to need a room with a view; it was perverse to be so self-sufficient.) So Pewter wanted to revisit these scenes of his growing up and not pit himself against the normality of vines growing on the wall outside, or of softness and colour and . . . and not make himself impossible to live with. And, really, it's not as if he preferred bare walls to walls draped in vine and moss and ivy. But he didn't want to have this sort of discussion any more. The house would, anyway, have been redecorated, successive new forms of life growing up in his room, the unexpected release of a breast not matching the face. Ah, with X, whom he's not allowed to name, and who never knew this house, the breast, the breast matched the face. And he thought now, looking beyond the closed front door: there'd be unknowable types growing up here. Or maybe just something daughterly and granddaughterly that a man his age shouldn't be thinking about. Enough. Time to go home.

*

He was back, reviving the life in his legs. He had gone back to a point from which to satisfy a woman he no longer lived with that he was looking at himself in a new way. At this point the image of something uncoiled came to mind; from this position he could be more generous about friends and acquaintances; and not draw comfort from the thought that if some of them were down on their luck, that meant he was ahead to that degree. He didn't really think that fitted him; what he was feeling was less crude than that, but perhaps it wasn't much less crude than that.

The three friends had set out their stall on the front steps of the house in Kilburn, still arguing over what wares they were going to sell. For they were in England, and hadn't Napoleon said something interesting about the English? So the three had to distinguish themselves by being truly superior shopkeepers.

Inside the house the family would be distracted for a few years more, needing time to complain of having given up familiar surroundings and people, given up status in one community, given up things like, yes, sunshine and . . . Though, at the same time, they had to be honest and admit they were pleased about certain things, pleased to be away from troublesome insects and cockroaches and lizards and woodslaves in the bathroom; and it was good living at the centre of things, the High Road – which the boys said was a Roman road – with shops that sold what you wanted; and not having to buy things you didn't want in order to get the things that were in short supply. And buying clothes off the peg meant that you didn't have to sew for the family and for neighbours; and that going to the doctor was free and it was good to know, too, that some of the doctors didn't speak English as well as you did. It was good too – someone said, though it seemed a selfish thing to say – it was good not having to run into the same people several times a day and to have to find something new to say to them each time, as if you were someone in a book, readily supplied with the words.

The boys on the steps protected the family inside from a sort of anxiety. Outside, their conversation was about the merits of Macmillan versus Gaitskell; pronouncing on bearded Bulganin and beardless Khrushchev; assessing Nehru and Jomo and Nkrumah, and deciding whether Portugal or Cyprus were underdeveloped countries and speculating whether that changed the status of the women in Portugal and Cyprus. On these steps the boys decided how to confront the fascist Mosley who had stood in the general election in Ladbroke Grove and had been humiliated there; and was said to be considering making another come-back in Kilburn. And the boys talked of making alliances with others who were targeted, like the Irish and the Jews; and they came down in favour of the Jews because the Jews owned their own homes and hence had more to defend.

If you had to join a persecuted group, Balham stressed, better to go with the one who's got a stake in the society; that way you get a chance to change the rules, to make the rules. Or you'd always be outmanoeuvred. So he had done just this; he had gone Jewish.

Back in St Caesare Pewter had had a clerical upbringing. Balham, in Jamaica, would have had the same, though he claimed to have rebelled. And Mark, who was mixed-race, had a choice of religions. So everyone knew all about the Exodus (even before the film of that name), Moses getting them to mark their door-posts with the blood of the lamb (a lot of lamb stew tonight, folks) so that the firstborn would be saved when the Lord 'smote the land of Egypt'. Bit rough on Egypt, but never mind. (Hang on in there, Nasser!) And rough on those who weren't firstborn, and on the girls. Pewter had a sister, Mark had a sister, Balham – well, Balham was reputed to have a mother living some-where in Cricklewood – so no one wanted their women-folk to be smitten in that way. If all this Passover thing was common knowledge, then what do you say about the *seder*, the *Haggada*?

Balham explained the ritual of unleavened bread and bitter herbs and crushed fruit and wine; much washing of hands and four cups of wine (and real wine, you know, none of this Cyprus sherry nonsense or some undrinkable home-brew) – and the children asking questions, and all that. But this was old stuff; he was into another ritual that took place in the best Jewish homes in Golders Green and

Edgware. Did it have a name? Ah, what's in a name, things got muddled this far from Egypt or what some call the Unholy Land. And you couldn't expect people in Golders Green, who lived so close to Kilburn, to be that Orthodox.

But on a certain night of the year, before they washed their hands and sat down to eat, they'd set an extra place, and anyone who turned up at that moment – made no difference who that person was; it could be Nasser himself, or an old tramp, or the Archbishop of Canterbury, Mr Fisher – that person would have to be seated at the table and given food and wine, and sung to and prayed over; and they would tell him stories of survival and he, in turn (or she) would have to tell his story – like singing for your supper. But that wouldn't be a hardship because a man or woman wandering the world would, anyway, have lots of stories to tell.

So far so good. Now everyone round the table is nicely sozzled on best Bordeaux; the stranger has made up his story and his reward is to have the pick of the women in the room – wife, daughter, makes no difference, he has to be accommodated. And he has to choose well for he's got only one chance at it; the religion has sanctioned coupling for just one night. More than that and you're into something else, heavy things like Sodom and Gomorrah and Licentiousness. Punishable by death at the hands of someone like a poor relative from the East End who didn't make it in the rag trade and resents this preferential treatment to strangers, particularly strangers of another tradition. Naturally, there had to be no trace of the stranger at breakfast; and, of course, he couldn't target the house and return on the next ritual occasion, because he'd no longer be a stranger, then, but a long-term lover; and there you were talking adultery, another thing punishable by Crazed Relative from East End. So the stranger would have to move on to find another Jewish home. And Balham, street-wise Balham, sitting here on the steps outside Pewter's mother's home in Kilburn, could tell the boys that he was now on to his fifth Jewish home.

And this is the story Pewter would tell the police: *Guten Abend, Schutzmann. Was ist los in Köln?* No no, no more pulling of rank. So he would use his own voice:
Bwoy, I ain't have no family left. But he didn't recognize this voice either. So he went on as he always did, trying not to be too self-conscious: *Went off for a . . . y'know, good reason. Always thinking you'd get back to, y'know . . . the right place. Obviously, not here. Bad timing. Idle curiosity, really. I've tracked down all the houses, you know. Hard to keep up with a family on the move. Who's tracking whom; who's pursuing? The boys, the boys from school would understand. This, Balham and Mark would say, is like – something in Dostoyevsky, something in Dickens. So, I find myself outside this house, outside that house, watching for a shadow, a movement. The game's gone stale, you say. And those inside the house are bored with it. They would just prefer you to move on as requested. Of course, I accept it with good grace, officer, as you can see. Just checking that everything is in order, that everyone's safe; that the country's in good hands. I'm OK, I'm OK. I'm fine.*

*

When she opened the door Pewter would be ready, making up for lost time. If she who greeted him wasn't his sister turning into her mother, she would still need to know, like his sister, like his mother, that his story was one of success; that the narrative of his life made sense. Even if she wasn't like the partner who he still isn't allowed to name, she would still need to know that he had uncoiled, that he had admitted the soft things into his life, the – ah! – unexpected release of a breast not matching the face, the cleverness of it . . . This was too much. And yes, there must be people inhabiting some of his rooms, his houses elsewhere, waiting to be amused, to be placated, to be avenged. Across the road, you say, as schoolboys, we learnt that the Siege of Leningrad lasted 900 days, millions dead, hundreds imprisoned later for cannibalism. Shostakovich beamed to the defenders, over loud-speakers, to keep up morale. Ah, this house rich in family, in expectation, might want *less* not more history. True, he did promise to do this or that when Macmillan and Mosley were alive to see it; when poor Oginga Odinga, fighting Kenyatta, fixed his teeth and came good in Kenya; when the Berlin Wall came down. But *distractions distractions*. Enough of him, enough of the old failing, self-obsession, self-absorption. What of *them* across the road: did they eat meat; had they been to Scotland? He couldn't help being curious. The people inside, yes, he understood, had to position themselves a little this way, a little that way. And for the duration there'd be no need to dwell on Balham and Mark, who had long gone to live in far-away places, and weren't available any more to come here and help protect the house, which was the last thing he remembered of the family.

17

Miss Vanesa's Research

I got stuck at the point where my mother shot Oswald Mosley dead. That Saturday afternoon in 1959, outside our house in Ladbroke Grove. This was just before the general election, Macmillan's 'You've Never Had It So Good' general election. Mosley brought his rabble to our house in Bevington Road, partly because of the public loos outside the house, which provided a space for meetings, and partly because his side-kick, Geoffrey Hamm, lived next door to us; but principally, I suspect, because the house was owned by a black family. So the joke that my mother attended Mosley's rally must be understood in that light. She was sitting at her first-floor window looking out. This was something she did, election rally or no election rally; indeed, this was something she used to do on Wellington Street, in St Caesare, in the years before England. On the Saturday in question my mother had already been sitting at her window, looking out, before the rally started. To shut your window now, or to absent yourself, would be to send the wrong sort of signal to the fascist. Though this is my thought process, not necessarily my mother's.

And after he said what he had to say, she had no choice but to shoot him. He was polite: the better-educated fascists were polite in those days, making us ambivalent about class. He was polite, he tipped his hat to her. But when she realized the import of his talk, she reached for her gun and killed him. She opened her handbag and took out her gun and killed him. She got up on the chair, reached for the gun where it was hidden on the lintel over the window, and killed him. And we had no idea that she knew my cousin, X, had hidden the gun there.

And then it seemed too neat: we were living in Ladbroke Grove, not in a film.

There's no reason to assume my mother would be a good shot; even though it was at close range. (For he had got up on a makeshift platform which brought him level with her, about four or five feet away; but it's better to think that she had wounded him.) So, let's say he had been hit, and fallen off his podium, concussed. Enter a black woman from the crowd, a no-nonsense sort of woman, from St Vincent. Or Antigua. A woman of a certain age. She, calmly – perhaps because of her nursing experience – waves away the crowds and bends down to give him the kiss of life. Priceless image of the black woman kissing the fascist in public, in front of his supporters. The cheers are ironic and embarrassed.

And what is my mother doing meanwhile? Ah, I failed her then; I fail her now. It's too late to get back to my Latin homework. Nearly half a century has passed. And yet . . .

II

I won't go to the meeting, of course: I chose a Sunday to emphasize the fact that it wasn't work; this would be a social call, a drink at the end of the day with a friend, an acquaintance, as with someone from work you hadn't seen in a bit, not since you left the place; someone you'd bumped into in the street and decided to have a drink with, a coffee, a hot chocolate, on the spur of the moment: the bookshop would be a good place for it. In town. Waterstone's.

'I thought you'd be in Paris.'

'Oh, I . . . come over from time to time. Lots of . . . y'know, bits 'n' pieces to . . . Ah. Stuff. What about you?'

'Oh, me?' Then something vague I don't listen to. (Interesting that Harold Bloom says that Shakespeare . . . Well. Melvyn Bragg says that Bloom says that Shakespearean characters don't really listen to each other, to one another; and that we don't, either. And that's one of the ways in which Shakespeare invented us. Nonsense, of course. Can you imagine Neanderthal man – man and woman – sitting there in the cave, after dark straining to look into each other's eyes, to understand the point that's being made –

'Pissingdown . . . Eh? No no. The rain. Wet.'

'Rain? Wet?'

'Bigwet. Not littlewet. No firething.'

'Gordon Bennett.'

'Bigrain. Waterwood.'

'Nag nag,' etc.

In any case, coming back to Shakespeare, I have a sense that Macbeth did, perhaps, listen to his wife. But then . . .)

I can confidently predict that the woman, my date, my arranged chance meeting for Sunday, will make no reference to my mother. She's a professional. We'd just be sitting upstairs in Waterstone's, in Sheffield, in the coffee shop, like any other odd couple, not talking books.

But I won't go to the meeting; I'll call her up, must have the number somewhere.

She had walked past me in the street, my mother; and there's no need to make too much of that; I was in something of a trance, and didn't myself recognize her until she had gone past, and said something: that's what caught my attention. And I recognized her because of the way she moved, drifting the way they do, not walking, not having to dodge people and traffic – though this was a traffic-free precinct – but still not having to deal with collisions and, 'sorry' and 'excuse me'. And that depressed me slightly. So I decided not to think about it.

But, on reflection, perhaps, it wasn't so bad; because she may have been confused. I don't like the notion of her being confused; a younger person being confused might be charming, in a sort of way – like that nice woman in her garden with her hat and gloves, ah! In Cambridge in April. Or in Montauroux or St Caesare or in a neighbouring island all the year round, practically: not the same woman, of course. But now, an older person being confused sets little alarm bells ringing. She never had those sorts of illnesses that we associate with an older person being confused.

Though, if she *were* confused in this instance, we could explain it away. We could say that she was visiting me in France, for, of course, the foolishness of boundaries, of geography, wouldn't matter to her. For, in effect, we were walking through a French street in Sheffield. Fargate. In Orchard Square. Taken over that day, as it is from time to time, by the French. From Breton Biscuits to the fruit and flower stalls at the other end – the usual garlic and fruit, lots of flowers, potted plants, the lot. I was actually standing at the Breton Biscuits stall, vaguely conscious, though not regretfully so, that I had given all that up; the sweet thing. A flag was mounted, stuck on the edge of the stall; a blue flag with the little pink stars dotted about, and behind the stall, the sturdy Frenchman in his white butcher's coat and white chef's cap, offering a tempting package at £1.35. £1.35 per 100 grammes of any mixture you fancied. (Would he pronounce the 's' in 'grammes'? I wondered.) Almonds, butter and jam; lots of chocolate. Chocolate waffles. Chocolate this, chocolate that. (I'd already drifted past the other stalls catering to other tastes. The sausages. Couscous. Cheese. As well as art-objects. And the nice range of soaps, which were almost art-objects. Soaps that put you in mind of that nice shop up the hill, in Fayance.) Anyway.

I was about to move off, again, not wanting to give the impression that I was considering chocolate; when the incident happened. He heard it, too, the Frenchman, though he wouldn't have known what it meant, wouldn't have known the idiom.

I imagined having to go to dinner (or more likely, tea at Waterstone's) with my acquaintance, a few days later, and having to conceal the fact that I saw my mother again; and that she had called me a 'tosser'. And I would have to make a joke of it and say that the Frenchman in the butcher's coat and cap had heard it and had asked me: 'What ees tosser?' – stressing the second syllable. So if I brought up the incident at all, I'd have to say something like: Isn't it good that we've become so cosmopolitan here in Sheffield, that you walk down Fargate on a Thursday morning; and instead of being conscious of, I don't know, Boots and M&S and WH Smith, on the other side, or the video place, and all that; instead of that, you're greeted with Breton Biscuits (complete with a blue flag and stars) and with a solid Frenchman behind the stall in his butcher's whatsit and his white cap offering you chocolates and biscuits at £1.35 a hundred grammes?

My mother could have been excused for thinking that she was visiting me in Paris – though she had yet to visit me in Paris. Then, the expletive would have been in French, for she had passed through that barrier, too, of language. And the expletive, in French, would have had no more force than the woman on *Chaine cinq* reading the News.

But, of course, this is my fantasy; for my mother, that

morning, in Sheffield, knew where I was heading; she knew I was heading for the pornographer. He is said to be the best one in town: first, he sits you in a high chair and makes you comfortable, the girl assistants excite you with this and that; then one of them does the mask thing to signal business. Now, you're on your back, looking up at the mirror set in the ceiling with humans talking dirty. It's like being in a private cinema. You can't help thinking there are, somewhere, poor people in the world, who don't have all this. But then, as the poet says, you've got only one life to live. You will say later – if you admit it at all – that you got no particular pleasure from this; and that paying for it was just a sign of the corruption of the times.

So, enough said about that.

'Tosser,' she says.

III

Meanwhile, things to do: phone calls. Duty call to RT in London. Call to XX (Oh, my Persian Princess of long ago!) in London. Just to hear her voice. Letter to Vanesa, in St Caesare.

Last time, the phone call to RT in Highgate wasn't as bad as I had feared; so maybe I could risk it. We had accepted, without too much fuss, that there was a problem (in the world? In England?) to be solved, and that he had come up with something close to a solution; so now he could be left alone to work on it; and I could forget his existence for the next few months, for a year, maybe; while he got on with it. So now, how about *attacking* Miss Vanesa, as the French say, as they set about a simple task, like washing up; or sweeping the floor. An e-mail to Miss Vanesa is certainly overdue.

But then you can't be honest with Vanesa and say: I just

don't feel like it, too stupid to talk of pressure, because you know and I know what pressure is, and yet this is pressure of a sort. Or, to be less precious about it, maybe you're just too far away, Vanesa (a nonsense, I accept, when we're talking about e-mail; so maybe you're just far away, in another sense. Though that doesn't sound . . .). So what do I mean? It's not just that it's miserable and damp here in Sheffield, and there's no sexual partner in sight. Or not even that I broke a tooth yesterday on a prune-thing, for Christ sake, some tasteless supermarket out-of-season travesty clocking up the air miles and making us guilty: *what we want is a government that brings back sensible rationing. In food. In the Health Service. In travel. Come back Harold Wilson, all is forgiven. What will the bloody tooth cost? Imagine a country without dentists; imagine the revolution gone wrong. Again.* Anyway, you can't be honest with Vanesa because you don't know her well enough; you can't be honest and say: it's a miserable April day here; it's a miserable nearly May-day here; I've been out for the paper, not that I read the paper any more; *but at least, it's in English.* And after a morning clearing out the old flat, getting the paper on the way back seemed an OK thing to do, a little reward. Catching up. But then the mood changed; probably because of my getting rained on both going and coming; still can't get the chill out of my bones. And the last thing I want to do, Miss Vanesa – you out there in the tropical sun, privileged – the last thing I want now is to write this unnecessary letter to you. And I'm doing it because you mentioned my mother. So what's a necessary letter, you might ask? For you like to present yourself as someone connected with the academy: what's a necessary letter? (*Remember that line in* King Lear *about the unnecessary Z!*) 'What's a necessary letter?' asks the woman with a neurological problem, over and over again. *And must she be a woman? And why is she always a woman?* someone asks, like this woman I'm due to meet, later. The answer is, she is not always a woman. *He* is not always a woman – though replete with womanly breasts. Forget my mood, Miss Vanesa, it's not personal. What's a necessary letter? I don't know? Maybe one to some woman from Eastern Europe who's been trafficked into prostitution (*rapes and beatings*) somewhere in Leeds or Nottingham. (Not, hopefully, in Sheffield.) *Nothing wrong with the prostitution, of course, it's the rapes and beatings; the control: 'pimp' is the four-letter word for which execution is too good for them. Too quick.* (I've been reading the Sunday papers.) 'Pimp' is so much worse than 'tosser'. Not that a letter would do any good; what you need is a weapon, state-of-the-art weapon, a Charles Bronson burner (for my purpose he is still alive and vigilanting). Or an Arnold Schwarzenegger terminator burning and terminating the pimps and pushers and traffickers out of . . . California. Without that you're helpless; without that, writing a letter to Miss Vanesa on her Caribbean island seems an effort you really can't be bothered to gee yourself up to make.

Miss Vanesa is doing research into what she calls my family: how kind of you, Miss Vanesa, to remind me of my debt to my mother – who, yes, like the woman you're researching, went to the Antigua Girls' School, and contributed to the *Antigua Girls' High School Magazine*, in 1932.

But then here's my mother, again, now contributing to the British Conservative Local Government campaign, of 2006!

The pressure to reclaim my mother comes from unexpected sources. My own neuroses are not interesting. Miss Vanesa's researches are sort of less telling. As a young actress in England in the sixties, she may have nearly played Harriette Wilson with a theatre group in Shepherd's Bush.

Harriette Wilson was mistress to the Duke of Wellington, the Iron Duke, conqueror of Napoleon at Waterloo. So now, why shouldn't she be researching my mother who, prior to coming to England, was thought to be the epitome of *style* on the island. Nothing wrong with that. But when David Cameron, the new, young Conservative lead, goes to my mother's old street in Ladbroke Grove, and stands in a certain spot, outside a certain house, and makes a claim, seventeen years after my mother's death, you can't pretend that nothing is happening here. So the first thing to do – ah, it's a Sunday morning in Sheffield – the first thing to do is to have a cup of tea, and not think about it.

And now, after a nice cup of tea, what? That's what she said, that woman, that other woman in Crouch End that time: (*young and pretty. Pretty young*) Now what? Now nothing nothing nothing. Nothing will come of . . . Thus we have memory to punish us *punish us punish us*. And, indeed, it's a relief to turn back to Miss Vanesa, for Miss Vanesa, far away on her Caribbean island, long-distanced and emotionally neutral, doesn't have the ability to unsettle us: hers is simply 'research'; literary archaeology. Her 'what then' or 'what nows' are an invitation to you to supply the neglected dialogue – dialogue for the young Harriette Wilson, or themes for the *Antigua Girls' High School Magazine* of long ago. But Master Cameron. Let's get this right.

The Cameron connection is scary. When, on his visit to Ladbroke Grove last week or the week before, campaigning for the local elections, he stood outside our house of long ago, in the same place where Mosley stood, all those years ago, and he invoked my mother, claiming her to be *his* mother, surely, someone, somewhere, was saying something to me. Cameron is said to have described the woman who came into his dream of a multicultural Britain and called him her son, a woman who – according to the newspaper, conferred on him legitimacy – this son from Eton and Oxford, trophy wife in tow – conferred on him the legitimacy of representing a many-ethnicked Britain. And the woman he had described was *my* mother. Her turn of phrase was my mother's. Her demand for a better environment was my mother's. Her fear that the streets were no longer safe for the innocent was my mother's. And – this is *my* experience – her belief that a lad most likely to do something about it (like Cameron), might be her son – *was* my mother. She had clearly not called *him* a tosser. Playing the lottery of dropping in on dreams, she had appeared to an idiot in Highgate thinking he might be me. She had appeared, briefly, in Sheffield, to show her disaffection: would nothing shame me – I could hear her say – into acting like a normal member of the family? I called up my brother in London, to get an exact description of my mother's face, to check on her particular turns of phrase, giving him the impression that I was thinking of writing something about the family. His image of her – his memory of her – didn't quite match mine. What was I to do? I couldn't very well check with David Cameron. So, here goes:

She makes her way to France, to Paris; the easy way. No need to be in coach eighteen on Eurostar to be the first ones out and to the head of the taxi queue outside the station. She's in Paris but she doesn't come to the flat because she would be imagining a different flat. I don't know she's in Paris because I haven't done enough to prepare Paris for family habitation. It took fifty years to do that for London – and before that members of the family fought wars to make London safe for anybody. So I don't expect her at my enforced haunts of bookshops and art galleries and restaurants and the street markets of the dixhuitième.

And then one day, for whatever reason, I find myself reading a story by one of my favourite writers. It's 'Miss Brill' by Katherine Mansfield. And I realize that Miss Brill is my mother. And here she is sitting in the park, now in Paris; she's superbly coiffured, like a Parisian lady of a certain age might be; and though it's night, the sky is lit, as if we're on stage; and there are noises off, like distant riots, in the French way. There's a sensation of activity. And – as in 'Miss Brill' – the young, impatient-to-be-alone couple drift into view and find my mother's presence irksome; and the young man says his crude piece. But my mother doesn't hear it, or ignores it, or dismisses it as being a human thing. Though a member of the family would need to deal with that, to put that right, to make Paris safe.

Would I test this story on the woman I'm due to meet at Waterstone's in *x* hours' time? She would ask me questions, or use silence, to make me modify it or abandon it. And yet I feel drawn to risking it, and seeing what happens. This makes the afternoon altogether more alive for me now, than trying to figure out what to say to Miss Vanesa about my mother's time at Antigua Girls' High School all those years ago.

Select Bibliography of E. A. Markham

POETRY COLLECTIONS

Love, Politics & Food (Von Hallett Publications, 1982)

Human Rites: Selected Poems 1970–1982
(Anvil Press Poetry, 1984)

Living in Disguise (Anvil Press Poetry, 1986)

Towards the End of a Century (Anvil Press Poetry, 1989)

Letter from Ulster & The Hugo Poems
(Littlewood Arc, 1993)

Misapprehensions (Anvil Press Poetry, 1995)

A Rough Climate (Anvil Press Poetry, 2002)

John Lewis & Co.
(Anvil Press Poetry, 2003)

Lambchops with Sally Goodman
The selected poems of
Paul St Vincent and Sally Goodman
(Salt Publishing, 2005)

SHORT STORY COLLECTIONS

Something Unusual (Ambit Books, 1986)

Ten Stories (PAVIC, 1994)

Taking the Drawing Room through Customs
(Peepal Tree Press, 2002)

Meet Me in Mozambique
(Tindal Street Press, 2005)

OTHER PROSE

A Papua New Guinea Sojourn: More Pleasures of Exile
Memoir (Carcanet, 1998)

Marking Time
Novel (Peepal Tree Press, 1999)

AS EDITOR
Merely a Matter of Colour
with Arnold Kingston (Q Books, 1973)
Hinterland:
Caribbean Poetry from the West Indies & Britain
(Bloodaxe Books, 1989)
Hugo Versus Montserrat
with Howard A. Fergus (Linda Lee Books, 1989)
The Penguin Book of Caribbean Short Stories
(Penguin, 1996)
Plant Care: A Festschrift for Mimi Khalvati
(Linda Lee Books, 2004)
Ten Hallam Poets
with Steve Earnshaw and Sean O'Brien
(Mews Press, 2005)

Versions of these stories have appeared in the following

'At Home with Miss Vanesa'
(extract) in *Poetry Review*, Autumn 2006

'Bookmarks for John La Rose'
in *Sable*, Autumn 2006, and *EnterText*

Acknowledgements

WITH THANKS TO

The three graces of Anglophone enlightenment in Paris,
(young) Sylvia Beach at Shakespeare & Company,
Odile Hellier at Village Voice Bookshop and
Penelope Fletcher Le Masson at The Red Wheelbarrow.

And the miracle-workers at Tindal Street Press,
in particular Emma Hargrave, Alan Mahar
and Penny Rendall.